EIDOLON

E.S. Yu

A NineStar Press Publication

Published by NineStar Press
P.O. Box 91792,
Albuquerque, New Mexico, 87199 USA.
www.ninestarpress.com

Eidolon

Printed in the USA
First Edition
August, 2018

Print ISBN: 978-1-949340-56-3

Also available in eBook, ISBN: 978-1-949340-52-5

Warning: This book contains depictions of violence, mentions of past rape/sexual assault, and suicidal ideation.

To my family, for all their love and support during the
difficult times in my life.

And to those who can't find a reason to get up in the
morning,
Who find themselves staring at the abyss and wondering
if they should just give in—
You are not alone.
Your pain is real, and valid, and it's hard.
But right now, I'm glad you're here.

ei·do·lon

1. *an idealized person or thing.*

2. *a specter or phantom; a spirit-image of a living or dead person.*

Part I

Marked for Death

Chapter One

THE CALL CAME, as it always did, out of the blue, making Vax choke and nearly spill his latte down his jacket. He reluctantly set his cup on the café table with a stifled sigh and, after another minute of buzzing, finally tapped the node in his ear. There was only one person who ever called him, and the call always meant bad news.

"You've reached Corporate Murder Services. How can I help you?" he answered.

"Very funny," a smooth voice said. "I have a new assignment for you. Get to my office."

"Now?" Vax massaged the bridge of his nose. For once, he'd managed to snag an unoccupied window table, and now he wouldn't get to enjoy the sunshine or the view. "I'll need thirty minutes to get there, give or take traffic."

"Fine. See you soon."

The call ended. Vax swallowed, his appetite suddenly gone. He downed the rest of his latte, got up from his seat, and texted for an AutoRide. Not for the first time, he thought about suggesting a text message next time, or even a video call, as being much more convenient than an in-person meeting; also not for the first time, he reminded himself glumly that that was never going to happen.

The world had to have been determined to hate him today; he got in the driverless car as it drove up, and just after it pulled away from the curb, the screen inside began broadcasting a news story about Cyrex's CEO.

"Over the weekend, Cyrex Corp CEO, Atali Norman, pledged five million dollars to support STEM programs in schools across the country..."

Vax immediately changed the channel to one that aired several bioaugment commercials—including the one for Cyrex's latest weight loss bioaug model that seemed to be everywhere lately—before reporting grim updates on the war overseas. He sighed, gazing morosely out the window at the passing traffic and the colorful screens on the street. Just the way he wanted to start his morning.

Cyrex's headquarters formed the tallest building in Orphis City, visible from miles away. All glass, as though inviting the world to come and look inside; it had no secrets to hide. It made Vax think of an obnoxiously shiny diamond in the center of Orphis's gleaming crown of wealthy, high-tech development, which was very photogenic and good for luring tourists to America's fastest-growing biotech hub, if not exactly an accurate representation of the city as a whole. Vax got out of the car as it pulled up and walked through the glass doors at the entrance.

The sleek, modern lobby bustled with people. Vax waved the microchip in his finger through security and stepped into the elevator. He kept his gaze averted as people in suits and lab coats got on and off with each stop, fixing his eyes on the glimpses of his own reflection in the glass, flickering in and out of existence, like a ghost.

At the top floor, he exited the elevator. He tapped the touch screen panel by the glass door that read *Atali Norman, CEO*, and the panel flashed green as the door unlocked with a click. Bracing himself, he pulled the door open and walked into the spacious office. Atali himself was standing by the floor-to-ceiling windows that provided a view of the entire city, talking to someone through his node as Vax entered.

"Honey, I know you're nervous about starting at a new school, but I guarantee that your classmates will be nice kids who want to become friends with you. Trust me, you have nothing to worry about. Getting *into* Exelor Academy was the hard part; everything else should be a piece of cake. And if anyone's mean to you? Just tell me, and I'll take it up with the school. I'm serious!" He turned around and caught sight of Vax. "Sorry, Cathy, I have to go. Call me back later if you're still anxious, okay? All right. Love you. See you later."

He ended the call with a press to his ear and turned to face Vax fully. Holographic text flashed in front of his eyes, projected from the transparent augment by his temple. The morning sunlight turned his blond hair into pallid silver, matching his pale skin, as he smiled.

"Hello, Vax. You're looking well."

Vax wasn't in the mood for small talk. "Who's the target?"

Atali sighed in mock disappointment. "Always business with you." He produced a microdrive from his pocket, which he inserted into the desk before tapping the touch screen desk surface. The windows behind him darkened and displayed a picture of a young, East Asian man with black hair and light-copper skin.

"Do you know who this is?" Atali asked.

Vax studied the picture more closely. The guy was quite good-looking—as much as Vax wished he could block that thought from his mind—but he didn't recognize him. "No, sir."

"That's Zai Lumero, age twenty-five. He's a journalist who writes for the *Daily Voice*, one of those independent news sites that aims to report on 'true issues' affecting people's lives." Atali spoke with the bored disdain of someone talking about an infestation of rats in a neighboring building. "He lives right in the city."

So Vax wouldn't be traveling this time. That was a bit disappointing, but he'd live. Journalist...what, had Lumero written something online that offended Atali? It seemed like overkill to Vax. Not that his opinion counted for anything, though.

"He's also the son of Lin Zhao Lumero, the current head of Meridian, Inc. Though he's been estranged from his family for a few years, due to his decision to become a justice crusader."

"Wait, the son of Meridian's CEO?" Vax echoed. Meridian might have been Cyrex's biggest competitor, but he didn't think Atali was reckless enough to order a hit against its CEO's son.

"Yes." Atali's lips thinned into a displeased line. "Unfortunate that he has such a prominent connection, but it can't be helped."

Oh. So this wasn't directly related to inter-corporation politics. Still... "How estranged are we talking about? This sounds like it could bring down a lot of heat."

"Do your job correctly, and that won't be an issue," Atali said, his voice turning icy.

Vax flinched at his tone and dropped his gaze. "Yes, sir."

"Ambush him in his apartment. Make it look like a home invasion gone wrong."

That was a first...and this assignment was sounding worse by the minute. "That doesn't sound like a good idea."

"Did I ask for your input?"

"No, sir," Vax muttered, "but you got it anyway."

Atali gave him a cool look. That was as much as Vax dared to push him.

"After you take care of him, take his computer, pod, anything he might've stored his information on, and destroy them somewhere far from his apartment, so no one can retrieve the information."

Because Atali was genuinely afraid of what Lumero had found, or because he thought it would divert attention from the murder? In any case, Vax wasn't being paid to care. He picked up the microdrive with Lumero's information from the desk and slipped it into his pocket.

"How soon do you need it done?"

"By the end of the week."

Vax tried not to look too disappointed. For a journalist with presumably minimal security, it was doable, though he would've liked more time. "Okay," he said.

"So," Atali said, in a pleasant tone now, "how have you been? Do anything fun lately?"

"No, sir." Vax stuffed his hands into his jacket pockets. He'd hoped the conversation would be strictly business; now he was stuck trying to figure out the least offensive thing to say that would allow him to exit.

"It's been a while. We should catch up once you've taken care of Lumero."

A wave of dread swept through Vax. He kept his eyes fixed on his shoes, trying to breathe through his nose, clenching his trembling hands in his pockets. *No, I'm fine not catching up. Really.*

He was aware of Atali slowly circling toward him, all of his senses instantly snapping alert as soon as Atali crossed an invisible threshold from *close* to *too close*. Without warning, Atali grabbed his chin and jerked it up and to the side, forcing him to meet his gaze. Vax winced at the sharp movement and the way Atali's thumb dug into his jaw, hard enough to bruise, his skin crawling at the unwanted contact.

"You're supposed to look at someone's eyes when they're talking to you."

"Yes, sir," he answered in a flat tone, struggling not to let his gaze slide away. He didn't want to make things worse, even though Atali's eyes were cold scalpels, flaying and dissecting him into pieces of pulpy flesh.

Atali held his jaw for a moment longer before releasing it. "Don't screw this up," he said, his voice cool and clipped with dismissal.

Vax exhaled, rubbing at where Atali had grabbed him. He could still feel the lingering pressure, like phantom fingerprints left behind on his jawbone.

"Yes, sir." He left as quickly as he could.

ZAI LUMERO HAD an uneventful life. Usually, he left his apartment in the morning, spent several hours at a café typing on his tablet—working remotely on articles for the *Voice*, Vax assumed—and occasionally went back to his apartment for a few hours at a time to make private calls. He broke for dinner at one of various hole-in-the-wall restaurants before heading back home, and then he spent the rest of the night typing on his tablet—still working?—before he went to sleep around eleven-o'-clock.

Very uneventful.

Also, Lumero either liked solitude, was a complete workaholic, or was lonely. He lived by himself, ate his meals by himself, didn't hit the bar or a club or anything at night, and never seemed to receive any visitors. It wasn't what Vax expected, considering that Zai always chatted with the café baristas with a bright, friendly smile. Well, at least there would be less of a problem with potential witnesses. Even better was the fact that Lumero didn't seem to have a home security system, as far as Vax could tell using the long-range scanner in his augment.

A day before his one-week deadline was up, Vax slipped into Lumero's apartment building in the afternoon, after

Lumero had left for lunch. He took care to keep his face turned away from the surveillance cameras. The lock on Lumero's door was standard, and it didn't take long to deactivate it with a lock decryptor and open the door. Since he had a few hours to kill before Lumero came home, based on his usual pattern, Vax took a quick look around.

Lumero's apartment appeared fairly new, with wallscreens that shifted between relaxing panoramas of beaches, jungle, and underwater scenery, and while not huge, it was larger than where Vax lived. It had comfortable furniture, but otherwise it looked sparse. There wasn't much in the way of decoration or obvious luxury, and there weren't many pictures of Lumero or his friends or family members, making the apartment feel strangely depersonalized.

There was only one digital picture frame, and it sat on top of Lumero's nightstand, probably of his family or friends. Vax avoided looking too closely.

You're just here to do a job.

A simple, ordinary job. He'd run through it a dozen times already in his head. Wait until Lumero returned home, and then take him out. Simple. He'd escape via the roof, go back to Cyrex, make his report, collect his paycheck, and hopefully be left alone for a while.

He settled behind the sofa, making sure he would be outside of Lumero's line of sight once he returned, and waited.

Outside the window, the sun slowly sank, bruising the sky red before it deepened to violet. Shadows bathed the apartment, though it wasn't a problem for Vax with his night-vision-enabled ocular bioaugs. He had plenty of time to check and double-check that his silenced gun was loaded and ready, to let any remaining nerves blur into the smoggy haze of minutes blending into each other as his gloved fingers ran absently over the gun. Nerves. He used to wonder whether they meant he was a poor assassin, but eventually he decided they meant he really didn't want to get caught—or see Atali's reaction if he failed.

He snapped alert when he heard a soft beep and a click as the front door opened. Zai Lumero stepped inside, shoulders sagging a little as he dropped his messenger bag on the ground with a *thump*, went to the fridge, and grabbed a bottle of something, all without noticing Vax was there.

Everything was lined up. He pointed his gun directly at Lumero's head, inhaled, and then pulled the trigger.

Lumero chose *just that second* to abruptly slump forward, dropping his head.

Fuck.

Lumero jumped as the bullet thudded into a wall. Vax readjusted and pulled the trigger again—

Lumero hit the ground, one hand to his ear, barking a command—

—and in the fraction of a second before Vax finished pulling the trigger, the lights came on and blinded him. His hand jerked. He didn't hear Lumero cry out, which meant he'd missed.

Again.

Before he could blink the colorful spots away from his vision, Lumero tackled him to the ground, trying to wrestle the gun from his hand—

Lumero's grip suddenly went slack.

"*Ethan?*" Lumero breathed, in a voice strangled with shock.

Vax wrenched his gun back, finger on the trigger, his hand moving to aim in the direction of Lumero's voice before his brain had a chance to process. *Ethan? Who the hell is...?*

He caught a flicker of movement out of the corner of his eye. Everything went white with blinding, agonizing pain, and—

—then—

Nothing.

Chapter Two

COLORS.

Indistinct shapes.

Light, and darkness.

Noise.

Silence.

There was...something. Something warm. But when he tried to grab it, it slipped through his fingers.

No, no, don't go, please—

And then—what? What was it? He couldn't remember.

Darkness.

Silence.

WARMTH.

"I want to marry you," someone murmured into his ear. Who? He didn't know. Soft fingers trailed down his throat, not to hurt him, just to touch him.

Laughter. *"Let's make it through graduation first."* Was that him? Was that him talking, laughing?

Everything was so fuzzy, so indistinct. The more he tried to make out the details, the more everything blurred and faded away from him.

No, please.

Don't go.

Please.

Then—
And then—nothing.
Darkness.
Silence.

CONSCIOUSNESS RETURNED TO Vax in pieces.

First he felt the pain, his head throbbing as though a tank had rolled over him. He was a floating, disembodied mass of agony. Slowly, he became aware of the rest of his body, every muscle stiff. He was lying on...something slightly softer than hard floor. A rug? He couldn't move his arms; his wrists were bound with something that felt like duct tape.

This wasn't good.

He heard footsteps approaching. Someone kneeled beside him. A voice sounded from far away, resolving into words. "Take it easy."

Vax's muscles seized up as he tried to move. He forced his eyes open. Something was wrong with his vision—everything was fuzzy, doubled, with weird splotches of color everywhere. He blinked hard. When his eyes adjusted, he could make out Zai Lumero's face above him. Too close.

"Get away from me," Vax snapped, trying to drown out the loud, terrified staccato of his heartbeat.

Zai recoiled, as though Vax's words had affected him. Vax awkwardly shuffled away from him, but his movements were clumsy and uncoordinated, his muscles still not entirely under his control. He hit something solid—the couch—and he reached up to try to pull himself into a sitting position with his bound wrists, breathing hard from the effort and adrenaline.

The entire time, Zai had stayed silent, watching him. Vax wished he would stop. God, his head hurt.

"What did you do to me?" Vax rasped. It was an effort to talk.

Zai took a slow breath. A minimal-sized copper-colored augment, matching his skin, traced his temple. A mixture of emotions flickered across his face, but Vax couldn't identify any of them.

"Electrical disruptor. I was aiming for your chest, but went too high. Though I don't know how it knocked you out, unless..." Zai's eyebrows drew together. "You have a neural implant that short-circuited?"

Vax frowned. Short-circuited...he hoped it hadn't been permanently damaged. And an electrical disruptor was an oddly specific weapon for a journalist to have. "How do you have something like that?"

Zai didn't answer. His fingers kept fidgeting in his lap. Now that Vax was looking at him, he noticed Zai seemed strangely lost.

"Who..." Zai swallowed hard. "Who are you?"

"I'm the mailman," he said, his voice heavy with sarcasm.

Zai stared at him. He was *definitely* slow to catch on to the obvious. Maybe it was the shock of being face-to-face with an assassin. But...he'd reacted with unexpected quickness when Vax had fired at him. Something wasn't adding up.

"You tried to kill me," Zai said, sounding dazed.

"It wasn't personal."

Zai frowned deeply. "But...you know who I am?"

Vax wasn't sure where the question was going. *Uh, yeah. That's how an assassination works.* "You're Zai Lumero. You write for the *Daily Voice*."

Zai rocked back on his heels, his expression oddly conflicted. Vax was starting to wonder if he had sustained some sort of concussion during their scuffle.

"Did Cyrex hire you?" Zai finally asked.

Vax narrowed his eyes. *How did he...?* "Why would you think that?"

"I've been digging up information on Cyrex that I guessed would attract the wrong kind of attention sooner or later."

It was probably too late for him to deny anything, then. Though it would only be a problem that Zai knew if he lived long enough to report it to anyone.

"If we're playing twenty questions," Vax went on, "then it's my turn. Why am I not in a jail cell yet?"

Another long, unnerving silence before Zai answered.

"I...wanted to talk to you."

Vax blinked, perplexed. "Why?" Zai had already guessed—correctly—who had sent Vax.

Zai looked at him, his lips pressed tightly together, and glanced away again.

"What's your name?" Zai's voice was so quiet it was barely a whisper.

Vax frowned. "You honestly expect me to answer that?"

Zai cringed. He seemed awfully sensitive for an investigative journalist.

"Please," he said, still in that same quiet, small voice. "I...I need to know."

He looked and sounded shell-shocked, which wasn't *that* strange given the circumstances, and yet...his behavior, the way he kept staring at Vax and then turning away, struck Vax as odd compared to the way Vax had observed him interacting with other people over the past week.

"Sorry, but I'm not telling you," Vax said.

Zai exhaled, his shoulders sagging. "Where are you...where are you from?"

Was this his journalistic instincts emerging at the strangest time possible, or had he completely lost his mind?

"*Fuck off* city. Why do you care?"

Zai jumped, an expression of shock flitting across his face. At Vax's language? That seemed...weird.

"I..." Zai's gaze slid away. "Just curious."

Vax looked at him. There was a strain in his voice. Vax couldn't shake the feeling that there was some reason for his odd, twitchy behavior other than discomfort because Vax had just tried to kill him. But...what?

"Who's Ethan?" Vax asked.

He thought he'd kept his tone casual, but Zai reacted as though he'd been stung by a giant wasp.

"No—no one." Before Vax could point out that he was a stunningly terrible liar, Zai swallowed hard and ground out, "He's...someone who died."

Oh?

"Why'd you call me by his name?" Vax went on.

Zai was silent for a long while. "It was...a mistake," he finally said.

Okay...

No other answer was forthcoming, but as curious as Vax was, he had other problems to deal with. He moved his wrists, trying to tug against the duct tape. No luck. He had a knife in his boot—assuming Zai hadn't found it and taken it away, but he didn't want to think about that—though it probably wouldn't saw through the tape that well, and besides, it was too big for him to use with his bound hands without stabbing himself.

"Are you going to keep me here forever?" he asked, his voice sharp.

Zai looked stunned for a second, as though he'd somehow completely forgotten about the duct tape.

"If I release you," he said slowly, "would you still try to kill me?"

"I told you, it's not personal."

Zai looked down. "That's funny. It feels *very* personal." He shook his head, seemingly at himself, and went on. "Listen. I don't know how much money Cyrex promised you—though I'm guessing it's more than my current bank savings—but they've gone without any sort of accountability for too long. They don't care whose lives they ruin as long as it helps their bottom line. But if you let me go, I can let the world know what they've been doing and stop them from hurting more people."

Zai was persuasive, Vax gave him that much. Still, that was thinking as though he had a choice. He didn't.

"Yeah, sorry. I answer only to Cyrex."

Zai winced as though Vax had stabbed him in the lung. "Kill me, and you won't find out where I've hidden all the backup copies of everything I've found, which will pass into the hands of my coworkers if I end up dead."

Vax paused...but technically, Atali hadn't said anything about *make sure Lumero's story doesn't run*. All he'd said was to kill Zai and destroy his personal computer. No way did Vax care enough to track down backup copies.

"I don't give a fuck about that either. All I'm being paid for is to kill you. If your story runs, that's Cyrex's problem, not mine."

Zai's eyes widened and then narrowed thoughtfully. "Well, that seems...counterproductive."

"Like I said, not my problem."

He studied the silver tape, turning his wrists around so he could see the other side. Where was... *Ah.* By holding his wrists awkwardly next to his face, he could just reach the edge of the tape with his teeth. He bit down, trying to pry the edge up and doing his best to ignore the awful taste of the tape.

"Hey—" Zai's voice became tense. "Don't—"

Vax let go of the duct tape for a second. "I have to kill you. It's not my decision."

Zai's face had a gray tinge, as though he was going to be sick. His hand darted to his pocket. "If you keep going, I'll—I'll zap you again."

Vax clenched his jaw, but he didn't have a choice. Failure was not an option. Though if he did fail and Atali wanted to blame him, Vax would simply say he had no idea Zai could knock out his neural. Totally not his fault.

Right, because that conversation's going to go over so *well,* he told himself sourly.

"And I'll wake up an hour later, and we'll have another chat?"

Zai's eyebrows drew together. "I really don't want to do this, but I can't—" He made a choked sound. "I can't—let you kill me."

"Sorry," was all Vax could say. *I'm not allowed to fail.* He started to move, even as he saw Zai's hand slip into his pocket.

White—

Darkness.

WHEN VAX WOKE again, with another pulsing headache and cramped muscles, his first thought was *This is really getting old.*

He was still in Zai Lumero's apartment, but light streamed into the room. Morning already? Though Zai himself was nowhere to be seen.

It took some time for his muscle control to return and for the pounding in his head to subside, and then it took more time to work the duct tape off his wrists with his teeth, the taste nearly making him throw up. At least he hadn't dreamed this time, though. He could still feel the melancholic ache in his chest from that damned recurring dream that wouldn't leave him alone. When he was done, Vax got to his feet and made a quick tour through the apartment. It looked as though a bunch of clothes were missing from the bedroom closet.

Vax sighed. *Great. Just great.*

The other problem he noticed was that his gun was gone—Zai must've taken it to try to hinder him. But he still had his knife, and buying a replacement gun online in a hurry shouldn't be too big of a problem. Not compared to the fact that Zai had fled, with at least several hours' head start.

He left the bedroom and sat down heavily on Zai's couch, rubbing his face. No way was he going to tell Atali about this. If luck was on his side, maybe he could find Zai and fix his mistake before Atali realized what had happened...

Yeah, right. Who was he kidding? There was no way he could locate Zai within a day, and by tomorrow, when he didn't report in, Atali would know something was up. Besides, for all he knew, maybe Zai had hightailed it out of the city—or the state, or even the country. Which is what any sane person would do if they'd just escaped an assassination attempt. In that case, Vax would never be able to find him...certainly not without Atali's help. Fear and dread churned in his stomach.

Stop it. Think positive. No use panicking until you're sure Zai Lumero isn't still in Orphis City.

Not that he was good at thinking positive even at the best of times.

Shaking his head, Vax tried to think of where Zai might have gone. He knew the various cafés and restaurants Zai frequented, so that was a start...only if Zai was unaware enough not to realize that those places might not be safe for him anymore.

Would Zai go to a family member or friend? Probably...unless he thought doing so would put the people he cared about in danger. Though, judging from the past week's surveillance, Zai didn't have any friends he saw in person frequently. He did have two younger sisters, Vax remembered from Atali's information. In any case, Vax had to begin somewhere.

Just as he'd started pulling up information on Zai's sisters on the internet, his node rang, making him jump and almost drop his pod. Atali was calling him? But...why? He couldn't know already...it wasn't possible.

With a trembling finger, Vax pressed his node to answer. "Y...yes?"

"I see you've taken a detour on your assignment."

The words were polite enough, but Atali's voice was cold enough to freeze the sun.

Vax swallowed hard, his mouth dry. "I...how did you...?"

"Zai Lumero just called HR and left a charming message. I don't suppose you want to know what he said."

It wasn't a question; Vax didn't have time to respond before he heard a recording of Zai's voice played back into his node.

"Yes, I would like to leave a complaint. I'd give Cyrex a zero out of ten for customer satisfaction for the totally unwanted assassination attempt. I don't know who

ordered the hit, but I will find out. I want you to know that I'm not afraid of you, or of any other criminal Cyrex sends after me. And if you're covering up something illegal, the truth will come out eventually. I can promise you that."

Vax sat back in shock. That was...a brazen message to leave. Not at all what he would've expected after seeing how shell-shocked Zai had been. Had something changed?

"So," Atali said, interrupting his thoughts, "explain to me how you managed to screw up *this* badly."

Vax flinched. "Look, I'm sorry—"

"I don't want *apologies*, Vax."

Vax closed his eyes and tried to take a deep breath. "He—he was able to knock me out via my neural. I didn't know he had access to disruptor tech. It wasn't my fault."

He expected a surprised silence, but Atali didn't even pause for a second before he replied. "Of course it was your fault. You had one task. *One.*"

Yeah, and by the way, I'm totally fine, not like my brain was fried or anything. Thanks for not asking, Vax thought.

"I'm sorry, okay? The point is, he's gone now—"

"Then find him."

"How?" said Vax, incredulous. "And even if I could, he'd just knock me out again."

"Do I have to spell everything out for you?" Atali's voice dripped with contempt. "Make sure he doesn't see you coming. Take the disruptor away from him. What am I paying you for if you can't overpower a journalist?"

Vax cringed. "I...got it, sir." He tried to take a breath. "Ah...should I come in to make sure the neural hasn't been damaged?"

"Unless you notice any symptoms, finish your assignment first."

Um...okay, then. "But...Zai Lumero could've left the state by now. Or even be on a plane headed out of the country."

"A journalist working on a story is like a dog with a bone. He's not going to leave the city."

"Okay..." That was assuming Zai valued his job more than his life, which was questionable, but Vax didn't have any better ideas. "That doesn't exactly narrow it down too much..."

"Since you are apparently so incompetent at your job," Atali said, with venom in his voice, not bothering to acknowledge the fact that Vax had never had to track down an escaped target before, "I had someone triangulate the origin of the call. If you're unlucky, he may have already left, but in any case, finding him is *your* problem. Find him. Kill him."

"Yes, sir."

Atali went on, "It has also come to my attention that Lumero has copies of his research that will pass into the hands of his colleagues if he dies. Make sure to get the access information to his copies and delete them before you kill him."

Vax blinked. "Uh...how did you find out about this just now?"

"Do you need to know in order to finish your job?"

"No, sir," Vax said, reluctantly. "But...Lumero's not going to just tell me his access information."

"Then beat it out of him."

The sour taste of bile rose to the back of his throat.

"No. We've been over this before. I'm not going to do that. Besides, it's probably not even going to work—"

"I don't care *what* you do, Vax. Just make sure his story doesn't run. If you don't, I will be very, very unhappy when you return. Oh, and if Lumero has reported you to the police, don't expect any help from me."

The call ended. Vax sank back on Zai's couch, rubbing his temples.

Something wasn't right.

It could have been a total coincidence that Atali learned of Zai's cloud drive around the same time Vax had...yet the timing made it seem as though he'd heard what Zai had told Vax earlier. But how the hell was that possible?

Did Atali have someone else bug Zai's apartment?

He scanned the rooms with his augment, but he couldn't find a single thing. But then, how else could he be under surveillance?

He rubbed his eyes again. Great. *Another* problem for him to solve. Things just kept getting better and better.

VAX HATED DEALING with this much uncertainty.

The coordinates Atali messaged to him encompassed several square miles on the south side of the city. He had to assume that Zai was still in the area somewhere, even though that was a big assumption to make. Zai could be staying in one of the four hotels or two hostels in the area, or he could be staying with a friend, in which case Vax had no idea where he might be. There were twenty-six restaurants in the area and three local grocery stores, which was way too much to survey at once, and Zai could just order takeout for every meal for the next week.

It was probably too much to hope that Zai might be careless enough to post his location on social media. Not that Vax was able to access Zai's uSpace account anyway— he vaguely considered the probability that Zai would accept a friend request from him if he made a fake account in a hurry, before deciding that the timing would make it too suspicious. Still, Vax kept an eye out.

He settled on watching the two Javawocky cafés in the area, as he'd seen Zai frequenting a Javawocky café near his apartment. A nagging voice in the back of his head told him that this was a waste of time; he had no proof that Zai was here. But there was no way he could report back to Atali admitting he didn't have a clue where Zai could be, so he had to hope something would turn up.

He didn't expect to catch a glimpse of Zai actually walking into the Javawocky café he'd been watching after only a few hours.

Vax blinked from his table at a neighboring café, sure he was hallucinating out of desperation. But no; it really was Zai Lumero. He exhaled sharply with relief. Apparently the need for Javawocky coffee trumped any sense of danger.

Zai sat at one of the outside tables with his coffee, browsing his tablet as he sipped. He took quite a while to finish; either his cup was bottomless, or he was really savoring that coffee. When he finally left nearly an hour later, Vax got up from his own seat and tailed him. Several times, Zai stopped and looked around, as though he thought someone might be following him; Vax stayed at a distance, ducking behind street corners or pretending to study windowscreens. Judging by Zai's unhurried pace, he hadn't seemed to notice any danger. Eventually, Zai made his way to a tiny one-star hotel and vanished inside. Vax waited until he saw a light flicker on in one of the rooms on the first story, and then he made his way to the roof of the opposite building to watch the room until Zai went to sleep.

The rational voice in Vax's head told him he still needed to survey the entire building and devise an escape plan and a less risky entry plan. All he knew was that the building was old and the windows had electronic locks according to his augment scan. But the paranoid voice in his head told him he couldn't afford to lose eyes on Zai Lumero now, and the paranoid voice won.

There was another question, though. How was he supposed to get the information Atali wanted, when his persuasive skills were nil? He agonized over his options, playing out possible conversations in his head until the sky had long since gone dark and the lights finally went out in Zai's room.

Time's up. Better move.

He went to examine the windows—only to find the window to Zai's room was open by a crack. *Huh.* That was quite careless. He quietly opened the window further and slipped into the dark room, closing the window behind him.

"Don't move," Zai suddenly said. Vax slowly turned to see Zai pointing a gun at him—the same gun he'd taken from Vax last night.

Well, *this* was a problem.

Vax stayed still, thinking fast. Zai had been expecting him? But he'd been careful about tailing him. Or...was it the call, the visit to Javawocky, the open window...

"Did you *lure* me here?" he said, surprised.

Zai's mouth was set in a grim line. "We had some unfinished business."

Whatever that was supposed to mean. Vax noticed that Zai's hands were shaking violently, despite his apparent bravado. "I can shoot you before you shoot me, so why don't you put the gun down?"

"If that's true, then you would've shot already," Zai fired back.

Unfortunately, Vax had nothing to say against that. Not because he had been completely bluffing, but because he wasn't allowed to shoot first, ask later this time.

"I'm here to negotiate," he said, through his teeth. *Negotiate.* That was such a slimy euphemism for what he was there to do. Something Atali would say.

Why did he have to think of that? It made him nauseous.

"You haven't shot me either," Vax went on, trying to bury that thought. "So I'm assuming you want something, too? Whatever the 'unfinished business' is."

Zai's eyes narrowed. "You first. What are you here to...*negotiate* for?"

"Your backup copies."

"I thought you didn't care."

"New orders," he said through his teeth.

Zai regarded him for a long moment. When he spoke, his voice was guarded. "And what are you going to do if I refuse to tell you?"

That was what he was afraid of.

"You don't want to know," was all he said. "I'd rather keep things simple. Just tell me where they are—"

"And then you'll kill me anyway, right?"

The sheer scorn in Zai's voice took him aback. This was not the same twitchy, uncertain young man he'd talked to the night before. Something had happened...or maybe Zai had adjusted to his new reality of being hunted by an assassin in record time.

Vax considered lying. *No, of course not. If you tell me they are, I'll let you live.* But he was pretty sure Zai wouldn't fall for that, even if he hadn't been a terrible liar to begin with.

"There are worse things than death that can happen to you," Vax replied. Damn it, he was not at all made for intimidation.

"Oh, yeah?" Zai didn't look at all afraid; if anything; he sounded even more incensed. "I'm starting to believe that."

Vax felt his eyebrows draw together. What the hell did *that* mean?

"How about this," Zai suddenly said. "I'll give you what you want if you tell me what *I* want to know."

Vax tried not to let his surprise show. This was a wildly unbalanced bargain, and Zai had to know it. He had to be playing some sort of mind game. Maybe he was stalling for time?

"I don't believe you," he said.

Zai gritted his teeth. "My backups are on AlphaDrive, account number 804520."

"Okay," said Vax. "Still don't believe you. And even if you're telling the truth, that means nothing to me without a password."

"If I tell you everything now, you're just going to kill me. I'll tell you the password after *you* talk."

Vax still didn't believe him, but he was starting to get desperate enough that he supposed he might as well hear Zai out.

"What do you want to know?" he asked, in a wary voice.

"I want to know about you."

"Me?" Vax would've chuckled with disbelief if Zai's expression hadn't been dead serious. "We've been over this already. For all I know, you're recording this conversation right now so you can send it to the police."

"I'm not." Zai carefully took one hand off the gun to pluck his nodes from his ears and jam them into his pants pockets. "I'm not wearing a hidden camera or recorder, either. I can strip down if you want to confirm for yourself."

"Uh." Vax blinked, momentarily distracted by the mental image of Zai taking his shirt off. He shook his head. "Say I believe you. If you're not trying to have me arrested, why are you so curious?"

"Because—"

The window suddenly shattered with a hail of gunfire.

Vax instinctively dropped to the ground—just as he saw Zai lunge toward him, and a brief moment of fear flashed through him as he realized he couldn't get away from the bullets *and* Zai at the same time—

He crashed into the ground behind the hotel room couch, with Zai on top of him, just as a spray of bullets thudded into the wall behind them.

Zai's dark eyes were intent on him. "Are you okay?" he asked.

Vax shoved him away before he abruptly realized that Zai had tried to push him out of the way of the bullets.

Except that made *no sense.*

"Why did you do that?" he rasped.

Zai's expression changed. He glanced at the bullet holes in the wall. "Better question: what the hell was that?"

Better question, indeed. Vax's mind raced. The bullets would've hit them both, so the shooter couldn't have been friendly to Zai. Did Zai have other enemies, and Vax happened to be acceptable collateral to the shooter?

Except what were the odds that someone else wanted Zai dead at this moment? They had to be pretty damn low.

Or...was the shooter *trying* to take both of them out? But that would mean...

"We need to get out of here," he said, half to himself. Those shots had probably drawn the attention of everyone in the entire hotel by now.

"Yeah, no kidding," Zai responded.

Vax couldn't escape through the window, or through the front entrance. He lunged for the door, ducking as he heard another gunshot. He managed to get the door open, and he waited for Zai to sprint through before he followed.

Some hotel guests and staff were already milling through the hall in a panic. Vax pushed past them, following Zai to the back of the building. Zai shoved the emergency door open. A shrill siren split the air, making Vax wince.

Zai took off in the opposite direction of where the bullets had come from. Vax ran after him, following Zai through the streets and up the stairs to a sky rail station where—by chance—a train was just pulling up, nearly empty at this hour of the night. He saw Zai enter a vacant car, and Vax darted toward the same car, slipping through the doors just before they closed. He grabbed the pole near where Zai had sat down as the train began to move.

Vax paused for a minute to catch his breath and collect his thoughts. He wanted so badly to believe the shooter had been some unrelated third party—maybe Zai was a really inflammatory journalist—yet the insistently rational voice in his head told him the odds of such a coincidence were miniscule. But if the shooter had been sent eliminate Vax along with Zai, that could only mean one thing—something Vax didn't want to believe.

What also bothered him was how public the whole thing had been. The shooter hadn't waited to get them on a deserted street. And how the hell had they been tracked? Had Vax been so focused on his target that he'd failed to notice he was being tailed as well?

Zai was trying to inch away. Vax drew his gun. "Don't move."

"Oh, for—" Zai reached into his pocket, his expression changing as he seemed to realize he'd forgotten his gun in the hotel room. "Two assassins after me in two days," he muttered to himself. "I didn't think my karma was *that* horrible." He held his hands up. "If I were you, I'd be more worried about whoever shot at you. Maybe it was Cyrex."

That was exactly the conclusion Vax was trying to avoid.

"Why would they shoot me *before* I finished the job?" he countered.

"I don't know, but I'd think a corporation sleazy enough to hire an assassin in the first place wouldn't think twice about double-crossing him."

Vax gritted his teeth. If that was true...well, it was his policy not to kill people if there was no paycheck involved. But he also knew that Zai was probably trying to talk himself out of the situation.

Still...

The train abruptly slowed, pitching Vax forward. He heard glass shatter, pain blazing a line across his left arm before he smashed into the floor.

"Hey!" Zai shouted. "*Hey!*"

The shriek of the wind rushing through the shattered window nearly drowned out Zai's voice. Swearing, Vax rolled over, his right hand going to the wound. It felt like a graze wound—bleeding, but not serious. The bullet had missed...barely.

"Still alive," he said, his mouth twisting as he raised his head to meet Zai's gaze. "Sorry to disappoint."

Except now it was clear: the shooter definitely wanted him dead.

"Okay," said Zai, who'd scrambled off his seat to crouch down on the floor. "Now, can you explain how the *hell* a sniper bullet found you on the train, *fifty feet off the ground*?"

That was the million-dollar question. Vax crawled to the side of the train and sat with his back to the wall, trying to get his breathing under control, trying to think.

How the hell did the shooter keep finding them? There was no way, even if the shooter saw them board a train and knew that train's route, the shooter could've had enough time to set up a sniper rifle and fire again. It made no sense, unless the assassin was able to track them remotely, somehow. But *how*?

Was there a tracker stuck to him?

He shrugged off his jacket and held it in front of him. "Scan mode: wireless transmitter, execute," he said, and scanned his jacket with his augment. He didn't see anything.

"What are you doing?" Zai asked.

"Making sure of something."

He turned his gaze to Zai. The scan swept over him, coming up clean.

Vax then inspected his pants, shirt, and shoes. He even physically patted himself down to cover the areas the scan couldn't reach. Still nothing. *Damn it.* He switched the scan off. He should've felt relieved, but he still couldn't shake the feeling that there had to be a tracker on him somewhere, or else nothing made sense...

Was it embedded in his body?

The thought sent a wave of nausea through him. He wished he could reject it out of hand—*No, there was no way Atali would do that*—but if it was true, that would mean...

Atali sent the shooter after him?

As punishment for his failure?

In a chilling way...it did make sense. He couldn't think of anyone else who could possibly want him dead—he only knew a handful of people, all Cyrex employees. And the only possible way for the shooter to have found him a second time was if the shooter could track him somehow, and he hadn't been tagged.

If the tracker *was* in his body...it had to be embedded either in his spine, in his brain, or in the augment next to his right eye. If it was in his spine or brain, he was fucked. He just had to trust that it would've been placed in a less complicated spot.

Vax reached down and unsheathed the knife from his boot. Zai's eyes widened—and then nearly bugged out of his head as Vax turned the knife toward his own head.

"Wait—what are you *doing*?"

"Just give me a sec." Damn, this would be easier with a mirror. Vax carefully felt around the side of his augment so he could slide the tip of the knife to the point where plastic joined skin.

At that moment, the train jolted again, and Vax nearly stabbed his own eye. He swore.

"No, seriously, what are you doing?" Zai insisted. "Whatever weird idea just popped into your head, could you save the blood and gore spectacle for later?"

Asking for help went against every instinct Vax had—*especially* from the guy he'd almost assassinated a day ago and who still had a grudge against him—but he didn't have any other choice if he wanted to remove the augment while keeping his eyes intact. And right now, the fear of having a tracker on him outweighed any other fear he had.

"I need your help," Vax said, through his teeth.

Zai blinked. "Excuse me?" he asked, as though he thought Vax were joking.

Vax pointed next to his right eye. "I need to get this augment out."

"Are you kidding me? Bioaugs need to be removed in a hospital, or else you could permanently injure yourself or even damage your nerves—"

"I think there might be a tracker in here," Vax cut in. "And if I don't get it out, I'm going to get my head blown off sooner or later. Now, can you help me or not?"

"Uh...okay?" He still sounded as though he thought Vax had lost his mind. That was fine. Vax just needed him to have steady enough hands to dig the augment out of him without making mincemeat out of his face.

Vax held the knife out to Zai, handle first. Zai stared at it.

"Just so you know," said Vax, "I can still subdue you even if you come at me with a knife."

Zai swallowed, approached him, and took the knife. Vax kept his back against the wall, his hands planted on the floor to keep himself steady. Zai leaned toward him. His face was close—close enough that Vax could see the dark smudges beneath his eyes and the stark red veins spiderwebbing across his sclera. He looked exhausted.

Light fingers prodded the side of his face, and Vax flinched. "Hurry up already."

"Okay, okay...you know, you should've at least sterilized—"

"Just *do it*!" he snapped.

The blade sank into his skin, and he grunted, screwing his eyes shut. He felt the bite of pain, but he felt the augment give way, too, bit by bit.

"Got it," Zai said.

Thank God. Vax exhaled and held his palm up. "Give it to me."

"Wait." Zai flipped the augment over, peering at the interior. "If there *is* a tracker in here...huh." Zai's eyes widened. "That *does* kind of look like a Cyrex-model GPS chip..."

"Okay, that's great, now give it to me so I can get rid of it—"

"Wait a second, is that...?" Zai's brow furrowed. "Weird. I wouldn't have expected a microcamera module in here too, based on the exterior..."

Vax stared at him. "*What*?"

He grabbed the blood-slicked augment from Zai's hands, along with his knife, and stared at it. Except, to him, the interior just looked like an incomprehensible collection of circuits and machinery.

No. There couldn't be a camera. Atali had never told him there was a camera function...

Figure that out later! Just get rid of it before the sniper shoots again!

Vax roughly wiped the blood off with the hem of his jacket, and then he drew his arm back and hurled the augment out the shattered window.

"Now what?" Zai asked.

Vax slipped his knife back into its sheath and jerked his thumb behind him. "Keep your head down and get in the next car."

They scooted along the floor, broken bits of glass crunching underfoot. Vax heaved the door shut behind them, cutting off the howling wind, and his ears rang in the sudden quiet.

Gunshots pierced the silence, making Vax flatten himself against the floor—though the sounds came from below their feet, beneath the sky rail.

So the shooter had been aiming at his augment after all. Vax exhaled, dragging himself to the wall and slumping against it. Now, hopefully, he was off their radar.

The elated relief soon wore off, and Vax looked at Zai across the car, realizing Zai was looking back at him warily.

"Are you going to try to shoot me again?" Zai said.

Vax heaved an exasperated sigh. "If I was, you'd be dead already. There's no point now."

Zai's eyes narrowed. "So you'll only kill people if you get paid for it?"

"Something like that."

Zai's eyes flicked to his face, then away. Again, that same pattern.

"Why did you try to push me away from the bullets?" Vax asked him.

"I—" Zai's mouth tightened. "It was...instinct. I wasn't thinking."

It sounded possible, if altruistic of him, but something in Zai's expression—the way he seemed as though he were swallowing some emotion—made Vax wonder if there was something else to it.

"Don't think too much of it," Zai went on. "Considering what you do—and what you *tried* to do—I wouldn't have lost any sleep if that shooter had succeeded."

"Uh-huh. You know, a simple 'you're welcome' would've been fine," said Vax.

Zai glared at him, but only briefly before looking away. Vax looked away as well—out the windows, at the buildings and screens flashing by.

Now what?

He hadn't had time to reflect on everything that was happening while they were escaping, but now he'd had a chance to catch his breath, to confront the fact that Atali wanted him dead.

After everything Vax had done for him, Atali wanted him dead.

He felt...betrayed. Not in a shocked, outraged way, but in a tired, disappointed way. Atali had warned him that if Vax screwed up, he would throw him under the bus, but Vax had been trying to fix his mistake. He could've fixed it. It wasn't fair to try to kill him before he'd fixed things.

Though when has Atali ever been fair?

Now he was on the run for his life, sitting across the train from the man he'd tried to kill, who kept staring at him when he thought Vax wasn't looking, and he had no idea what he was supposed to do next.

Stay alive. That was a reasonable goal. But to do that, he'd have to leave Orphis City, the closest thing he had to a home—and even then, Cyrex had global resources. Vax wasn't confident enough to bet he could stay out of Cyrex's crosshairs forever, and there was little chance Atali would rest until he was found.

And even if he could stay under the radar...what would he do? He had no idea.

"Let me see if I've got this right," Zai suddenly said. "Whoever shot at us...was tracking you through your bioaug, which came from Cyrex, which means they're also working for Cyrex?"

"Yes," said Vax.

"Meaning you've been replaced, and Cyrex has turned on you."

"Yes, thank you for stating the obvious," said Vax, sarcastically.

"You seem pretty calm for someone who was nearly killed by your own employer. Or are all assassins used to living with that risk?"

Vax glanced at him. Calm? Not really. More like he was numb after running on adrenaline for so long. "You're pretty calm, too, all things considered."

"Yeah, well...my life got a whole lot stranger when you showed up. Guess I'm still in shock." Though Zai sounded more deadpan than shocked. His eyes drifted to a spot to the side of Vax's head. "Is that going to be okay?"

"What?" Vax remembered he was bleeding from where Zai had excised his augment. "Oh, um...yeah," he said, slightly disoriented by the question. "I've got a healing augment."

"Figures," said Zai, his eyes narrowing.

"What figures?" Vax asked, not understanding his reaction.

"That an assassin would have an expensive bioaug that makes it harder for people to kill him."

Vax decided not to respond to Zai's goading tone. The night had been exhausting enough.

"If you want to not die, you should probably leave the city and lay low for a while," Vax offered after a moment of silence.

"What, you're giving me survival advice now?" Zai said, incredulous. "In any case, I can't. I've got to find out what Cyrex is hiding."

Vax hesitated, and then shrugged. "It's your death warrant." The sky rail slowed as it approached a station, and he got to his feet, clutching the train pole and debating with himself whether to get off here.

"Wait."

He turned back to give Zai a questioning glance. "What?"

"I—"

Zai met his gaze and abruptly looked away again, swallowing whatever he wanted to say. Why the hell was this guy so twitchy?

"I might...need your help." Zai spoke as though a dentist was in the middle of yanking a tooth out of his mouth.

Vax blinked at him, sure he'd misunderstood. "Come again?"

Zai blew out a breath. "Look, Cyrex isn't going to stop trying to kill us, so the only way to make sure neither of us ends up 'disappeared' is to strike back at them."

"How? By killing Atali Norman?" Vax tried not to let on how much that idea rattled him.

Zai's lip curled. "*No*. Unlike some people, *I* don't advocate murder."

"That's great for you, but if that's the case, then what are you suggesting?"

"Help me stay alive long enough to uncover whatever Cyrex's big dark secret is and expose it to the world. It'll shake up the management and put Cyrex under so much scrutiny, there's no way they can keep hiring assassins under the table."

"So...what, you're asking me to be your...bodyguard?" He couldn't quite believe Zai was suggesting this after having made his dislike for Vax clear. Guarding a nest of angry wasps would probably be more pleasant.

Zai's mouth twisted, as though he'd just tasted something sour.

"For the record, I hate having to depend on a professional killer as much as you hate having to depend on me, but we don't have much of a choice here. My odds of surviving by myself against whoever Cyrex can buy the services of are not great, and you'll have a target on your back for at least as long as Cyrex is operational."

Vax opened his mouth to argue that what Zai was proposing was ridiculous, but he couldn't find a loophole in Zai's logic. He closed his mouth and gritted his teeth.

"How do I know you won't sell me out to Cyrex in exchange for a guarantee of your safety?"

Zai stared at him. Then he burst into sharp, humorless laughter.

"What?" Vax asked. "What's so funny?"

"Wow. Just...wow." Zai wiped at his eyes. "You know I didn't even think of that until you brought it up?"

Vax silently swore to himself.

"Anyway, to answer your question: One, I wouldn't trust anything Cyrex says. They could sign a document promising I'd be safe in exchange for whatever, and I could still end up with a bullet in my head the next day. I can't sue them for breach of contract if I'm dead. Nor do I want to spend the rest of my life paranoid that Cyrex will finally get me. And two, even though I don't like you, I'm not a completely heartless bastard, and I don't want to be responsible for your death."

Vax wasn't sure he believed the second part. The first part, though, sounded reasonable. "And...I'm just supposed to take you at your word?"

Zai rolled his eyes. "Of the two of us, *you're* the criminal, so...yes."

The sky rail came to a stop, the doors opening to the station. He could step out right at that moment. Walk away from Zai, from Cyrex and Atali and everything that had happened.

And...do what, exactly? He had no direction, no plan, and no clean credentials. Zai's offer at least bought him something to do, and some time to think about what to do next. And it would be a lie to say he wasn't interested in bringing Atali down.

The doors closed, and he exhaled.

"Fine," he said at last, meeting Zai's gaze. "I'll help you. As long as you're sure you can deliver."

"Oh, I will," Zai said through his teeth. "I'm not going to let an organization that hires *contract killers* get away from me."

It was clear that Zai didn't trust him. That was fine. All Vax needed was to see that Zai remained alive long enough to get Cyrex off his back. To get *Atali* off his back. And then, if he was lucky, he wouldn't have to see Zai Lumero ever again.

Part II

The Man Who Didn't Exist

Chapter Three

"WELCOME TO THE bunker," Zai said, as he opened the door to his new temporary living space.

Vax looked around. This apartment was considerably older and more cramped than Zai's last one, with a door that opened into a bedroom area that was just big enough for a bed and not much else. The furniture was minimal: a worn couch, a coffee table, a plastic square dining table, and two fold-out chairs. The dim, yellowish light revealed water stains blooming across the ceiling and weird splotches of color covering the carpet. The air smelled musty and stale.

"Nice taste," he said sarcastically.

"Thanks," Zai returned with equal sarcasm as he closed the door. "So, there's a bed and a couch..."

"I'll take the couch."

Zai raised an eyebrow. "Wow, I didn't expect you to be *that* polite."

Vax ignored the jab. "The couch is closer to the door. If someone breaks in, of the two of us, who do you think will be in a better position to do something?"

Zai held his hands up. "Hey, *I'm* not complaining." He went to the kitchen area and started opening cupboards. "You have any allergies? If you're vegetarian or vegan, or if you keep kosher or halal...well, I'm not saying you're totally screwed, but you'll probably get bored fast with the limited options. It's mostly frozen stuff, dried snacks, and self-heating meals here."

"I'm good, thanks," he replied. Halal? It wasn't the first time someone assumed he was Muslim, though it sounded more like Zai was just going through a laundry list of possible dietary restrictions. That was...considerate of him. "Remind me how you happened to have a safe house stocked with food just lying around, again?"

"It's not mine." Zai turned and tossed him a tub of self-heating instant noodles; he caught it. "I...called in a favor."

"A favor," Vax echoed, curious. "Like, a family connections favor?"

Zai glanced at him. "Nice guess, but...no. Hell, if my parents found out about what happened these past two days, they'd have me bundled off to some nuclear bomb shelter in the middle of Greenland or something before you can say 'Cyrex.'"

Vax raised his eyebrows. "I thought you weren't on good terms with them."

Zai gave him another, longer look. "What are you, a stalker?"

Vax blinked. "I was...told some things about you. I thought they were public knowledge."

Zai snorted. "Not exactly. I'm not *that* famous, thank God. And there's a difference between your parents being mad at you versus your parents being okay with their child getting murdered. I mean, unless your parents really suck."

Vax didn't have any experience with parents to compare that to, so he stayed quiet. After making sure his wounds were clean and healing properly, he sat at the table and dug into his beef-flavored noodles. He searched for the time in the corner of his vision before he remembered that he didn't have his augment anymore, which meant he'd have to look at his pod to check exactly which ungodly hour of the morning it was. This was going to take some getting used to.

It was only once he'd almost finished that he realized Zai was staring at him again from across the table. "What?"

Zai started and shook his head, as though rousing himself from a trance. "It's just...my life has taken a turn into complete and utter insanity. *You* showed up—" He broke off for a second, as though he was struggling with something, "—*and* you tried to kill me, and now we're eating instant noodles like it's no big deal."

"Well...enemy of my enemy, right?" Vax said.

"Right," Zai muttered.

"Besides, you were the one who wanted to talk to me at the hotel. You never finished answering why, by the way."

Zai twitched. He set his container down and, after a moment, said, "You were right. I...*was* trying to learn more about you, so I could later report you to the police. But I guess that's a moot point now."

Vax had thought as much, although... "It doesn't have anything to do with why you keep staring at me? Or...whoever 'Ethan' was?"

Zai jerked, violently. Whoever Ethan had been, he must have been important to Zai—but Vax couldn't tell if it was in a positive or negative way. Maybe he'd done something bad to Zai and that was why Zai seemed to hate Vax, on top of the fact that Vax had admittedly tried to kill him. Then again, Zai had tried to shield him from gunfire...

"He doesn't have anything to do with this," said Zai, his voice coldly hostile. "He's *dead*."

"All right," said Vax, frowning. He wasn't sure he believed him, but Zai clearly wasn't willing to talk about this Ethan guy.

Zai asked, "So, are you finally going to tell me your name? Or do I have to call you 'Hey you' the whole time?"

"It's Vax," Vax said.

Zai frowned. "Just...Vax?"

"You have a problem with that?"

"All right, then...*Vax*." Zai said his name as though he thought it was obviously code for something. "What's your real name?"

Vax bristled. "This isn't an interview."

"Hey, you know *my* name, so I think it's only fair that I know yours."

"That *is* my name," Vax protested.

Zai's eyes narrowed with skepticism.

"Fine," he said, though he sounded unconvinced. "Where are you really from?"

"The city," Vax said after a pause. That was the only answer he could really give. "Same as you."

"Born and raised, or...?"

"Does it matter?"

Their eyes met again. Zai's mouth tightened, but his expression was unreadable.

"Guess I shouldn't be surprised that getting information from a criminal is like wringing blood from a stone, right?"

Vax shrugged. Whatever would get Zai to stop asking for personal details.

"Okay, then..." Zai's voice turned cool. "How long have you been working as a contract killer?"

That question made Vax freeze.

"A while," he managed to say.

Zai rolled his eyes. "And we live on planet Earth. Could you be any more vague?"

"Why do you want to know?" Vax hedged.

"Besides general curiosity?" Zai eyed him. "You seem kind of...young to be a contract killer."

Vax considered that. "How old do you think I am?"

Zai seemed taken aback. "I don't know...twenty-something?"

"There's a big difference between twenty-one and twenty-nine."

"Well, how should I know?" When Vax didn't reply, Zai went on, "Fine...how old *are* you?"

"Blood from a stone, remember?" Vax said, through his teeth.

Zai glared at him. "Okay, fine, I give up. Happy?"

"Ecstatic," he said sarcastically.

"Just one more thing: how did you end up with a tracking chip in your bioaug?"

Ah. Now that was a question he wanted to know the answer to, as well.

"I don't know," he said, aware of how inadequate and ridiculous the truth sounded. His fingers tightened around his container. "If I'd known about it earlier, I would've removed it."

Zai gave him a dubious look. "How the hell could Cyrex have tagged you with a GPS tracker without you knowing?"

Well...there were ways, even if Vax didn't like any of them. The *how* didn't bother him so much as the *why.*

And what was up with that camera? What was the point of having a function he never used and never even saw any access to when he'd tinkered with the settings for his augment? Unless...

Sudden nausea surged through him. No. He refused to believe Atali had had him monitored. He would walk off a roof in horrified humiliation.

Zai's voice cut through his thoughts. "Were they planning on killing you off that early on?"

Vax stared at the remainder of his noodles swimming in beef broth. *Don't think about the camera. Don't think about the camera.* He tried to focus on Zai's question. "I...I really didn't think they wanted me dead." Though maybe Atali had decided it was more important to sever Cyrex from Zai's attempted murder than to keep his investment alive. He shuddered slightly.

"Really?" Zai sounded surprised and almost darkly amused. "The assassin didn't see the backstab coming? That's the last thing I would've expected."

Vax rubbed his forehead. "It's not the backstab that's surprising, it's—never mind."

"No, I want to hear this," Zai said, still sounding amused.

Vax narrowed his eyes, giving Zai a cool glare. Zai gazed back, undaunted. Finally, Vax said, "Not that it's any of your business, but I was paying off a debt to Cyrex. That's why I didn't think they would try to kill me—it's kind of a poor business strategy to kill off your debtors."

"You're in debt to Cyrex?" Zai looked surprised. "Wait, let me guess—it was in exchange for your bioaugs."

"No."

Zai looked skeptical. "Sure it wasn't. It's not like healing augments cost more than a neurosurgical procedure and neurals cost about five times that. Whatever you get paid for murdering people, it can't be *that* much."

Well...if Zai didn't want to believe him, there was probably nothing Vax could say that would convince him.

"Is that a common thing?" Zai asked. "Assassins having neurals? It kind of sounds like those conspiracy theories about criminals having black market cognition-enhancing implants might be on to something."

"If I had a cognition-enhancing implant, I wouldn't have been duped by my employer," said Vax, sourly. He sipped his noodle broth. "As for other people, I have no idea. I don't have much of a social life."

Zai's lips flattened into a thin line, but he didn't respond. He looked like he wanted to ask what Vax's neural was for, but had just enough tact not to do so. Which was fine. It was private anyway, and Vax didn't like remembering why he'd needed his neural and what it had failed to do.

Vax occupied himself with finishing the rest of his noodles, and silence fell. When he was done, he pushed the tub aside.

"So, I've got a question," he said.

Zai snorted. "You spend all this time avoiding *my* questions and now you want me to answer *your* question?"

"You can be spiteful and refuse to answer, if you want," he said, sardonically.

Zai poked around in his tub before setting it aside. "Fine, I'll hear you out. What's your question?"

"Why were you prepared for me when I was at your apartment?"

Zai's lips pursed. "'Prepared' is overselling it. Let's just say I've been going through a paranoid spell recently. I mean, I've been hounding every major bioaug company for product safety, safe working conditions, and labor violations for a while now, and pissed-off corporate managers can resort to making unpleasant threats, but these last few months I started to think at least one of those threats might not be a bluff. Assassination attempts weren't quite on my list of expected dangers, but..." Zai gave him a cool look. "Clearly my paranoia paid off."

Vax frowned to himself. "So...no one tipped you off or anything?"

"Uh, no. Otherwise I wouldn't have sat around waiting for you to show up and nearly blow my head off. Thanks for that, by the way," Zai added sarcastically. "I didn't need that traumatic experience in my life."

Vax gritted his teeth. "I told you, it wasn't personal."

"Like that makes a difference?"

Vax leaned back in his chair. He couldn't exactly fault Zai for still being upset with him.

"So...what is this information you've found that's pissed Cyrex off so bad they want you dead?"

Zai raised an eyebrow. "Oh, *now* you want to know."

"Well, since we're apparently stuck with each other for a while"—Vax didn't bother to try to hide the irritation in his voice—"*and* I think it's safe to say my employment prospects with Cyrex are fucked, yeah, color me curious."

"Fine." Zai took a deep breath. "I've been trying to get Cyrex ever since that foreign factory of theirs blew up four years ago, killing over a dozen people and injuring many more. There was strong evidence that unsafe working conditions were a major factor—because why would Cyrex care about the safety of foreign workers in a poor country that borders the war zone—but not a damn thing happened to Cyrex except that they had to pay a pathetically small fine, and not a penny of compensation money went to the victims or their families. They blamed the incident on a subsidiary, but c'mon, *everyone* knows Cyrex controls all aspects of their product manufacturing, subsidiaries or no. I was pretty sure a company like that had to have more shady dealings up its sleeve, but—and I hate to say this—Cyrex has been annoyingly good at covering their tracks. For a while, my editor thought I was on a wild goose chase. And then..."

"Then?"

"Last week, an accountant for Cyrex named Celia Duquette emailed me. She'd noticed some small discrepancies in the R&D budget for a while. I would've thought it was embezzlement, but she proposed to me that the missing funds were going into some kind of side project that had not been submitted to the Augmentation Regulatory Committee.”

Celia...the name sounded vaguely familiar to Vax. He didn't think he'd met her before, though.

“She came to me because of my background with bioaugs and Meridian, but her story sounded kind of out-there—she claimed Cyrex was developing bioaugs that could brainwash people.”

Vax blinked. “Really?” It sounded like the stuff of science fiction...or something Integrity, the leading anti-augmentation group, would use as proof that bioaugmentation as a whole was “evil.”

“Yeah, I know.” Zai shrugged. “Even for me, that was a bit much. I didn't believe her, but I promised I'd take a look at the evidence she claimed to have.” Zai eyed him. “And then you tried to kill me, which means at least *some* part of it has to be true after all.”

Way to go, Atali, Vax thought to himself. Not that he'd ever get a chance to gloat, though.

“What happened to the evidence?” he asked.

Zai produced a pod from his jacket and set it on the table. It projected images of nine faces in the air.

“These are, supposedly, nine individuals who were connected to the accounting irregularities.” He tapped his pod, and a few names and dates appeared below the photos. “I've been trying to figure out who these people were. Of the ones I managed to track down, they all seemed to be homeless, either without families or not in contact with them, before they disappeared some years ago. So far, I haven't been able to find anything else they have in common, other than the fact that they all look to be in their twenties or thirties.”

Vax studied the pictures. “So, what, these people received brainwashing neurals or something?”

"Or something. I mean, I still doubt that Celia could've been right about the purpose of the project."

"Okay, then. What's your next step?"

"Ideally? Find someone from this list who's willing to talk. These people *have* to be important somehow. I just don't know how." Zai switched off the projector and put his pod away. He sighed. "The problem is, I've been searching for over a week and I can't find anything about these people, other than what some of their names were. No clue if they're dead or alive—inquiries to the police didn't reveal anything. And here's another thing: the last person on this list disappeared over four years ago. Before that, people seemed to be disappearing sequentially within several months of each other. So, there are two possibilities: either Cyrex quit and is now trying to cover up any evidence that this program, or whatever it is, existed, or there have been more people who got sucked in that my contact wasn't aware of. The question is, which answer is the right one?" Zai leaned back. "Unfortunately it's kind of hard to figure out if there are more people who fit this profile, considering no one seems to care if homeless people go missing."

Vax considered what he said. "Sounds like you've got your work cut out for you."

Zai made a face. "Like I said, I was half convinced this was another dead end, until you showed up. I know now that I've got to be onto something, but I'm still no closer to finding any answers."

"What about the employee who contacted you?"

"She was fired, and then she...fell out of contact." Zai sighed. "I mean, sure, it was a mugging gone wrong, but the timing was suspicious enough that if I were a conspiracy theorist, I would've sworn it was some sort of hit—"

Zai stopped abruptly. It took Vax a moment to realize Zai was staring at him with narrowed eyes.

"No. No way," Zai breathed. "You *didn't*."

"What?"

Zai suddenly got to his feet and approached him, and Vax flung his hands out instinctively as his heart rate spiked, his muscles tensing, preparing to fight. Zai bumped against Vax's hands, but he barely seemed to notice, let alone care.

"You *bastard*," Zai spat. "You killed an innocent woman and orphaned her daughter? What the *fuck* is wrong with you?"

"I—what? I didn't kill her," Vax stammered, confused.

"Sure you didn't," said Zai, with sarcastic contempt. "Just like you didn't try to kill me, right?"

"This might shock you," said Vax, "but I'm probably not the only assassin who's ever worked in Orphis City."

"Even if that's true, you've killed plenty of people like her, haven't you?"

"What do you want me to say?" Vax said, exasperated, not knowing what Zai wanted from him. "I'm an assassin. You asked for my help. Why is any of this news to you?"

Zai shoved his hands back, looking hardly pacified. "Unbelievable. You're unbelievable," he seethed, and then stalked off.

Vax rubbed the back of his head. At this rate, it would be a miracle if the two of them didn't kill each other before Cyrex found them.

THE COUCH WAS so cramped that Vax could only fit on it if he curled up on his side, bent his knees, or let his legs dangle off the armrest. The cushions were uncomfortably hard, and the upholstery was distractingly coarse. Oh, well. It was probably still better than sleeping on the floor. He removed his nodes from his ears and left his handgun on the coffee table within easy reach before glancing at both the front door and the door to the bedroom. He'd probably be safe, regardless of where a threat might come from.

Despite his attempts to remain vigilant, along with the intermittent noises coming from elsewhere in the apartment building, exhaustion hit him like a black tidal wave, dragging him under into a restless sleep. He dreamed he was running, surrounded by gunfire, the constant whir of flying drones, the acrid smell of smoke, and the stench of blood.

Then Atali's face appeared, looming over it all.

Where are you going, Vax? Do you really think you can run? From me?

"You—you tried to kill me," Vax stammered.

Have you forgotten what you would have been without me? Nothing. I know where you are, and when I find you—

Vax woke with a start when he heard Zai's voice coming from the bedroom. Zai's voice was low, but the walls were thin, and Vax was able to make out his words.

"Hey. I've...run into some trouble lately, and I need to keep a low profile for a while. Just letting you know so you don't think I'm dead if you don't hear from me for a bit. Unless I'm actually dead. In which case, tell the police Cyrex had something to with it." A pause. "I wasn't trying to be funny." Another pause. "I can't really get into the details right now, but...look, something weird happened, okay? Something...I don't even know how to explain. I think I might be losing my mind. Just..." A sigh. "Anyway, I need you to cover for me in case Mom starts asking questions. Tell Ree not to worry, okay? And seriously, don't freak out. I know what I'm doing...more or less. All right. I promise."

The bedroom door opened. When Zai caught sight of Vax on the couch, he froze for a second.

"Surprise, I'm still here," Vax said sardonically.

"I knew that," Zai muttered. He went into the kitchen and placed his tablet on the counter. He'd set it to broadcast the news out loud, and holographic text also scrolled in front of his eyes from his augment as he grabbed food from the fridge and began eating.

Vax stood, stretching his stiff joints, and followed him to dig out a frozen breakfast roll from the fridge. A crease had appeared between Zai's eyebrows, as though he were focusing intently on the news, so Vax decided not to interrupt. The news sounded mundane—Cyrex's stock rose again, some pop star got married to her long-time girlfriend, Integrity was trying to reach the top of the trending social media hashtags list with #liveaugmentfree, and some violent crimes happened the night before. No news about the shooting of the sky rail, though, oddly enough.

When the announcer started reporting on the status of the war, Zai visibly tensed.

"When will this fucking thing ever end?" Zai muttered.

Vax glanced at him over his roll. "Not a fan?"

"No." Zai's head swiveled around to face him, his eyes narrowed. "Don't tell me you're a war supporter," he said through his teeth.

"Whoa." Vax held his hands up. "I'm just asking. Personally, I don't really have an opinion. What's your deal?"

He thought he sounded neutral, but the more he spoke, the more pissed-off Zai's expression became. "We have no legitimate reason to be over there, fighting for some other country's sovereignty, and—" Zai's fingers curled into fists, his knuckles paling. "It's taken—people—I cared about," he said, practically spitting the words out.

Vax couldn't exactly argue against that as a reason to hate the war. "I thought only people who couldn't pay the exemption fee were drafted," he said. "I didn't know you knew many people like that."

Zai didn't reply. He listened further to the news while more holographic text scrolled rapidly in front of his eyes before musing out loud, "So…Cyrex paid off the local media not to report on the sniper shots last night?"

"Probably." Though the highly public nature of the whole thing still bothered Vax. It wasn't Atali's style. What made him desperate enough to hire a sniper to try to kill Vax?

Zai finally switched the news off and turned to face Vax, with a look on his face as though he were going to interrogate him. Again.

"Funny thing I noticed this morning: I went to check on my AlphaDrive account, and the whole account had been deleted."

Vax frowned. "Wait…that was actually a real account?"

"It was a dummy account, obviously," Zai said.

Oh. That made sense.

"So it's not like I'm heartbroken or anything, since I still have all my original files. Still, it's pretty suspicious that the day after I tell you the account number, the entire account disappears, isn't it?" It took Vax a moment to realize Zai was looking at him as though he expected Vax to have an answer.

"What? You never gave me the password, remember?" When Zai kept glaring at him, Vax sighed with exasperation. "No, I *don't* know how to hack into accounts. I don't know the first thing about internet hacking. And what reason would I have for hacking your account, anyway?"

"Okay, well, assuming you didn't do it"—though Zai's tone suggested that he wasn't quite willing to let go of the possibility, for reasons Vax couldn't fathom—"there's only one other option I can think of, and that's that your hidden camera was streaming to someone at Cyrex who hired hackers to take care of it."

Vax looked away. He really, *really* didn't want to think about that camera.

"Which brings me to my next question: who's your boss?"

"My boss?" Vax echoed.

"Yeah. You know, the person who tells you who to kill. I'm assuming not *all* of Cyrex knows that an assassin's on their payroll. And I'd like to know who specifically I'm up against."

Fair enough. "It's Atali Norman."

That disturbed Zai's composure. He blinked. "You're joking."

"No, I'm not," Vax said, with a frown.

"He's the *CEO*."

"No, really?" Vax couldn't help the sarcasm. "I had no idea!"

Zai gave him a sharp look. "He's a *philanthropist*."

Something inside Vax snapped at that word. "Oh yeah, he's a philanthropist who donates to charities and always talks about 'helping people' and all that crap he doesn't actually believe. Damn, I guess that revokes his 'right to hire an assassin' card. Because everyone knows that someone who smiles that much for the camera and poses for pictures with underprivileged students can't *possibly* be a bad person, right? He can't *possibly* be doing it just for PR, right? He can't *possibly* have a personal assassin on hand to do all his dirty work for him while he keeps his own hands pristine, *right*? I mean, what makes *you* think you know what kind of person he really is, anyway?"

His hands had balled into fists, his fingernails biting into his palms, and he was breathing hard, as though he'd just run a marathon. Zai's expression was unreadable.

"And *you* know what kind of person he really is?" Zai asked.

His tone was mild, but the question sounded skeptical, and that only pissed off Vax even further.

"You think I'm lying?" he said, through his teeth.

"I didn't say that."

Vax knew he was somewhat lacking in the social intuition department, but he wasn't completely clueless. "You don't believe me. What, you don't trust an assassin but you'll trust the person who hired him? Because he's well-dressed and well-spoken and has degrees from the most prestigious universities in the country?"

Maybe he shouldn't have been so surprised. Zai and Atali weren't that different in terms of background, after all; both came from wealthy families and graduated from expensive schools.

What he said gave Zai pause, though.

"All right," Zai finally said. "But if what you're saying is true..."

If? Vax's jaw clenched, though he didn't say anything.

Zai tapped his fingers against the table, his blunt fingernails clacking against the plastic surface. "That would mean Atali Norman at least knows about the disappeared people, doesn't it?"

Vax shrugged. "Well, it's not like you can just call him and ask him."

Zai frowned. "You don't seem that surprised about the idea that Norman could be involved."

"Yeah, because he's a control freak," said Vax, flatly. "The surprise would be if he *didn't* know what was going on."

Zai was still frowning, his fingers still tapping on the table. "If he really was involved, though...I'd need a hell of a lot of proof."

Here we go again. "Because the word of an assassin doesn't count for anything?" Vax said bitterly.

"That's not exactly what I meant. He's the CEO—someone in that position won't go down easily. Unless I've got rock-solid evidence, he'll find some loophole and then hit me with a suit for libel." Zai grimaced. "Which would *really* suck."

He seemed to think for a moment. Then, he got up from his seat and pulled on his jacket.

"Uh...where are you going?" Vax asked. "Cyrex *just tried* to kill both of us yesterday."

"Cyrex might have a lot of money and resources, but they can't watch the entire city." Zai sounded so unconcerned he almost sounded bored. "And they have no idea where we are."

"Even so, you don't think lying low for a few days *might* be a good idea?"

"You worry too much," said Zai. "Now, come on."

Trying not to curse, Vax grabbed the handgun from the coffee table and double-checked the magazine. "Where are we going, and why?"

"I have a list of people I need to talk to. You're coming along to make sure no one *else* tries to shoot me in the head."

"And you couldn't have your conversations on the phone because...?"

"It's harder to turn away a journalist in person, believe me. And some of these people might not have a listed phone number."

With that cryptic comment, Zai opened the door.

Chapter Four

DESPITE ZAI'S CONFIDENCE, part of Vax expected to see last night's mystery assassin right outside the doorway, or the apartment building, waiting for them. But no one was there, and as they set off down the sidewalk without drawing a second glance from passersby, he exhaled the breath he'd been holding.

It was a bright, sunny day, almost mockingly cheerful, as though absolutely nothing out of the ordinary had happened the night before. The streets bustled with people talking through their nodes or scanning newsfeeds from their augments, holographic text scrolling in front of their eyes.

Attempts to ask Zai where precisely they were going only got him "You'll see when we get there" for an unhelpful answer, so Vax settled for following him in silence and watching for anyone who might be tailing them. If he'd still had his augment, he could've scanned for weapons; as it was, he had to rely on his augmented vision alone.

Throughout the day, Zai visited various apartment buildings, introducing himself and asking about one of the people on his list. The responses he got were all along the same lines:

"Sorry, I hadn't heard from her for years before she disappeared."

"He probably just got drunk one night and fell in the river."

"I tried to tell the police, but they didn't care. It's been seven years—what's there left to find?"

If Zai was disappointed by the lack of leads, he didn't show it; he merely kept forging ahead. Vax wouldn't have thought Zai would have the patience to keep repeating the same questions, over and over, always in a calm, professional tone, but that was what he did.

In the evening, they stopped by a soup kitchen.

"Uh...what are we doing here?" Vax muttered to Zai.

"My job." Zai gave his shoulder a pat, making him start. "Try to blend in. Hopefully we won't be here for too long, but you never know."

"Wait, what are you going to—?"

Zai set off without waiting for him to finish. Vax rubbed his forehead, trying not to curse under his breath.

The soup kitchen was crowded, which meant no one spared a second glance at them, but also meant it was harder to keep track of potential threats, not to mention it would be hard to escape the room a hurry. Crowded areas always made him twitchy; he kept flinching whenever someone brushed against him.

Focus, he told himself. Staying close enough to Zai to be able to reach him quickly while trying not to make it look like he was shadowing him was harder than it sounded. Zai kept glancing around the cafeteria, as though he were looking for someone, but he seemed unable to find whoever he was looking for, and he settled for chatting with the patrons instead.

Somewhat to Vax's surprise, Zai was all pleasant smiles and warm greetings as he introduced himself and engaged the diners in small talk. He seemed to listen with genuine sympathy as some of them started talking about their plights, and even jotted down notes on occasion. Vax watched, stupefied by how Zai managed to transform from the surly interrogator he'd been earlier into a charming conversationalist.

Though he couldn't help thinking that Zai did have a very nice smile.

At some point, the elderly man Zai was talking to looked up and caught sight of Vax staring. Vax started and quickly turned away, taking a sip from the cup of water in his hands, but it was too late. He heard the man tell Zai in a low voice, "I think that guy over there is staring at you. He might be from the CIA."

Zai chuckled. "Nah, I don't think so. I get stared at a lot, you know. He's probably starstruck by my good looks."

Vax choked, nearly inhaling water into his lungs.

After Zai was done, he casually walked to where Vax was, hands tucked into his pockets. Without looking at him, he muttered, "If you keep staring, you're going to draw attention."

"I know that," Vax muttered in return, through his teeth. "It wasn't on purpose—"

"Wait." Vax risked a glance at him; Zai was staring at something across the room, his brow furrowed. "Hold that thought."

He started walking away at a steady but leisurely pace, making his way to where a dark-haired woman was sitting with her meal. Vax followed him after a pause and sat a table away.

"Hi," said Zai, in a friendly voice. "My name is Zai, and I'm a writer for the *Daily Voice*. You are...?"

"What do you want?" the woman replied curtly, without answering his question.

Tough crowd, Vax thought. He wondered how Zai would handle it.

From where he was sitting, he could see Zai pull out his pod and project a holographic picture of one of the nine missing people—a woman with deep-brown skin and long black hair.

"I heard you were friends with Elisa Delgado," Zai said.

That made the woman hesitate. "Have you seen her?"

"No, but—"

"Then I got nothing to say to you." The woman stood up to leave.

"I'm trying to find out what happened to her," Zai said.

She paused.

"But to do that, I'll need your help," Zai added softly.

She turned to face him again, but her expression was still skeptical. "Why do you care? Journalists don't write about people no one wants to read about. People like us."

Zai didn't look stunned or defensive; instead, his expression grew more somber and sympathetic.

"But that's not right, is it?" he said. "It's not right if someone disappears and no one cares, not even the police. If there was foul play involved, the world deserves to know what happened."

She didn't reply, but she didn't disagree with him, either.

"If there's anything you know," said Zai, "it would be very helpful, Miss...?"

"Rosa Molina."

"Rosa." Zai smiled reassuringly. "When was the last time you saw Elisa?"

Rosa exhaled, the tension leaving her as her shoulders fell. "Five years ago."

"Did she tell you anything before she disappeared?"

"She told me that she wasn't supposed to tell me anything." Rosa passed a hand over her face. "But she said... she said she was going to 'get better.'"

"Get better?" Zai echoed. "Was she...ill?"

Rosa's fingers fidgeted with her cup of water. "You could say that. She'd...struggled with depression for most of her life."

Rosa straightened, narrowing her eyes as though she expected Zai to say something hostile. Instead, Zai made a note on his tablet. "So...she expected treatment?"

"That's what I thought. But whenever I tried to ask her if that was what it was, she refused to say anything else."

Frowning, Zai jotted down notes on his tablet. "And you're sure you don't know where she might have gone?"

Rosa shook her head. "Just that it was somewhere in the city, and she got a free sky rail credit to get to wherever she needed to go."

"Okay. How did she hear about this...treatment, or whatever it was?"

"I don't even know," Rosa said with frustration. "I think she was contacted by some person over the internet, but she wouldn't tell me who it was. That's why I thought the whole thing seemed really shady." Her hands clenched around her cup. "I know she was desperate for treatment—so desperate that she ignored the obvious red flags."

Vax sipped water from his cup, swallowing hard in unexpected empathy. He knew what that kind of desperation felt like.

Zai's frown deepened. "Did you ever see her talking with someone who looked like a recruiter? Or anyone else suspicious?"

"Can't say I have. At some point, she gave me a number to message, after I bugged her enough, because I wanted to look into it, but I never got a response. I think the number was deactivated."

"Hm. Could you tell me what number she gave you?" Once Rosa finished, Zai went on, "Did she ever mention anything regarding Cyrex?"

Rosa's eyebrows lifted. "Well, she was a fan...she thought the CEO was great for donating to charities and stuff. Why do you ask?"

"Just wondering if she might have had contact with anyone from the company," said Zai.

Rosa snorted. "It's not like she could afford their fancy bioaugs, no matter how much she wanted them."

If Zai felt frustrated by the lack of information he was getting, he didn't show it. "All right. Is there anything else you can tell me about what might've happened to Elisa?"

Rosa shook her head again. "I tried reporting it to the police, but they wouldn't take me seriously," she said bitterly. "I don't know what kind of scam Elisa got pulled into, and I know that after five years, she's probably dead...but I wish I knew what happened to her, you know?"

"I know." The gentleness in Zai's voice stunned Vax. "I...lost someone I cared about years ago, too. I knew what happened to him..." Zai abruptly faltered for a moment before he shook his head and went on. "But it was so sudden. It's hard when people disappear from your life like that, and you don't even get a chance to say goodbye."

Rosa nodded slowly. "Yeah."

"One last thing. Can you tell me something about her? What kind of person she was, what her dreams were?"

That question seemed to take Rosa aback. "Well...she always said she wanted to run her own business. It was kind of a running joke between us for a while, since she'd change her mind about what kind of business she wanted to run every other week. She liked the idea of a coffee shop, but I told her, 'There's a Javawocky on every street corner, how are you going to make it?' She never gave up hope that she could one day save enough money to go back to school..." She trailed off. In a quiet voice, she said, "I know it's a long shot, but...if you find anything, will you let me know?"

"Of course I will. I promise."

"Thank you," Rosa whispered.

ONCE THEY'D FINISHED talking to Rosa and returned to the apartment, Zai collapsed into a chair and fell into a brooding silence as he reread his notes—the first sign of dissatisfaction from him all day.

Vax quietly cleared his throat. "Seems like there's not a lot of information out there."

Zai glanced at him. "If all these disappearances are related, then there has to be something connecting them— some trail that will lead back to Cyrex. A common recruitment method, a place they all visited, *something*." He sighed, rubbing his eyes. "Like I said, Cyrex has been annoyingly good at covering its tracks. But it's not possible to get rid of everything," he muttered, seemingly half to himself. "I just have to find where they've slipped up and left evidence behind."

At least his determination hadn't suffered a blow.

Zai seemed to notice his staring. "What?"

"You're good at manipulating people," said Vax.

Zai gave him a sideways look. "I prefer to say I'm good at *persuading* people."

Vax wasn't sure he saw the difference, and the way Zai could effortlessly charm people mesmerized him, yet also reminded him uncomfortably of Atali. He shifted on his feet. "Do you actually mean what you say to people? Or is it all just...white lies to get what you want?"

Zai raised an eyebrow. "I can promise you I'm not planning on going behind your back and hiring an assassin to kill you."

Vax gritted his teeth. "That's not what I asked."

"You were comparing me to Atali Norman, weren't you? Which, I mean—he's a middle-aged married CEO with secret homicidal tendencies, according to you, and I'm not." Zai eyed him. "Why are you so concerned, anyway?"

Maybe because Vax had a bad history with people who seemed nice at first and later turned on him. Then again, to be fair, Zai at least hadn't made any pretense of liking him from the start.

"No reason," he said, his mouth a bit dry. He swallowed, crossing the room to sit in the chair opposite Zai, and asked instead, half-sardonically, half-seriously, "Ever considered becoming a lawyer?"

"Hell, no." Zai made a face. "I mean, I know there are public interest lawyers who champion social causes, but by now I've seen too many asshole corporate lawyers for law school to seem at all appealing. Plus, law school sounds like a nightmare."

"Well, you'd probably make a killing if you did change careers."

Zai suddenly went quiet.

"I knew someone, once, who wanted to go to law school," he said, his voice oddly uneven. "Not to make a killing, but because he thought he could really help people that way."

Vax watched him, not understanding the sudden heaviness that had descended on him.

"Out of curiosity, what led you to decide to become a journalist? Or were you always such a justice-crusading Good Samaritan?" he asked.

Zai stared at him. Then he burst out laughing.

Vax frowned. "What?"

Zai shook his head. "Good Samaritan?" he echoed, with a snort. "My parents *wish*. I was always a terrible influence."

Vax blinked. "Seriously?"

"Seriously." Zai paused. "Before I got to college, I always slacked off at school, drove my parents crazy, didn't care about anything other than getting laid with the hottest girls and guys in class."

Zai's sudden openness to friendly conversation was refreshing. "What changed in college?" Vax asked.

"I...met someone." Zai wasn't looking at him. "He opened my eyes to how privileged I'd been and how much things sucked for the rest of the world. And because of that...I eventually decided to become a journalist."

Vax wondered who this person was. Maybe the mysterious Ethan? But a gloomy silence settled over Zai, and after debating with himself, Vax chose to leave him in peace, at least for the moment.

"How'd you end up estranged from your family?" Vax found himself asking instead.

"Estranged from my parents," Zai corrected. "I wrote a piece on how Meridian was underpaying its facility workers, which pissed them off."

Yeah, that'll do it, Vax thought. He had to admire Zai's guts for tackling that kind of subject, though. "Is it hard?" he asked. "Being estranged from them."

Zai gave him an odd look. "It's...not exactly as serious as it sounds. They still call me once in a while, trying to get me to apologize and promise never to do it again."

"And you won't?"

Zai shrugged. "Someone once convinced me to try to be honest with the people who are close to me. And the honest truth is I'm not sorry, and I can't promise not to pull something like that again." He leaned back in his chair, regarding him. "For someone who tries to keep his own background as mysterious as possible, you're really interested in asking about other people's personal lives."

Vax could feel the weight of Zai's unspoken question hanging in the air, daring him to ignore it. He exhaled, slowly. "You seem happy to talk about yourself."

"I've got to find a way to fill the silence somehow, and besides, I don't have anything to hide."

"If that's the case," Vax said, "why do you keep refusing to answer when I try to ask you why you always give me these weird looks? Seems to me like you *do* have something to hide."

Zai's entire body tensed.

"Am I wrong?" Vax pressed.

"For *fuck's sake*," Zai suddenly snapped, "will you cut me some *fucking slack* for not *dealing* very well with the fact that you *look like the love of my life*?"

Vax stared at him. "What?"

The color in Zai's face changed, and he looked away. A muscle twitched in his jaw as he swallowed thickly, his hands clenching and stiffly unclenching.

"Is his name Ethan?" Vax asked.

Zai's shoulders sagged, the tension in him breaking.

"Yes," he whispered, after a long pause. "His...his name was Ethan. Ethan Tromer."

Was. "And...he's the guy who died?"

Zai nodded once.

"I'm sorry."

Zai stared at him as though he'd spoken Martian. Vax frowned. Did he say something wrong? "What?" Vax asked.

"You're an assassin, and you're sorry my boyfriend's dead?"

"Yes? Why wouldn't I be?"

"You kill people for a living," Zai said, his voice suddenly cold. "Lives don't have any meaning to you."

"I'm just...sorry for your loss, that's all," Vax repeated, not knowing what else to say. "And I'm sorry I remind you of him."

Zai kept staring at him, and Vax fought the instinct to flinch under his icy glare. Then, without a word, Zai retreated to the bedroom and shut the door.

What the hell is his *problem?* Vax wondered.

SEEKING ANSWERS, VAX turned to the internet. A quick search of "Zai Lumero" brought up links to Zai's *Daily Voice* articles, a mostly empty PicShare page, and his Jabber account, @Zaixzl—Vax couldn't help wondering if Zai had mashed his keyboard to get that handle—which, at a glance, seemed to consist mostly of acerbic arguments between him and people who strongly disagreed with him. Trying to follow the most recent conversations felt like wading through a verbal battlefield full of angry words and weaponized contempt, and though Vax wasn't shocked by Zai's tone, he was a little amazed by Zai's apparently boundless energy in engaging with bigots and critics. And despite—or perhaps because of—his strong opinions, he had quite a few followers.

Vax tried searching Zai's Jabber account for the name "Ethan," but nothing came up. In fact, the account was only a little more than three years old, and it seemed to be more of a professional than a personal account.

He skimmed Zai's most popular articles. The piece on Meridian was at the top of the list, and Vax glanced over it. No wonder Zai's parents had been upset with him; it was pretty critical. Mostly Zai wrote about bioaugs and reported on the major bioaug companies. There were a few passionate anti-war opinion pieces in there, as well, that generated a lot of controversy in the comments.

In any case, Vax was disappointed that he'd learned nothing he didn't already know. He still had a hard time reconciling the hostile, combative Zai with the one he observed conversing sympathetically with homeless people at the soup kitchen.

As the night wore on and Vax settled down to sleep, he noticed that light still spilled out from the edges of the bedroom door. Apparently Zai was working late. He tried to ignore the light, as the last thing he wanted was another confrontation with Zai while he may still be touchy about the subject of his dead boyfriend, but after an hour, Vax still couldn't sleep. He checked the time on his pod—1:10 in the morning. With an inward sigh, he got up, braced himself, and knocked on the door.

No response.

Vax knocked again, more loudly. "Zai?" he tentatively called.

Still no response.

Vax hesitated, but vague worry started to outweigh the certainty that Zai would blow up at him for intruding, so he opened the door and stepped into the room.

He found Zai slumped over awkwardly on the bed, as though he'd fallen asleep while in the middle of working on his tablet. He hadn't even removed his nodes. There was no way that position could have been comfortable.

"Um...hey." When that elicited no response, Vax nudged his shoulder. "Zai."

Zai grunted. Vax wasn't sure whether that meant he was awake or not.

"You should probably get some sleep," Vax went on, awkwardly.

"Nn," Zai murmured, sitting up and sagging against the wall. His eyes didn't open, but his eyebrows drew together. "Don't...leave this time, Ethan."

Vax froze.

Clearly Zai was dreaming. Or he was so sleep-deprived he was starting to hallucinate that Vax sounded like Ethan. Vax tried to slowly inch away, but Zai's hand groped in the air, found his sleeve, and latched on.

"Please," Zai whispered. "Please stay. You promised you'd come home."

Vax wavered, but it seemed crueler to keep up the pretense. "You're dreaming, Zai. You need to wake up."

Zai shook his head slowly. "Just...talk to me," he mumbled.

What the hell was he supposed to do? He felt as though he'd intruded into a private space and he should back out. And yet...

Zai still hadn't let go of his sleeve. Sighing, Vax drew closer.

"I'm not the person you think I am," he said. When Zai didn't respond, he hesitantly went on. "But I'm sure that... that Ethan never wanted for you to be this sad without him."

Still no response. Maybe Zai had fallen back asleep. Vax gently, cautiously removed Zai's fingers from his sleeve.

"I didn't mean to," Zai whispered, without warning. Vax paused. "But when you were gone...suddenly, everything seemed so hard. Going back to school. Getting out of bed. Eating. Living. I don't know what happened."

Vax swallowed hard. The more Zai talked, the more keenly Vax felt completely out of his element.

"You...really need to sleep, okay? You'll feel better in the morning." *I hope.*

Zai didn't protest this time as Vax quietly made his way to the door and switched off the light. When he settled back onto the couch, though, he found himself staring at the ceiling with an aching, empty feeling in his chest.

Sleep was a long time coming.

Chapter Five

IF ZAI REMEMBERED what happened last night, he didn't make any mention of it the next morning, to Vax's relief. Or maybe he'd forgotten the whole thing, which was equally fine.

He'd also apparently decided not to speak to Vax at all. Vax wasn't sure which was worse. Obviously the situation was awkward, and Vax couldn't blame Zai for that, but...he'd genuinely enjoyed it when Zai relaxed long enough to provide Vax with a window into his life, and he'd hoped their relationship could remain that civil.

Well...of all the disappointments he'd experienced, this hardly rated as the worst.

They went for more interviews. Slowly, Vax learned more bits and pieces about the people who'd disappeared, making them more than just names and faces. Natalya Zelenko had immigrated to the country in the hopes of finding a better job. Tyson Alexander had had a hard time readjusting to civilian life after returning from the war. Lanh Huynh had been discharged from the psychiatric hospital and found an outpatient program that seemed to be working. But Zai still seemed no closer to discovering what had happened to them.

On the way back, Zai suddenly said, "I have a theory."

It was the first thing he'd said to Vax all day, and Vax tried not to sound too eager as he asked, "What kind of theory?"

"Maybe Cyrex lured these people by promising them a free bioaug," said Zai. "Most of these people seem to have been interested in bioaugs, to a certain extent. According to Rosa, Elisa Delgado said she would be 'getting better' soon, and a lot of our missing people seem to have had mental health issues..."

Vax didn't know a more delicate way to ask the question on his mind. "I thought that wasn't exactly unusual for homeless people."

"Yeah, but my point is, what if Cyrex directly targeted them by promising them bioaugs that could cure their mental illnesses?"

Vax frowned. "Those don't exist." He was certain he would've heard of such things.

"They don't," Zai agreed, "but they could've been told it was experimental, a secret clinical trial or something. It's not exactly a new idea," he added. "Before laws were passed making it illegal, there were a handful of high-profile cases of companies and unethical researchers luring people into their studies by promising them free bioaugs. Which is the problem when most bioaugs are so expensive that only the wealthy can afford them."

Vax didn't expect Zai to be so critical. "Uh...you're one of 'the wealthy' too, aren't you?"

"Yeah, and I know I'm privileged. But at least I don't use my bioaugs for a harmful purpose," Zai said, shooting him a glare.

Inwardly, Vax sighed. He tried to change the topic back to something that would redirect Zai's aggravation. "So you're saying Cyrex purposefully targeted homeless people with mental illnesses?"

"Maybe." Zai's expression darkened. "As if they specifically wanted the people who would be least likely to be missed. It's sickening."

Vax's stomach lurched. He hadn't expected to care much about Zai's crusade—he knew, obviously, that Cyrex had illegal activities, and he wasn't interested in more details—but the idea of Cyrex preying on people with mental illnesses struck a nerve in him.

"There's still no clue as to where those nine people went or what happened to them, though," he said.

"I know," Zai muttered. "I can't *believe* it's been impossible to figure out how these people were recruited."

It did seem difficult for Zai's investigation to move forward without that missing link.

"What did Cyrex do, kill off the recruiter? Or use multiple crowd-sourced recruiters?" He rubbed his eyes, but then abruptly frowned and pressed his node. "Play voice mail," he said.

As Zai listened, his eyebrows lifted in surprise.

"We need to get back," he said, once he'd finished.

"We're almost there," said Vax. "What happened?"

"A lead...I think," Zai muttered without elaborating.

When they returned, Zai sat at the kitchen table, tapped on his tablet screen, and waited. Then the tablet projected a video screen into the air, showing the face of a young, dark-haired, bronze-skinned woman with a nervous expression.

"Are you Jane Shaw?" he asked.

She frowned. "Who is this?"

"My name is Zai Lumero, and I'm a journalist. I heard you contacted Rosa Molina to ask about Elisa Delgado."

She seemed to hesitate. "Right, Rosa mentioned you. She said you were investigating this case."

"You told her you work for Cyrex?"

"I do, but..." Jane paused again, and then she shook her head. "I...I don't know if I should be talking to you anymore. If someone at Cyrex hears that I'm talking to you, I'd lose my job, and..."

"Jane." Zai's voice was gentle. "No one has to know that you've talked to me, I can promise you that. Besides, you've met Rosa. You must have seen how much she wants to know what happened to her friend. There were others, too—others who have friends and family members who'd want to know what happened to them. Anything you can tell me would help give them some peace."

She glanced over her shoulder. Vax hoped it was just a nervous reflex, not that she was actually in danger of being overheard.

"Elisa Delgado was part of a project," Jane began, in a low voice. "The purpose of it was to augment the capabilities of the human brain—enhanced memory, enhanced neural processing speed, things like that—and also to induce brainwashing in order to create superior spies and military for the war."

That confirmed what Zai's previous source had told him, at least...though Vax still thought the idea of brainwashing neural augments sounded ridiculous.

"Huh." Zai's eyebrows knit. "Did the project get very far? I didn't think current neuroscience research was advanced enough for that kind of augmentation."

"Well, that's the thing—the project had a lot of failures." Jane's voice lowered further. "That's how nine people died."

Not that Vax had had much hope they were alive and living in secret somewhere else on the globe, but that was still sobering to hear.

"So they *are* dead," Zai echoed.

Jane nodded.

"Did the project stop four years ago, or is it still ongoing?"

"It stopped. The number of dead bodies was getting too high, so someone high up pulled the plug on the funding."

"Who knew what was going on? And who was in charge of it?" Zai went on.

"Not many knew, other than the scientists involved. Even the upper management in the company didn't know, because the project was kept so secret. I'm a secretary for one of the scientists—I only found out when I was looking into some reports to the ARC and stumbled across some information I wasn't supposed to see." She hesitated before shaking her head. "If I told you their names, they'd know it was me. No, sorry, I can't."

Zai looked disappointed, but he didn't press further. "What happened to the bodies?" he asked.

"They were buried. Secretly, of course."

"Do you know where?"

"Well...I think I might know where at least one of them is."

Zai's eyes widened slightly. "Where?"

"I...I can't tell you over the internet. But I can show you where it is in person."

That doesn't sound suspicious at all, Vax thought sarcastically to himself.

Zai's gaze became unfocused, as though he was actually considering it. But all he said was "Thank you for the information. I'll be in touch."

The video closed. Zai sat quietly for a moment before he started typing onto the tablet.

"Do you believe her?" Vax asked.

Zai glanced up, startled, as though he'd forgotten Vax was there. "Well...it's a little weird that she didn't want to name any of the people involved, but other than that, I don't see much reason not to."

"Don't you find it kind of suspicious, though?" Vax pressed. "It's only been two days since the shooter."

"The voice message I listened to earlier was from Rosa—she called to say she met Jane, who had information for me. Unless you're saying *she's* the assassin...or the assassin was somehow able to follow us yesterday." Zai gave him a pointed look.

Vax hadn't noticed anyone following them, but he wasn't arrogant enough to believe, with 100 percent certainty, that they'd gone completely unnoticed. Who knew what resources Atali had that he'd never bothered sharing with Vax, after all.

"Plus, she said something very similar to what Celia said," Zai went on.

That was true...however, the timing of it still bothered Vax.

"Still...are you sure Jane Shaw is even a real person?" Vax asked. "Or that she actually works for Cyrex?"

Zai rolled his eyes. "Believe it or not, I *was* going to check that after calling her. What are you, a backseat-journalist?"

Vax bit his lower lip and didn't reply. If he were in the other assassin's place, he would try to lure Zai into the open to save himself the effort of having to track him down, and that's what made him anxious.

Maybe Cyrex's HR had no idea who Jane Shaw was, and he could put that worry from his mind. But one call later—during which Zai posed as Jane Shaw's new landlord, inquiring about her employment—the HR person confirmed that Jane Shaw was indeed an employee who had worked at Cyrex for the past five years.

"There," said Zai, after ending the call. "Jane Shaw is a real person, not an alias. Unless you think a Cyrex secretary has been moonlighting as an assassin."

Vax had no idea how Zai could be so nonchalant right now. "Seriously? You were paranoid enough to think you might be attacked by an assassin in your own home before all of this happened, and now you don't even think she could've faked her credentials?"

Zai waved a hand, still infuriatingly calm. "Well, if that turns out to be the case, that's what I have you for, right?"

"I see one *minor* problem with your plan," Vax deadpanned, "and it's that luring you to a deserted location would be a great way to pick you off with a sniper rifle. Or did you forget what happened a few days ago?"

"I remember," Zai returned, equally deadpan. "But weren't they technically aiming at you?"

Vax opened his mouth, and then closed it again. "Well...okay, but why would that make a difference?"

Zai shrugged. "You're way more dangerous than I am," he said, blandly. "Maybe that's why they had to drop you with a sniper shot, regardless of how flashy it is."

Vax doubted it was because of how *dangerous* he was—even a dangerous person was vulnerable when they were asleep or caught off guard. "So you're saying...what, you don't think you'll be shot by a sniper because you're not a physical threat?"

Zai drummed his fingers against the table. "I might be new to this whole world of underground crime and hitmen, but look—I'm not famous, but I'm also not a complete nobody. If it *looked* like I'd been assassinated, you can bet your expensive bioaugments that my family would be beyond pissed off and do everything they could to figure out what had happened. And they would have the resources to pour into a thorough investigation. Correct me if I'm wrong, but that's not the kind of attention Cyrex would want, right? I mean, even you at least tried to go for the home-robbery-gone-wrong angle."

Vax hated to admit that Zai had a point, but that much was true.

"Still," he said, frowning, "that's a massive gamble to take. Cyrex is cautious, yeah, but you can't be sure they haven't decided you've become a big enough liability that they'd rather just kill you ASAP and deal with the rest later. Or even get rid of your body permanently, so no one could prove anything. Plus, they could engineer evidence to implicate some random person for the crime."

Zai shrugged. "Predicting how people will act or react is usually my thing. I'm not saying I'm a one hundred percent accurate mind reader, but I think it's a risk worth taking."

Vax begged to differ. He preferred a much, *much* lower margin of risk, and to him, human behavior was the most unpredictable variable of all. Whatever people-reading skill Zai had, Vax wasn't inclined to trust it completely—especially since, as Zai himself admitted, he didn't have all that much experience with criminals.

"Plus, you're forgetting one other thing," Zai went on, "which is that they don't just need me dead—they need to destroy whatever information I have. What if I planned to dump everything on the internet as a failsafe in case I die?"

"Maybe they're gambling on the idea that you're not that thorough?" Vax knew it was a weak argument, but Cyrex had already shown, by using a sniper, that they were willing to take messy risks.

Zai glanced at him. "You're really taking this 'help me not die' thing seriously," he commented.

Vax frowned at him, not understanding why Zai was saying that. "You were the one who asked me to."

Zai gave him a blank look, as though he hadn't expected that response.

"Yeah, but I didn't think you'd be so...enthusiastically paranoid."

"Says the guy who's been targeted for assassination," Vax muttered, fighting the urge to drop his face into his palm. "Seriously, how did someone like you find himself in the middle of such a life-threatening investigation?"

"I guess I'm spending most of my time these days chasing ghosts," Zai muttered, half to himself.

Vax turned to meet his gaze, though Zai blinked and quickly looked away. He suddenly had the feeling that Zai wasn't just referring to the nine people he was investigating for his article.

"Ghosts," Vax echoed. "Why not living people?"

Zai's lips pressed into a critical line. "What can I say? I'm stuck in the past. Or so everyone thinks."

"Are you?" Vax asked, tentatively.

Zai's mouth twisted. "No...well, in a way, but not like..." A sigh escaped from him, and when he continued, his tone was barbed. "Look, I don't expect you to understand, but...when I lost him, it was like my whole world...broke apart. Call me spoiled and sheltered, but back then, I thought the world was fair. I didn't think death was a real thing that could happen to people I cared about. Afterward, I had to rethink everything I'd believed in. I *did* try to move on—" He shook his head. "I *have* moved on. I've dated other people. I mean, it's been four years, for crying out loud. I *know* he's dead, and he's not coming back. Even so...I guess all of that still haunts me, sometimes. Because I never got to say goodbye, and—"

He stopped, as though he'd choked on his words. Vax's skin prickled, and he averted his gaze. Once again, he felt like he'd stumbled across something that hadn't been meant for him to see. Zai's plea from the other night echoed in his head: *You promised you'd come home.*

"Never mind," said Zai, his voice rough. "Forget what I said."

"You must have loved him a lot," Vax said, quietly.

Zai gave him a weird look. "Yeah...I did."

He didn't know what that felt like, having someone who loved him that much. He wished he knew.

I want to marry you.

He pushed that ghostly echo out of his head.

"What was he like?" he asked.

Zai still had that strange, uncomfortable expression on his face, as though he might bolt. Finally, he sighed.

"Well...uh..." He ran a hand through his hair, eyes losing focus, as though he were caught up in a memory. "For one...he never swore. Ever."

Vax's eyebrows rose. "Seriously?"

"Seriously. I used to tease him about it." Zai's mouth slid into a wistful smile that suddenly made him look a few years younger. "God, he was *such* a goody-two-shoes. Didn't swear, didn't drink, didn't party, just stayed in his room or in the library, studying all the time."

That was hard for Vax to imagine.

Zai paused. "He didn't have any bioaugs, either. Not even ocular ones. It wasn't because he was part of the anti-aug movement, though; his family just believed in getting bioaugs only if there was a medical need for it."

Vax was starting to wonder if Zai was purposely latching on to everything about Ethan Tromer that made him the polar opposite of Vax.

"He was...so smart. Not that he was a prodigy—he was just super organized and disciplined and hard-working. He was one of those geeks who actually enjoyed school because he liked to learn new things, and he liked solving problems. In his free time, he was a total nerd." Zai said that word affectionately, as a compliment. "He was really into fantasy and sci-fi movies, and murder mysteries, too. He was...kind of shy around strangers, but when you got to know him, he could be sarcastic as hell. He was so humble, though; he never bragged or thought of himself as better than others. And he was kind. Always trying to help other people, if he could. Always caring about other people's problems. Always trying to give back, and never asking for anything in return."

Could he walk on water, too? Vax kept quiet, though.

"All he ever wanted was to do good," Zai said quietly, his gaze falling to the floor. "And then he was killed in the war."

War hero? Vax could think of far worse deaths. But he kept that thought to himself, too.

"It just—it wasn't fair." Zai's hands clenched into fists. "He didn't *want* to fight in the war—didn't even agree with it in the first place, because hell, who does?—but he couldn't pay the exemption fee to get out of the draft. So he went to serve his country. Then he was gone, and it was like...the world didn't care. He was just another *statistic*." Zai spat out the word, letting it hang in the air. "Another casualty of war out of thousands. Good for a local news story to make people teary-eyed and rail about how terrible war is for a few days, and that was all. The Earth kept spinning. The war kept going. It was like his death, his life, meant nothing at all." His fingers relaxed, and he turned his palms up. "He was always close with his family. His parents and sister are some of the kindest people I've ever known. They were devastated by his death, and they didn't—they didn't deserve that. *He* didn't deserve that."

Some bitter part of Vax wanted to say, *Too bad, sometimes life sucks that way. It's not* supposed *to be fair.* But maybe that was because it made him strangely jealous to hear about someone who'd been missed...who'd been dearly loved. Or maybe he just wanted to know that there were others who'd suffered as much bad luck as he had, for the sake of his own petty selfishness.

Zai exhaled, his shoulders slumping a little, as though the breath he'd been holding was all that had kept him upright. "You asked me, before, why I became a journalist. I guess I made that decision in part because...he inspired me. And I wanted to...honor him, somehow."

"I see." It sounded like Zai practically worshipped the guy.

Zai shook his head and cleared his throat. "I don't...know why I'm telling you all of this. I mean, what do you care, right? You see dead people all the time."

"Well...not *all* the time..."

Zai looked at him. "Oh, what, Cyrex doesn't need someone whacked every hour?"

"No," said Vax, appalled. "Nowhere close."

"In that case, what does an assassin do when he's not assassinating?"

Vax shrugged. "Read. Watch TV. Surf the internet. Hit the gym. Visit the aquarium..." And some days, he spent hours trying to find a reason to get out of bed or leave his apartment.

Zai blinked. "You...visit the aquarium."

"Sometimes."

"You're an assassin, and you visit the aquarium."

"What do those things have to do with each other?" Vax said irritably. "What, you think I go there to murder the fish?"

"No, it's just..." Zai shook his head. "Why?"

"Because it's relaxing? Because I like looking at fish swimming in tanks? Will you stop looking at me like I'm a goddamned alien? It's not *that* weird, okay?"

Zai jumped at his tone. "I just...I don't know, thought you'd spend your free time in a murder dungeon, or something."

Vax raised an eyebrow. "What the fuck is a *murder dungeon*?"

"I don't *know*. Never mind."

Vax hesitated, and then said, "You know I do it for the money, right? It's just a job."

Zai's head snapped around, his mouth curling. "Oh, right, of course. You just *kill people* for money. No big deal or anything."

God, the arrogant moral superiority in Zai's voice was unbelievable.

"Hey, fuck you," Vax spat, trying not to snarl at him. "You don't know a damn thing about me."

That made Zai laugh coldly. "No, I don't. What was it? You graduated from petty thief to professional murderer? You had a tragic childhood that screwed you up? Your family member is dying of a terminal illness and there's no other way to get enough money? Look, I'm actually—*gasp*—sympathetic to the reasons that drive people to crime for money, but what the *fuck* justifies killing innocent people as a job, huh? What made you decide you wanted to be a killer, instead of *literally* anything else?"

Vax glared at him, breathing heavily, clenching his hands into fists and trying not to punch Zai in the face. Someone clearly never told Zai that it was a bad idea to piss off an assassin.

Zai's mouth twisted. "What? Can't even answer?"

"I didn't *want*—I didn't *choose* this," Vax ground out.

Zai's eyebrow arched with mocking skepticism. "Oh, *sure*. Did someone put a gun to your head and say, 'Become an assassin or I'll kill you'? A company like Cyrex doesn't pick an incompetent nobody to do their dirty work. You must've been neck-deep in blood long before they ever found you."

Vax's jaw tightened painfully.

"Weren't you?" Zai hissed.

"I don't know—I don't fucking *know*, okay?" Vax exploded without thinking.

The room suddenly went deathly quiet. Zai was giving him a strange look.

"What do you mean—you *don't know*?"

Shit. Vax looked away, his jaw clenched.

"I was...injured, a few years back," he said. "I don't remember anything before that."

When Zai didn't respond right away, Vax glanced at him. Zai's eyes were wide with shock, as though he was frozen.

"You...don't remember...*anything*...before that?" he whispered.

"That's what I said."

"How many—" Zai stopped as abruptly as though he'd run into a wall. "No. Never mind."

Never mind? Zai's usual journalist's curiosity was just...gone?

Vax peered at him. "Are you...okay?"

Zai was looking down, his hands white-knuckled, breathing in and out with harsh, barely controlled breaths.

"I'm...fine," he answered, his voice hoarse and jagged. By his standards, that was a poor excuse for a lie.

Vax watched him uncertainly for a while. When he remained silent, Vax asked again, "Seriously, are you okay? Why the hell are you so freaked out?"

"I was...just...surprised by what you said, that's all," Zai managed to say, his tone flat.

Unease and suspicion gnawed at Vax. "That's not all, is it?"

"Yes, it *is* all," Zai snapped.

God damn, this guy could out-stubborn a brick wall.

"All right," said Vax. "You hate me and don't trust me, fine. I get it. And you hate that I look like your dead boyfriend, because you hate that I've killed people while he was some kind of goddamned saint. I mean, I'm sorry, but I didn't *ask* to look like him—"

"You know what? You're right." Zai's voice was cold. "What was I thinking, comparing the two of you? He was a far better man than you ever could be."

Vax ground his teeth. Much as it irritated him, he had no response to that. It wasn't like he wanted to insult a dead man he'd never met before.

"Listen," he said, "I'm the last person who would force someone else to talk about something they don't want to, but I want to understand why you keep—having these weird reactions. Is that too much to ask?"

Zai didn't answer. His eyes narrowed. "How do I know you're telling the truth, anyway?"

Vax exhaled with a hiss of breath and massaged the bridge of his nose. *For fuck's sake.* "And what, exactly, am I supposed to get out of lying to you about having amnesia?"

"I don't know," Zai grudgingly admitted, "but doesn't it seem really statistically unlikely that you got a bump on the head, and the only thing affected is your memory of your past? That's *really* precise head trauma."

Vax bristled at his skepticism. "I know that, believe it or not. But 'statistically unlikely' doesn't mean *impossible*."

"If you have complete amnesia, how'd you know you were an assassin?"

"I...have the skills for it," Vax said, feeling awkward. "Also, Atali—Atali Norman—filled me in."

Zai's eyebrows lifted in surprise. "He knew you?"

"Apparently."

"You worked for him before your memory loss?" Zai guessed.

"So I'm told."

"If you *are* telling the truth, why didn't you ever bring this up before? Why have you been hiding this information all this time?"

"What was I supposed to say? 'Hi, my name is Vax, and I have amnesia'?" Vax glanced away, swallowing hard. "I didn't tell you because it's *humiliating*. Not because I have some sinister ulterior motive."

Zai sat back, frowning deeply, as though he were lost in thought. Vax hoped he would stop asking questions already. He hated having to discuss his amnesia—hated being reminded that there were blank spaces in his brain where normal people had memories. He had no childhood, no knowledge of where he'd come from or who his family had been. He wasn't even sure what his race was. He had no idea why or how he'd learned half the things he knew, like how to handle a gun or how to speak Arabic or how neurons worked, and thinking about it all depressed him and made him feel like an alien in his own body.

"And you've never, I don't know, tried to figure out who you were?"

"Considering what I do for a living, I couldn't exactly put a picture of my face on the internet with, 'Call this number if you know who I am!'" Vax rubbed his face with his hands. "I didn't answer your questions before because I *couldn't*. Now you know why, so can you please stop asking?"

Zai opened his mouth, but then closed it. "Okay. Fine," he said, in a flat tone. "Whatever. I've got more important things to worry about—like finding some dead bodies."

If they're there at all. But Vax didn't voice his protest this time. If Zai didn't trust him, there was nothing else he could do except tag along and hope Zai was right and he wasn't going to get himself killed.

Chapter Six

"I STILL THINK this is a trap," Vax muttered. The cold night air scraped against his exposed skin as they walked from the sky rail station to the river.

Zai glanced at him, an eyebrow raised. "For someone who makes a living by killing people, you're the most risk-averse person I've ever met."

Vax kneaded his forehead. *What, do you think I did my job by charging in blind and firing bullets everywhere?*

"Asking us to meet her by the river? At night? You realize that nothing could scream 'This is a setup!' louder, right?"

Not to mention the location she'd given them was on the edge of the city proper, near an empty parking garage and a few ramshackle properties that hadn't been bought by enterprising developers yet.

"To be fair, the river does seem like a logical place to get rid of a dead body," said Zai.

Vax bit his lower lip. *Not if you know Atali Norman.* While he still wasn't entirely sure how much Atali was involved with the project, there was no way, absolutely no way Atali would allow evidence of a crime to be buried near the river. He didn't like to leave any trace of wrongdoing behind.

"I have full faith in your ability to get us out of a potential ambush alive," said Zai. "Because if not, we're already dead men walking."

Vax wasn't so sure that was supposed to be much of a compliment. "I'm sorry to disappoint you, but there's *still* nothing I can do against a sniper rifle."

"You're such a pessimist."

Vax scowled. "Says the guy who called us 'dead men walking.'"

The coordinates Jane had given them lay ahead, on the riverbank, overgrown with reeds. Nearby, a steel pedestrian bridge spanned the river. Zai stopped by the corner of the last building next to the river to peer at the supposed meeting spot. Vax withdrew his gun, switched the safety off, and kept it by his side.

"It's her. She's there," said Zai. He gave Vax a look. "What were you saying about snipers again?"

Vax regretted not having his augment with its long-range weapons scanner anymore. He gritted his teeth. "She could've hired a decoy. Or maybe she isn't the sniper, but she was hired by the sniper as bait. Or maybe she's going to draw on you and shoot as soon as you step into the open. Are you sure you want to risk any of that?"

Zai gazed at the lone figure standing by the river. "Like I said, I don't think any of that will happen, and I trust Rosa. But the bottom line is, I *have* to know whether she has the information I need or not."

At least no one could fault Zai's dedication to his job.

Vax muttered to him, "If this goes south, you run. I'll hold her off."

Zai had an incredulous expression on his face, though Vax wasn't sure what part of what he said was so hard to believe. "Why?"

Vax gave him a confused look. "Because I have a gun, and you don't?"

Zai gave him another weird look before setting off toward Jane. Vax shook his head before following. Sometimes, he really didn't get Zai.

"Hey!" Zai waved at her once she was within earshot. Without missing a beat, he gestured to Vax and said, "This is my coworker on the *Daily Voice*. He's here to film everything."

That was when Vax saw her hand plunge into her purse, bringing out something with a metallic gleam.

He was faster. He pulled the trigger, aiming for her chest. She dropped to the ground and then popped back up to fire back at him. He ducked and charged forward, barreling her into the ground, trying to give Zai time to run.

"Move!" he yelled at Zai. He couldn't turn to check, but he heard rapid footsteps fleeing.

Vax had never fought for his life before, not against a real danger. The most he'd done was train in the virtual reality gym, but this was different. He aimed for her arms, trying to get her to drop her gun, but with a jerk, she dodged the bullet. Jane's reflexes were faster than a normal human's—*Wait, does she have a spinal bioaug with augmented reflexes, too? But I thought I had the only prototype—*

He was so caught up in his thoughts that she managed to hook her foot around his ankle and throw him to the ground. His gun slipped from his hands. Before he could get up, she was already on top of him, her gun pointed straight between his eyes.

"You're working with Zai Lumero?" she asked flatly.

He didn't answer that. "Who are you?" he said instead.

The gun pressed hard against his forehead, making him wince. "You've cost me Lumero," she said, her voice still cold. "Tell me where he's gone, and I'll spare your life."

Vax let out a harsh, barking laugh. "You really expect me to believe that? Or are you going to tell me you had nothing to do with trying to shoot me with a sniper rifle?"

"My orders are to bring you in alive if possible, dead if not," she said. "Trust me, bringing you in dead would be so much easier."

Vax frowned. "You'll forgive me if I don't believe that you actually want to bring me in alive."

"The first time was...different."

Vax stilled. *Different? What the hell is that supposed to mean?*

"Now where is Lumero?"

"What makes you think I'd know where he is?" he hedged.

Her eyes narrowed. She moved the gun down, and he heard it fire as pain exploded through his abdomen, making him scream.

"I don't have to bring you back in one piece," she said. "Lie to me again, and I'll blow your knee out next."

"Keep...shooting...and you'll kill me," he said, through his teeth.

"I'm sure Mr. Norman will find some way to patch you up."

Vax's blood ran cold. *No.* Bleeding to death would be better.

He tried to push through the fog of pain. He slapped the gun pointed at his face to the side. The bang as it went off almost ripped his eardrums apart. He twisted beneath her and threw her off as hard as he could.

He saw her land on the bridge, but all he could hear was a tinny ringing sound in his ears.

No time to worry. He lunged toward her, grabbing her gun and clumsily rolling to his feet. He pulled the trigger three times.

The pain was throwing off his aim, because one bullet went through her shoulder, another hit her in the side, and the third one missed. The impact threw her back, but she didn't even open her mouth to cry out before she was getting back on her feet, good arm pulling a combat knife from her boot, apparently unconcerned with the bloodstains blooming through her jacket.

What the hell? A chilling thought came to him: *Does she have pain inhibitors?*

He had to end this, fast.

He pulled the trigger again, twice. She lunged to the side. It had to be pain inhibitors; she shouldn't be able to react that quickly with two gunshot wounds. *He* couldn't react that quickly at this point. As she rolled to her feet, he charged her, shoving her against the railing and off the bridge.

Jane tumbled down, hitting the water with a distant splash.

Vax slumped against the ground, breathing hard. At least his hearing had recovered. His hand went to the gunshot wound on his abdomen, and he winced. The black fabric of his jacket obscured the blood, but he could feel it was soaked. *Shit.* He reached behind him, finding a gaping exit wound on his lower back.

The good news was the bullet had passed straight through, so he didn't have to worry about it being stuck inside him. The bad news was the bullet must have hit something important, because he was now losing blood faster than his augment could clot. He hadn't had an opportunity to test how well his healing augment did with a gunshot wound before, so he just had to trust that everything was going to be fine.

Because the alternative was...very bad news.

Focus. It was probably too much to hope that Jane didn't know how to swim. He had to scramble before she swam back to shore and finished him off. Vax got to his feet, unsteadily, and tried to run back to the sky rail station, though he was forced to settle for an awkward jog.

He made it to a parking garage before he was forced to catch his breath for a second, leaning against a concrete pillar, all too aware that he was wasting time. She could emerge from the river at any time. She could—

"What the hell took you—Jesus *Christ.*" Zai stepped out from the parking garage, his eyes wide. "How badly are you hurt?"

"What—" Vax stared at him. "What the hell are you still doing here?"

"Waiting for you. Obviously. Do you need an ambulance, or—"

"It's—fine," Vax ground out. "We need to get out of here. Before she comes back."

"She's coming back?"

"*Zai,*" he hissed through his teeth.

Zai's mouth snapped shut, and he started running.

Vax followed him as best as he could, concentrating on the sound of his footsteps and the dull ache in his legs as he jogged after Zai, trying to keep the pain at bay. He put pressure on the wound, stifling a grunt. *Why isn't it healing fast enough?*

Zai turned to look at him, his eyes narrowing. "We need to call nine-one-one."

"No!" Vax grabbed his arm, nearly losing his balance. "No, you can't do that—"

"This is ridiculous, you're losing a lot of blood—"

"I have a healing augment, remember?"

"Healing augs don't make you *invincible,*" Zai shot back.

"It's *fine*," Vax repeated.

Zai didn't look convinced. "Then I'll text for a lift back before you collapse on me."

The two minutes it took for the AutoRide to arrive were an eternity. As they waited, Vax focused on the way the cold night air burned his lungs as he breathed harshly. Inhale, exhale. Inhale, exhale. The pain wasn't getting any better. Vax squeezed his eyes shut. How long would it take for Jane to swim out of the river and track them down? Not long enough. *Please let the car get here soon...*

The car pulled up, and Vax was dimly aware of Zai helping him into the backseat. He slumped against the window, trying to keep the blood from getting on the inside of the car. *Can't leave any trace...can't leave anything...*

It seemed to take forever for the car to get to their destination; Zai kept swearing every time they had to stop at a red light or wait for traffic. Finally, the door opened, and Zai practically dragged him onto the sidewalk.

The world lurched, and the ground slipped out from under him. He heard Zai curse as he fell, collapsing against a brick wall. Zai's voice sounded so far away.

"Hey! *Hey*! Stay with me here..."

"Just...go..." he slurred.

"Shut up." Something pressed harder against his bleeding wound, making him groan. "We had a deal, remember? You can't die on me. You *can't*."

What do you want from me? Vax wanted to cry out. Zai was alive. He'd done his part, hadn't he? What more did Zai want? He was so tired...so tired of it all. So tired of being used and then discarded, like a person—a *thing*—that didn't matter. No one cared. The only person who knew him had tried to have him killed. There was no one who cared if he lived or died. And he was tired. *So let me die.*

"Hey...Vax." Zai's voice was softer now. Shaking, blood-slicked hands held his face. "I can't do this without you. Please. Just...hang on a little longer. Everything's going to be okay, I promise."

The kind words lulled him, drawing him in, but they didn't soothe his pain. "Can't..." he whispered. "Don't... want..."

"You can. You will. Look at me. Vax, look at me."

He tried. Everything blurred together, details occasionally coming into focus before slipping away again. Brown eyes, looking intently at him.

"I need you to do this. For me. I need you, Vax." His eyes were so gentle. Almost as if... "Promise. Promise you'll do it for me."

Vax tasted salt on his lip. "Tired..."

"I know. I know you are. And I'm sorry. Only a little bit longer, okay? Only a little longer. Just stay with me."

More salt. Something soft stroked his hair.

"It's okay. It's okay...just hang on..."

Vax felt Zai haul him to his feet with a grunt. He nearly blacked out, and all he could catch were fragments as he wavered on the edge of consciousness. Door. Yellow light, linoleum floor. Elevator. Low ceilings and a narrow hallway. Falling onto the hard couch, and bone-deep relief at not having to move anymore.

He heard voices. Zai was talking to someone. Who? Police? Paramedics? Zai sounded agitated, but Vax's comprehension was starting to slip. Everything was going fuzzy and black...

"Hey. Hey, hey. Look at me."

A cold hand touched his face. He forced his eyes open, with difficulty. Tried to concentrate on Zai's face, fading in and out of focus.

"Listen, this is going to hurt like hell, okay? And I'm really sorry."

He didn't understand what was going on. Hands were pushing his shirt up, and even through his agonized, mostly-unconscious haze, icy terror set in. He tried to push the hands away, but he was too weak. *No. No!*

"It's okay!" Zai's voice sounded distant. "It's okay...you're going to be okay..."

Lies. People always lied to him. He didn't know why, but they did. He'd trusted Atali once, and look how that turned out: biggest fucking mistake of his life.

Smooth fingers moved across his skin. He didn't trust those fingers, but he couldn't fight against the hands, so he gave in. He'd lost ownership of his body a long time ago, and there was nothing left he could do. *Please don't hurt me. Please don't hurt me too much.*

He wasn't prepared for the liquid fire that doused his abdomen and *holy fuck—*

REALITY DRIFTED TOWARD and away from him like the tide.

Sometimes he thought he was walking through a lightless tunnel. Corpses littered the ground, all bloody, gaping wounds revealing bone and organs. He was the only one alive, and he didn't know where he was walking to.

It was so dark. The emptiness wrapped around him like a blanket, squeezing the breath from his lungs and crushing him.

Sometimes he was aware of a voice speaking to him in a low tone. He couldn't make out all the words, but he clung to them, because he needed to know there was someone else here with him. That he wasn't alone.

"...can't...in pain...sorry..."

"...not him...but still..."

"Don't die...please don't die..."

AT FIRST, WHEN consciousness came back to him, he felt...fine. Weak, but fine. Then he tried to sit up, and it felt like someone reached into his stomach and lit him on fire.

"*Aahngh*," he groaned.

Footsteps. Zai's voice, close by. "How do you feel?"

"Like...I'd rather be dead," he croaked.

Zai gave a dry laugh. "Well thank God you aren't. Here." A plastic bottle in his hand; Zai wrapped his fingers around it. "Can you drink?"

Vax tried. He managed to get a little down. He grimaced at the smell of dried blood on his hands. "Shit. I look like a butcher."

Zai passed him a damp towel. Vax set the water bottle aside and took it, wiping his hands and face, which was sticky with dried salt. Much better.

"Thanks. I..." Vax blinked hard, trying to get his vision to focus. "How long...was I out?"

"About..." Zai's eyes glanced to the corner, and he did a double take. "Eight hours. Felt like forever, though."

Vax glanced at his abdomen, which now had a gauze bandage covering it. "You did this?"

"Um...yeah." Zai coughed. "I had to call my sister for instructions, and she was practically screaming in my ear about how everything was supposed to be sterilized with something *other* than a bottle of whiskey and only a doctor should do it...but hey, you're alive, right?"

"Yeah." Vax closed his eyes. "Thank you. You could've...left me to die."

"Yeah, well..." Zai cleared his throat. "I didn't...think you would actually risk your life to save mine."

"You're on an important mission," Vax said, his words starting to slur a little with exhaustion. "Can't...let Cyrex win."

"Thanks for that," Zai said quietly.

"Hn."

Everything went hazy, and he drifted off again.

He woke some time later to the smell of baked beans.

"You awake?"

Vax took a deep breath and rubbed his face, stubble rasping against his palms. He still felt weak, but the pain seemed to be gone for good this time. "Yeah."

"You've lost a lot of blood." Zai thrust a can and spoon into his hands. "Eat."

"Yes, Doctor," Vax said sarcastically. He hadn't realized how hungry he was until he put a spoonful of beans into his mouth, and it suddenly tasted like the best thing he'd ever had in his life.

Zai snorted as he perched on the edge of the coffee table. "My sister would be horrified if she ever heard you call me that." After a pause, he said, hesitantly, "Do you mind if I...look at the wound?"

Vax swallowed his mouthful of beans. "Why?"

Zai looked a bit startled. "To make sure it isn't infected or anything."

"Um...I know what an infected wound looks like," said Vax, wryly. "I can take care of it myself."

"Right," Zai muttered.

Silence passed as Vax finished the can of beans. Zai finally said, "So...what happened out there?"

Vax grimaced. "She's got the same reflexes, plus pain inhibitors and better combat training." Or maybe he just sucked. That was a possibility, too.

"Pain inhibitors," Zai echoed. "Aren't those only for people who have medical conditions that cause chronic pain?"

Vax shrugged. "There are always...*creative* uses for bioaugs."

Zai looked troubled for a moment before he shook his head. "If you're an assassin, what's wrong with your combat skills?"

"Nothing's *wrong*," said Vax. He was trained; he could take down the average person who came at him. "I don't usually have to go hand-to-hand against people, that's all."

Zai looked stunned. "You don't?"

Between that and the "murder dungeon," Vax was starting to wonder if Zai knew what assassinations entailed at all.

"Yeah, well, the important part is, we're still alive...for now." After he set the empty can aside with the spoon, he leaned back against the armrest of the couch and met Zai's gaze. In a quiet voice, he said, "Thanks...again."

Zai glanced away. "Just...repaying the favor. Again."

"Because you still need me to keep you alive, right?" Vax said, in a dry voice.

Zai gave him a long look.

"I...can't deny that," he said, at last. "But I'm also...not a heartless bastard, you know. I couldn't just...watch you die."

Vax blinked at that.

"Because I...look like Ethan?" he asked, tentatively.

Zai's mouth tightened, and he had trouble meeting Vax's gaze again. "Well...I wouldn't abandon a dying stranger, no matter what he looked like. That's just... wrong."

Vax was quiet, trying to understand. He'd assumed he had been a means to an end, simply worth more to Zai alive than dead. He'd assumed the same thing with Atali, and Atali decided to get rid of him as soon as he became a liability. It was hard for him to wrap his mind around Zai's words and believe them—not because he was sure Zai was lying, but because the idea that he was worth something other than for pure utilitarian value made him feel...strange.

"You're a good person," he said.

Zai's expression flickered with surprise and a shadow of something Vax couldn't identify.

"I..." Zai shook his head. "I'm just a normal person, trying to do the right thing. Sometimes, I'm not even sure what that is," he murmured, as though speaking to himself.

"I mean it. Everything you've been doing, trying to investigate Cyrex—you care about people you've never even met. And you put your neck on the line to save my life. You're...a really nice guy," said Vax, his voice soft.

Zai's mouth twitched into a ghost of a smile for one moment. Then, abruptly, his smile faltered, and he looked away, coughing.

"Yeah, well..." He cleared his throat. "Uh...I guess it's late. You should probably get some rest."

"Sure, um...see you tomorrow?"

"Yeah, see you," Zai said, to the floor. He got up and went into the bedroom, closing the door without looking at Vax once.

Puzzled, Vax wrapped his arms around his knees, staring at the spot on the coffee table where Zai had been sitting. There was a strange, dull ache in his chest, as though someone had stabbed him and left the knife inside.

Was he losing his mind? Spending so much time with Zai that he was starting to...to think that...?

Shaking his head at himself, he grabbed the blanket, spread it over himself, and curled up on the couch, closing his eyes.

Chapter Seven

THE AWKWARDNESS WAS still there the next morning, as soon as Zai opened the bedroom door and he and Vax locked eyes. He looked away immediately, and Vax felt the same confused, phantom twinge before Zai cleared his throat, speaking carefully.

"How are you feeling?"

Vax had inspected the wound while he was in the bathroom to shave and wash the blood out of his clothes.

"It doesn't look like there's any infection," he said.

"So...how are you feeling?" Zai repeated.

Vax frowned a little. "Um...fine...I guess?"

Zai nodded, as though that answer satisfied him. He cleared his throat again, still without making eye contact. "I guess I...owe you an apology," he said.

Vax stared at him, totally caught off guard. "For what?"

"You wouldn't have almost bled to death if I hadn't dragged you to that ambush, which you'd been against from the start. It's one thing if I'm risking my own life, but it's another to risk someone else's. So...I'm sorry."

Vax hadn't expected Zai to apologize. "Uh...well, you saved my life, so I think we can call it even."

Zai shook his head with a frustrated expression.

"I wouldn't have had to if we hadn't gone. It was an unnecessary risk, and I didn't get anything out of it. Worse— it's probably safe to say that all the information was a bust...which brings us all the way back to square one." He sighed, his shoulders sagging. "I'm not even sure if any of that information from Celia Duquette is true at this point. If Jane—assuming that's her real name—was comfortable telling us about that, it's probably fake, right?"

"I'd think so. She probably found out what Celia Duquette knew and told you the same thing to make you believe her." A thought suddenly occurred to him. Zai had believed Vax was the one who had killed her, but...was it possible that Jane had, instead?

"And she's still out there, somewhere, planning her next move to try to kill us," Zai went on. "I mean, at least she doesn't know where we are, but I'm not sure either of us can survive in one piece if we run into her again. No offense."

"None taken," said Vax.

Zai dragged his hands through his hair and frowned to himself. "I don't get it, though. Rosa was the one who told me about her, and Cyrex's HR confirmed she was an employee."

Vax cleared his throat. "Have you considered that the entire thing was a setup?"

Zai looked at him. "You've said that before, but still...that's an elaborate setup."

"Not really. All it would take is for her to know what you're investigating, make an educated guess at who you'd talk to, and persuade them to pass along false information. As for Cyrex's HR, well, she works for Atali. It'd be easy for him to pull the strings."

Zai didn't look particularly shocked, but he still seemed uneasy.

"I think it's time for another talk with Rosa," he said.

THEY RETURNED TO the soup kitchen they'd visited. This time, Zai didn't chat with any of the other visitors; he made a beeline for Rosa as soon as he saw her.

"You left a voice mail for me two days ago about someone named Jane Shaw," he said without preamble.

She looked at him with surprise. "Yeah. Was she helpful?"

"Actually, no. She turned out to be an assassin who almost killed me."

And almost killed me, Vax silently added from where he was observing a table away.

Rosa laughed—only to stop when she realized Zai wasn't laughing with her. "Wait...you're serious?"

"The point is, she wasn't who she said she was, and she doesn't want this investigation to go forward."

"I...wow, really?" She was still staring as though she expected him to say he was joking. "Oh my God, I'm so sorry, I had no idea...an *assassin*?"

"How did you meet her?" Zai asked.

"Well...she showed up at the employment agency I visited yesterday, asking about Elisa. I thought it was kind of a weird coincidence, since you'd talked to me the day before. I mentioned your name to her, thinking you guys could compare notes." Rosa shook her head. "My God, I am so sorry. I thought she wanted to help."

Zai sighed. "Don't worry about it. It's not your fault I've made some pretty powerful enemies."

"You're saying that whoever made Elisa disappear is trying to kill you?" Rosa asked, her eyes wide.

"Could you please not say that quite so loudly?" Zai kept his own voice low. "Maybe. I don't know. Right now, I've got three assassination attempts on my head and not a lot of information to show for it. If there's anything else you can tell me about, ah, Jane Shaw, or anything else you remember about where Elisa might've gone, I'd really appreciate it."

Rosa paused. "I don't think there's anything more I can tell you about Jane. She said she worked for Cyrex, and that's it. She didn't say much about herself. When I asked her how she found me, she said she found some emergency contact info in an old file on Elisa. But I do remember Elisa said something weird one time..."

Zai suddenly perked up. "Oh?"

"Yeah. A few days before she disappeared, she kept muttering, 'Before, before, before' to herself. Except she stressed it weirdly, like, 'Be-*fore*, be-*fore*.'" Rosa shrugged. "I'm sorry. I have no idea what it might mean."

Vax frowned to himself. Be-*fore*...as in...no, it had to be a coincidence...right?

"That's okay." Zai looked disappointed, but he gave her a tired smile. "It might be something, it might be nothing, but every little bit helps."

Vax kept quiet as they left. Once they'd walked a block away from the soup kitchen, Zai exhaled.

"So much for getting more information. 'Before'...any idea what that means?"

Vax hesitated. "I'm...not sure..."

Zai glanced at him. "Wait, do you know something?"

"I'm not sure," Vax repeated, staring at the concrete sidewalk. He glanced around them. No one looked their way; the street was full of busy people intent on their destinations. "I'll tell you later."

When they got back, Zai shut the door and turned to him impatiently. "Okay. What do you know?"

"I..." The more Vax thought it through, the more it sounded like sheer coincidence. "I don't know. It's probably nothing."

"Just tell me what you're thinking."

Vax sighed. "Well, there's a lab at Cyrex's northern building called B4. You know...basement level four. B4...get it?" He shrugged. "It's probably coincidence, though."

Zai didn't look quite so ready to dismiss it. "How do you know about that lab?"

"I've...been there before. But I've never seen any of those nine people there," he added. He winced. "Well...not that I can remember, at least."

"Hmm..." Zai's brow furrowed. "What did you visit the lab for?"

"Uh..." Vax swallowed. "It's where I get my bioaugs."

Zai looked at him. "So...it's some kind of bioaug lab."

"Yeah."

"But even if Elisa had been saying 'B4,' it's not like that's the only building with a basement level four."

"Yeah, I know," Vax admitted. "It was a long shot..."

"But maybe we should check it out."

Vax blinked at him. "Um...what?"

"We're on a deadline." Zai's mouth was set in a grim line. "It looks like Jane's not going to give up until we're dead. Which means it's time for something more drastic."

"What, getting ambushed by an assassin for the second time wasn't drastic enough for you?"

Zai ignored his comment. "The best thing to do right now is to get concrete evidence of what happened to those nine people. Right now, I've gotten nothing except multiple assassination attempts. I don't know why I haven't been able to find whoever recruited those people, but I've tried everything I can think of and I'm running out of options."

"So you're actually suggesting that we break into Cyrex's lab?"

For a moment, Vax had the feeble hope that Zai would burst into laughter and say "Gotcha! Just messing with you." But Zai only gazed back calmly at him, his expression dead serious.

"Do you know what a *terrible* idea that is?" Vax said, feeling like he was stating the obvious. "There are security measures all over the place. Besides, it's not like you're going to find dead bodies in the lab by peeking in there."

"Aren't you supposed to be an expert in breaking into secure places?"

"Uh, *no*?" Vax said, taken aback. "Whatever gave you that idea?"

"You're an assassin," said Zai, as though the answer were self-evident.

"I'm not a thief or a *burglar*." He hadn't typically been required to break into somewhere secure to get to his targets.

"You broke into my apartment," said Zai, accusingly.

"In case you haven't noticed, your apartment doesn't exactly have state-of-the-art security." Vax rubbed his forehead. "Please tell me that changes your plan."

"Not really." Zai held his hands up, as though to ward off Vax's protests. "Hear me out, okay? I have it on good authority that all of Cyrex's most secure information is kept off-cloud and as close to unhackable from the outside as possible. That means the only way to get to that information is to see it in person. And it doesn't hurt to take a peek at the top-secret lab along the way, just in case. You never know what they might leave lying around..."

"Okay, but here's one major flaw in your plan: Do you not realize that all of their computers are obviously password-locked? Or have you forgotten to tell me that you moonlight as a computer hacker?"

"Well, as it so happens, Integrity's been trying to hack Cyrex's systems for a while now—they've found a flaw in the security camera control system, but they can't crack Cyrex's server from the outside, so they've been trying to get someone inside Cyrex's labs forever. All I have to do is volunteer myself for the job, and they can do the rest."

Vax looked at him. "Are you serious? I didn't know you knew Integrity. I didn't know you even *liked* Integrity."

He had no opinion on augment-free philosophies in general, but Integrity always struck him as...extreme. Going beyond the issues of bioaug prices and accessibility, they used scare-mongering tactics and sketchy, cherry-picked "science" to blame augments for causing everything from Alzheimer's to autism, and they kept claiming augments would "steal" or "warp" people's humanity...whatever that was supposed to mean.

"Situations like these are kind of the point of making friends with people you don't like," Zai said. "After all, without them, we wouldn't be in this apartment right now."

That answered one question, and their odds admittedly looked better if Zai had Integrity's help. Still...

"But how are we supposed to get in?" Vax asked, exasperated. "I have a microchip—"

Zai's expression lit up. "You do?"

"Yeah, except I'd ping the system as soon as I swiped in," Vax went on sourly. "Which means I can't use it. Also, I don't have security clearance for any of the labs, so it's useless."

"Oh. Bummer." Though Zai didn't look as crushed as Vax had hoped. "Well, that's okay. There's still a way."

"And if we get caught? How do you plan on finishing your article from jail?"

"Then we don't get caught, and even if we do, no one's going to jail. Relax."

"How can you be so sure?" Vax asked, incredulous. "Unless you know how to charm the security drones into ignoring us?"

Zai eyed him. "I thought you'd be more excited about this kind of thing."

"Forgive me for not jumping for joy at what sounds like a suicide run."

Zai waved dismissively. "Don't be so dramatic. It's not a suicide run—I have a plan."

"Okay..." Vax folded his arms, still skeptical. "What kind of plan would that be?"

VAX WAS CONVINCED Zai's plan was going to go horribly wrong.

There was no possible way, for starters, that Zai could simply talk his way into the lab. They'd spent two days staking out the lab and observing its exterior security—two days that Vax argued weren't nearly enough, while Zai, as usual, disagreed—before making their move, and Vax still couldn't see how this was going to happen. He hung around outside the building, watching as Zai approached the receptionist, and listened through the open channel in his node. He was certain she would call for a guard and have him thrown out.

"Hi!" Zai said brightly, giving the receptionist a smile.

"Oh—hi!" She sounded flustered, for some reason.

"I'm here for a job interview."

"Job interview?" the receptionist repeated. "It's after-hours—are you sure you got the time right?"

"I'm sure I did—I checked and double-checked. Dr. Hussain said he was really busy and wouldn't have time until the evening."

"All right, then..." The receptionist sounded hesitant, but she went on. "I'll need you to sign in here before you can get a visitor's pass."

"Sure thing," said Zai without hesitation and with another wide, dazzling smile. Vax didn't miss the way Zai's hand brushed against hers as he took a tablet from her. The receptionist blushed, and Vax resisted the urge to groan aloud.

Zai finished writing on the tablet and handed it back. The receptionist looked it over. "Thank you so much, Mr....uh...Yu?"

"Yue," Zai supplied. He flashed her an apologetic grin. "Yeah, not the easiest Mandarin last name to pronounce, sorry."

"No, I think it sounds beautiful. Uh..." The receptionist cleared her throat and handed him a card. "Here's your visitor's pass. Dr. Hussain works on the seventh floor. Um...good luck."

"Thank you so much. You've been such a great help," Zai gushed.

"Ah...my pleasure. Hope to see you again soon."

"You too," said Zai with one last smile.

Vax watched as Zai disappeared inside. All right, he had to admit Zai was good. Listening to Zai flirt with the receptionist had annoyed him, though. Did he have to sound so enthusiastic?

Shaking his head, Vax walked to the back of the building, next to the emergency exit, and waited. The drive that Zai received from Integrity that contained a program to hack and download files from Cyrex's computers sat in his pocket in case Zai couldn't pass through security with it, which meant Zai needed to get him in. He still didn't believe this was going to work. What, was Zai going to flirt with a security guard to get the access chip?

About fifteen minutes later, the door opened, and Zai popped his head out. He flashed the access chip. "See?" he said. "You worry too much."

Vax stared at him. "You did *not* talk a guard into giving you the access chip."

"Want to bet?"

Though Vax was sorely tempted to ask for more detail, they were on a timetable. One of these days, he *really* needed to figure out how Zai could simply talk people into doing things.

Zai glanced at him. "Someone's in a bad mood."

"We don't have long before someone will notice the cameras are frozen, remember?"

"Yes, sir, Captain Sourpuss, sir."

Vax resisted the temptation to roll his eyes as they made their way down the emergency stairwell to level B4. He motioned to Zai to wait as he put his ear against the door, listening for a passing guard.

Faint footsteps approached, and Vax held his breath. They passed by the door, and then faded. Vax counted two minutes before slowly, silently opening the door to survey the area.

Clear.

They emerged into the sterile white hallway. It was silent and deserted, but that didn't soothe Vax's unease. Other than ducking into one of the rooms, there was nowhere to hide if a guard turned a corner at one of the ends. Even their soft, careful footsteps sounded too loud to Vax's ears.

Zai tried to peer through the darkened windows. "What's with these tinted windows? I can't see anything through them," he whispered.

"Yeah, it's something called 'secrecy.'"

Zai frowned. "The labs at Meridian don't look like this. Whatever's going on here has to be either military-sponsored research or illegal."

Oh? Vax had assumed the windows were standard, but then again, he'd never had any comparison.

In any case, he could've told Zai what was behind the darkened windows. That was the room where the doctors performed operations. That was a recuperating room. That was an examination room. That was testing room A...

Vax's back throbbed dully, and he absently reached up to touch his spinal augment at the back of his neck, fingertips brushing against hard synthetic skin where his vertebrae should've been. He had to fight not to glance at the security cameras on the ceiling, reminding himself that Zai's mysterious friends at Integrity were taking care of them. Still, paranoia itched at him. They had to hurry.

"We need to get into somewhere with a computer," said Zai, interrupting his thoughts. "Either a lab or someone's office. Actually, a lab. I want to take pictures."

"What kind of lab?" Vax asked him.

Zai gave him a look. "What kinds of labs do they have here?"

"Well, that's an operating room—"

"What? Where?"

Vax pointed him to the room, and Zai swiped the security access chip at the door and opened it. He followed Zai into the darkened room and closed the door.

"Whoa." Zai whipped out his pod and began snapping pictures. "A state-of-the-art bioaug operating room inside a research lab? That's not suspicious at all..."

Vax bit back the urge to ask if Zai always talked to himself this much while breaking into secure facilities.

"You happen to know if they have any other medical equipment on this floor?" Zai asked, still snapping away, zooming in on the monitors and machines next to the operating table.

"There's another room with an MRI—"

"An MRI?" Zai echoed, giving him a sharp look. "You sure?"

"It's some kind of brain imaging machine, anyway." Vax glanced back at him. "What? What's that look for?"

"I have to get a picture of this," was all Zai muttered, springing for the door. "Which room is it?"

"Across the hall and to the left." Vax followed him to the brain imaging room.

"Hmm." Zai once again took pictures of the machine, his brow furrowed. "You know, it's funny that they have an MRI here when, according to their website, all the neural augment research is done in their main building."

Vax said nothing. It felt strange, being here without having a doctor in a white coat next to him, giving him instructions.

"Where's the next stop?" Zai asked.

Vax snapped out of his reverie. "Shouldn't we look for a computer?"

"All right. Where are the offices?" Zai opened the door; then Vax heard a quiet clatter and the sound of the door swinging shut. He glanced over to see that Zai had dropped the chip inside the room.

"Crap," Zai hissed from the other side of the door.

I've got it, Vax was about to tell him, as he bent to retrieve the chip, when he heard a tapping sound coming from somewhere down the hall. It sounded ominously like footsteps.

"Excuse me," a rough voice called out. "Who are you?"

Vax's heart stopped.

"Oh, thank goodness you're here," Zai exclaimed, without missing a beat. "I was supposed to meet Dr. Hussain here? For a job interview? I think I took a wrong turn somewhere, and now I'm completely lost."

Vax was trapped inside the MRI room; if he opened the door now, it would be over for both him and Zai.

"How did you get in here?" the security guard asked, suspiciously.

Vax's hand slowly inched toward his gun.

"Someone let me in, when I explained what I was here for. Wait...am I not supposed to be here?" Zai's feigned uncertainty would've completely convinced Vax if he hadn't known better.

"Come with me," the guard said.

"Oh God, I hope I'm not in trouble..."

They began to walk away, their footsteps echoing against the floor.

Vax stayed where he was, torn. Should he follow them to make sure Zai was okay? What if the guard recognized him and was under orders to get rid of him in any way possible?

Then again, he had the drive with the hacking program and the access chip, and if Zai was capable of talking his way out of the situation, he'd probably want Vax to look for more information.

Why did I ever agree to this? Vax silently groaned to himself.

Screw it; he couldn't, in good conscience, continue without knowing Zai wasn't going to get arrested or murdered. He crept out of the room and began following the faint sound of footsteps and voices, trying to stay quiet. At least Zai was still talking the entire time.

Zai and the guard passed through a door. Vax was waiting until their voices had almost faded before he followed—until he heard the door open again on its own, with the nearly silent whir of an approaching security drone.

Damn it.

Of *course* today, of all days, the drones were deviating from their usual exterior routes to make an internal sweep. Or maybe their routes had been changed because the security guard had picked up Zai. Vax cursed silently. He should've thought of that possibility. Had they realized who Zai was? He hoped it was just normal protocol.

Vax glanced around wildly for somewhere to hide. The closest room was an office belonging to Dr. Amanda Fields.

He quickly opened it with the access chip and darted inside, quietly shutting the door behind him. Vax flattened himself against the wall as the whirring came closer. *No, no, no, don't come this way.* Would it come inside? He didn't know enough about how the security drones were programmed. It could probably scan for him through the door. He wasn't breathing, but his heartbeat sounded like a drum, hammering so loudly against his ribs he was convinced the drone could detect it.

Closer.

Vax quietly drew his own gun and aimed it at the door, his palms cold and clammy. This was a horrible idea. He should never have let Zai talk him into coming here. Even if he managed to shoot the drone, the lab's security would be instantly alerted, and it would be game over for him.

Closer...

Vax watched the light seeping from below the door. A shadow moved across it.

And...kept moving.

Vax didn't breathe until the whirring grew faint. Then, he finally let himself take a breath, put his gun away, and looked around the office.

A computer sat on the desk by the wall. Well, this was his chance to finish what they'd come here for. He just hoped Zai was okay.

Now to see if this thing actually works.

He plugged the drive into the computer. The screen instantly flashed, letters and numbers appearing in code he didn't recognize. At the bottom, he saw "in progress, please wait."

When the hacking program finally finished, the computer screen shifted to the desktop. He sucked in a breath. *Wow. Who knew that Integrity actually has a competent hacker?*

A window popped up. *Please enter the path to the folder to download.*

He wasn't a computer security expert at all, but he couldn't help thinking there had to be a safeguard against randomly copying files. He left the window alone for now, the cursor blinking.

He poked around the server for a bit. There was a folder named "Project VAX," and he frowned. *"Project"? What the hell?*

When he opened it, he found eleven sub-folders, named numerically from "01" to "11."

Well that's helpful, he thought sarcastically to himself.

He opened the folder named "01" and found some video files, plus documents full of notes. One file named "Subject 01" caught his attention. He opened it—and found a picture of a familiar-looking face.

It was one of the faces of Zai's nine missing people.

Wait...no way...

Heartbeat pulsing in his ears, he quickly went through the other folders. Each of them contained a picture of one of the missing people. Then he got to "10"...

The face was his own.

He sat back in the chair, staring at the screen for a long moment. *No. No way. I would've* known *if I were part of some experiment with other people involved...*

Unless Atali had simply decided not to tell him anything. He was becoming less and less sure that Atali had told him the whole truth, and that thought terrified him.

But what the hell was "Project VAX"?

There was still folder "11." He opened that folder—and found a picture of the other assassin. Jane Shaw...or whatever her real name was.

But that meant...she was also part of this? She was also an assassin...and Atali had done the same kinds of experiments on her that he did on Vax? And Vax hadn't known about her this entire time?

Vax's head was spinning. *What the hell is all of this?* The answers were right in front of him, but he didn't have time to search through all the files, or else he'd be here all night.

The window was still there. *Please enter the path to the folder to download.*

He chewed on his lower lip for a moment, and then typed the path to the "Project VAX" folder and pressed the Enter key. As the program began working, he looked at Dr. Fields's emails. The email program was already logged in to her account. After thinking for a minute, he typed "Project VAX" into the search box and pressed the return key. Maybe he could find an explanation here.

The search returned only a handful of emails. Maybe they used some other codename for the project? The oldest one dated back over seven years ago. There were a few more from four years ago. He clicked on one of them with an attached file.

Here is the information you requested. Do not forward this email to or share its contents with anyone. Do not reproduce this file without permission, and destroy this email immediately when you finish reading.

It was lucky for him that the doctor hadn't followed those instructions. He opened the file, curious as to what top-secret information was inside.

Shock froze him, at first.

Then, his next thought was: *I am such an idiot.*

You look like the love of my life, Zai had said. All those strange, searching looks.

I'm sorry I remind you of him, and, *You hate that I look like him*, Vax had said, like some clueless, blithering moron.

He should've put it together. But the possibility hadn't even occurred him until he was staring at the picture for himself. The face on the screen—it was his face. *His face.* Except it had a different name.

Tromer, Ethan David.

The height listed—it was the same as his. Date of birth…Ethan Tromer would be twenty-five years old, and Vax had always put his best guess of his own age as somewhere in his twenties.

He scrutinized the face on the screen, looking for any difference, no matter how miniscule. Ethan Tromer's face was slightly rounder, as though he'd been better fed than Vax was, but that was it.

But…no, there had to be a difference. Otherwise, Zai would have said so, right? Especially once Vax had told him about his amnesia? There had to be some kind of different birthmark or scar or his voice—

Voice. He remembered that night when he'd found Zai half asleep. *Just talk to me*, Zai had said. Vax had thought he was simply delusional at that point, but...what if he hadn't been?

But...but Zai had said that Ethan Tromer was dead, hadn't he? He had to have some reason for saying that. A dead body couldn't be faked...or at least, was unlikely to be faked...

But then why else would there be a file here, on a Cyrex server, for a supposedly dead soldier who just happened to have the exact same face as him? And...

I want to marry you.

He'd convinced himself that that had been nothing more than a recurring dream, to spare himself the crushing disappointment of not being able to remember anything else, but...what if it hadn't been a dream? What if it really had been a shred of a memory?

His heartbeat pounded in his ears, and his hands were shaking, slick with cold sweat.

All this time. Zai had had the answer, and it had been sitting right in front of him, *all this time.* And—what, Zai had hidden it? Refused to tell him? Kept poking and prodding Vax for personal information he already knew, but Vax didn't, as though it were some—demented kind of game to him?

But *why?*

He tried to go through everything he remembered Zai saying, in his head, when it hit him. Not the answer to that question, but something else. He staggered back from the screen, unable to breathe. The world was twisting, turning inside out, reforming into something completely unrecognizable in front of him.

Oh my God, I'm...I'm him?

The person Zai couldn't talk about without getting a wistful, heartbroken, yearning look in his eyes. *Mr. Walked-on-Water*. The guy Vax had been fucking *jealous* of, because of how much Zai had obviously loved him.

Ethan Tromer.

He pressed his trembling fingertips to his brow. No, this was...it was too much. Something weak and helpless welled up inside him, a raw, wordless pain.

He'd thought that, if he ever uncovered his past, it would be the happiest moment of his life. So why did he feel...betrayed, instead? And betrayed by whom? Atali? Zai?

Himself?

A window suddenly popped up on the screen, blotting out the picture. "Error: Download interrupted. Unable to continue. Retrying in 5 seconds..."

Vax stared at the screen. Footsteps pounded outside in the hallway. He snatched the drive off the computer—just as the door slammed open, and he looked up to find himself staring at the muzzle of a gun. Security. *Shit.* He should have been thinking about how to escape, how to get out of here—

But he couldn't *think*. Not with that picture, and that name—*Tromer, Ethan David*—drowning out everything else in his head.

"Hands over your head!" the security guard barked.

He did so, even though all he could think was *No*. No, he had to get out of here. Had to escape. Had to talk to Zai.

I have to talk to Zai...

"You." The guard's eyes narrowed, recognizing him from the times he'd come into the lab.

"I have a right to be here," Vax said, trying to sound more confident than he felt. It wasn't working. His eyes darted around the room, taking stock. Computer, wired into the wall. Swivel chair, next to him. He took a small step back.

"Not after hours, you don't." The guard took one hand off his gun and moved it toward his ear node.

He had to move *now*.

He kicked the swivel chair toward the guard and ducked. The gun went off with a bang, the bullet thudding into the wall behind him, and the guard yelped as the chair collided with him. Vax lunged forward, wrestling the gun from the guard's hands and knocking him on the temple with the butt of the gun. The guard slumped to the ground, going still.

Vax crouched down and placed two fingers against the pulse point on the guard's neck. Still alive.

He let out the breath he'd been holding, but he had to hurry. The gunshot would've drawn the attention of anyone else nearby. Keeping the gun with him, he ran from the office and down the hall, toward the emergency stairwell.

He slammed the access chip into the slot by the door, overriding the emergency alarm. He shoved the door open, raced up the stairs to the ground floor, and slipped through the door that led outside. He didn't stop running until, a dozen blocks later, his adrenaline suddenly dropped and exhaustion hit him like a wall. He staggered into an alley and sank to the concrete, with a brick wall at his back. His head fell into his hands, bowed by the weight of the truth.

Ethan Tromer.

I'm Ethan Tromer.

Chapter Eight

ZAI ANSWERED THE door seconds after Vax rang the doorbell. Relief crossed his expression once he saw Vax.

"Oh, thank God. I was afraid you'd gotten shot to hell again. I wanted to wait for you, but the guard was watching me when I left."

Vax just stood there, staring at him. Zai was looking back at him as though he were Vax the assassin. As though he didn't *know*.

As though all this time, he hadn't known.

Zai frowned. "What is it?"

Vax stepped inside without a word. When the door closed firmly behind him, he spun to face Zai.

"You said Ethan Tromer died in the war. Did you ever see his body?"

"Excuse me?" Zai was staring at him with blank surprise. "Why are you asking that?"

"Because all this time, you've been going on about how much I looked like Ethan Tromer, but I thought you only meant I looked like his biological relative. I didn't know you meant I looked like the *exact same person*."

Zai flinched. "I..."

"But it's not just that I look like him." Vax narrowed his eyes with certainty. "My voice—it's also the same. *Isn't it*?"

He took Zai's silence as assent.

"And your freak-out when I mentioned my amnesia. That was the last confirmation, wasn't it? You already knew then that I *was* Ethan—"

"I don't *know anything*," Zai exploded. His voice shook. "What was I supposed to think? That my boyfriend—who died in a war halfway around the world—has somehow been alive for the past four years, with amnesia? Or that, out of the billions of people on this planet, someone else just *happens* to look like him? Hell, there are even websites and apps dedicated to that kind of thing—"

"But was there a body?" Vax asked harshly.

Zai jerked, wincing. When he didn't answer, Vax asked him again, "*Was there a body?*"

"There—there was a bomb," Zai stammered. "There was nothing left to bury...only charred bones...that was what they'd said..."

So, in other words, there hadn't been a body. Not for certain.

"You could've *told* me," Vax said.

"Told you *what*? 'Hey, you *might* be my supposedly dead boyfriend, there's just the question of how the hell you managed to survive with no one knowing, but none of us can figure it out because you conveniently have *amnesia*'?" Zai shook his head and added bitterly, "And you're fine with the life you have now, aren't you?"

"Fine? *Fine*?" Vax repeated incredulously. "You think I'm *fine*? Walking around with a huge chunk of my life that's *missing*? Being forced to work for a manipulative, sadistic bastard? Having to fucking *kill people* for a living because I *literally* can't remember anything else? You think I'm *fine* like this?"

Zai stared at him. Suddenly, Vax wasn't angry anymore—he was exhausted, and aching with loneliness and loss. His head spun with confusion, he didn't know who he was or who he was supposed to be, and he was staring at the person who had once loved Ethan Tromer—who had loved *him*—more than anything else in the world.

Vax surged forward and kissed him.

It lasted only a second before Zai pushed him back, eyes wide. "What—what are you *doing*?"

The rejection hit him like an icy slap. He stood there, blinking hard, his pulse beating wildly out of control. "I...I thought..."

I thought you'd be happy. Because I'm Ethan Tromer, and you said you loved him. I need to remember...I need something to make sense. I need something good, to chase away all the bad.

"I'm sorry, but—" Zai slowly backed away from him. "Even though you look like Ethan—even though you *sound* like Ethan—you *can't* be him. I don't care how it all seems. He died in the war, and people don't just die and come back to life. And besides that..." Zai's eyes narrowed. "Ethan could never have become an assassin. He would've *died* rather than harm innocent people. Even if he'd lost all his memories, he would've remembered that much."

Vax dropped his gaze, shoulders slumped, struggling to breathe. Nothing made sense anymore; his head was spinning, and he was dizzy with vertigo.

"I don't know who you are." Those six words punched a hole through Vax's gut, like cold lead bullets. "But you're not him, okay? There's just no way it's possible."

Zai turned and started walking toward the bedroom door.

Vax's chest constricted. *No, please don't go.* Raising his head, he mumbled, "You wanted to marry me."

Zai froze midstep. He slowly turned his head to face Vax. "What...what did you say?" he whispered, his eyes wide.

Vax swallowed. "You said that...didn't you? I don't know when, or where, but...you said that."

He almost regretted bringing it up; Zai looked as though Vax had shot him straight through the heart. And then Zai's expression darkened with fury.

"How..." Zai walked back over to him until they were face to face. His voice shook with anger. "How do you know that? How the *hell do you know about that*?"

"I don't..." Vax shook his head. "I don't know. I just...do."

"No. No, you can't possibly know that," Zai snarled. "The man I said that to, the man I loved...he's long dead."

Zai walked through the door and slammed it shut behind him.

And Vax was alone.

THE CLICK OF a doorknob turning woke Vax up. Zai was standing in the bedroom doorway, watching him with an unreadable expression.

"Zai?" he said, his heartbeat thudding in his ears.

Slowly, wordlessly, Zai came over to the couch. Vax sat up, tensing, unsure as to what was going on. Zai leaned close to him and kissed him—though it was less a kiss and more just a meeting of their lips that pressed Vax back against the couch.

"Wait," said Vax, his breaths coming fast and shallow. "What are you..."

"I'm doing what you want," Zai murmured. "Isn't this what you want?"

Was it? His heart beat like a trapped bird in his chest, and he couldn't tell whether it was from longing, fear, or both.

"What's wrong? Don't you want to remember?"

"I..." He wanted to. He wanted to remember; he wanted it so badly. He'd been lost for so long in a wandering, groundless existence, and he was tired of it. Tired of being lost and alone.

Zai kissed him again, but gently this time, softly, and Vax closed his eyes. He felt Zai's fingers trail down his throat, like a doubling of that memory, and why couldn't he remember anything more? Why was it that whenever he tried, he ran into a wall of blankness?

"Maybe you'd remember if you had something...more." Zai's hand drifted to his stomach, and then lower—

"No!" Vax shoved him back and stood up from the couch, his pulse racing. *"Don't touch me."*

"Why not?" Zai looked genuinely hurt. "I thought you wanted what we used to have."

Confusion, guilt, and shame welled up inside him. "I don't—not like—"

"Guess you're not interested, then." Zai turned his back on Vax and started walking away.

"No, wait—"

Vax lunged for his arm in a panic. The momentum caused him to stumble too far forward, pinning Zai against the wall. Zai gazed at him levelly.

"What do you want?" Zai said.

"I just want—"

Someone to care about me.

"What makes you think you deserve that?" Zai asked, in a harsh voice.

"Don't—don't ask me that," said Vax.

"What makes you think you deserve that?" Zai repeated.

"Stop it—"

"What makes you think—"

Vax kissed him, desperately. Zai groaned against his mouth, clawing at his back as Vax's fingers dug deeply into his hips.

"Don't..."

"Don't what?"

"You're hurting me," Zai whispered.

Vax jerked back and stared at him. "I didn't mean—I'm sorry—"

"It's what you want, isn't it?" Zai's fingernails sank painfully into his neck. "You want to hurt me. You want to kill me. You want to take everything I have."

"No, I—*no*—"

"*You want this!*" Zai snarled.

Zai kissed him again, hard, but this time Vax tasted blood, pouring into his mouth, so thick he was suffocating on the metallic stench and what the fuck—what the *fuck*—

Vax tore out of sleep, panting harshly, limbs flailing before he finally got the blanket off him and remembered where he was. On the couch at Zai's safe house. Trying to stay clear of Cyrex's sight. Trying to sleep.

Zai was nowhere to be seen. The bedroom door remained closed, and he was presumably asleep on the other side of it.

Vax lay his head back down, still breathing hard.

What the *fuck* kind of dream was that?

The violence of it made him shudder, nauseous. God, he would never—he wasn't *like* that. He wasn't like—

He rubbed his eyes with the heels of his hands and took deep breaths. *It was just a dream. Just a weird dream. Forget it.*

He groped for the blanket that had fallen to the floor, pulled it back over himself, and turned on his side, curling into a ball and waiting for his heartbeat to slow back down to normal.

His chest ached with all the things he'd wanted but given up on ever having. For one brief, shining moment, his hopes had been resurrected—only to be snuffed out, leaving him with nothing again. Was he Ethan Tromer? Was he someone completely different? Was this all just a really bad coincidence? Was this too messed up to be coincidence?

Wasn't this too messed up to be coincidence?

But if this wasn't a coincidence, how did he go from being a dead man—as Zai kept insisting—to a live one? *People don't just die and come back to life.*

He had no idea. Not a clue. There were too many pieces missing, and what was there didn't make any sense.

I want to marry you.

He couldn't remember any names or faces, no context, no reasons, only that one sentence and how it had made him feel. Warm.

Happy.

He squeezed his eyes shut and burrowed his head under the blanket, praying for sleep.

HE DIDN'T REMEMBER when he'd fallen asleep, but when he finally got up, his eyes felt like sandpaper, and heavy, as though they'd been bruised, and his limbs ached with a leaden weight. He didn't feel like he'd gotten any rest at all.

He barely saw Zai at all the next day. Once in a while, Zai slipped out of the bedroom to grab some food from the kitchen, but he always kept his head down, refusing to look at Vax, and then shuffled back to the bedroom and closed the door.

Meanwhile, Vax aimlessly surfed the internet on his pod or disassembled and reassembled his gun or paced around the room or even played his solitaire app. He couldn't leave, and yet he was starting to feel like he'd go stir-crazy if he stayed.

He wanted to talk to Zai badly, but he didn't know what to say.

An internet search of "Ethan Tromer" brought up a nonpublic uSpace profile, as well as an obituary. Vax hesitated for a long while—the idea of reading his own obituary seemed weird—but finally, curiosity won, and he clicked the link.

There was a picture of him again. This one was different, though—his hair was a bit longer, framing his face with a shaggy mop, and he wore thick-rimmed glasses. No bioaugs, Vax remembered Zai saying—what was it, last week? It already felt like a lifetime ago.

He was also smiling.

Vax couldn't take his eyes off the picture. He was smiling. He looked *happy*. That was...such an alien thought, he couldn't wrap his mind around it.

Finally, he started reading the obituary.

"*Ethan Tromer, son of Safiya Bahur and Daniel Tromer, brother of Rachel Tromer. Ethan was a humble, kind, and caring person who always put others before himself. He spent his summers volunteering his time in his community, dedicating himself to helping those who were less fortunate than he was. A bright and hardworking student, Ethan had been attending Orphis College on scholarship, where he was completing a major in history and pre-law studies, before he was called on to serve his country...*"

He couldn't. Couldn't keep going. Reading it was too surreal, and he couldn't recognize himself in the saccharine descriptions.

The truth was, Ethan Tromer didn't feel like a real person to him, but rather like some kind of mystical saint who was far beyond his reach. He didn't feel right, trying to claim Ethan Tromer's life as his own, yet at the same time, he'd been dying for so long to have *something* from his past to cling to.

And even if nothing sounded familiar, there were parts that made sense. He kept rereading *son of Safiya Bahur* over and over again. That would explain why he knew Arabic and clear the aching confusion he'd always had about his race, confusion that led to embarrassment when people asked him or made assumptions and he wasn't sure how to answer. It couldn't just be a coincidence...right?

Sometime in the evening, Zai emerged from the bedroom, shuffled to the kitchen, and grabbed what looked like a bottle of vodka from a cupboard. He then sat on the other side of the couch from Vax, still without looking at him, and drank straight from the bottle. Vax watched him, unsure of what was going to happen next.

"How did you know?" Zai suddenly asked, in a quiet voice.

"Know...what?"

"About...you, and Ethan."

Maybe this would convince him. "I went into one of the offices and started searching the computer. I found an email with a file on Ethan Tromer attached, including a picture."

Zai didn't say anything for a moment. "That could mean anything," he said.

"Like what?"

"Cyrex has ties with the military. There could be any number of reasons why they'd request files for individual soldiers."

Vax fell silent. Clearly Zai wasn't willing to entertain the idea that finding Ethan's file on Cyrex's servers meant anything.

"You know how many times I've thought about what I would give to have Ethan back?" Without waiting for an answer, Zai went on. "An arm, a leg, every penny I owned, my own *life*." He sighed. "Well. They say be careful what you wish for, right?"

Vax didn't know what to say to that.

"You told me you didn't remember anything." An edge of lazy accusation laced Zai's voice. "Or have you been lying this entire time?"

"I—I wasn't *lying*, I just—" Vax's hands tightened. "It was just a fragment. Not enough to make any sense, until now. I didn't think it was relevant, so I...didn't bring it up."

Zai didn't answer. Maybe he found Vax's explanation reasonable. Or maybe not, but he wasn't saying so.

"Well, then," Zai drawled, after another long drink of vodka, "let's pretend, for the moment, that you *are* Ethan after all, if you say you remembered the part where I said I wanted to marry you."

Vax pressed his lips together at Zai's tone. "Sorry to disappoint."

Zai took another swig. Then he held the bottle in front of him, studying it as though it contained a clue to some kind of treasure.

"You know what the worst part is?" he said. His voice had changed, becoming hoarse, raspy, unbalanced, as though his defensive walls were slowly peeling away. "I actually...actually planned the wedding. In my head."

Vax's mouth felt dry. "You...did?"

"Yeah. So fucking stupid, right?" Zai shook his head at himself. "It wasn't—like me at all. Hell, I never even wanted to get married before. But I was dumb and in love, and I thought—no, I was *sure* we were going to have a long, happy future together. And I still had access to my family's money back then. It was going to be a hell of a party. After that— you were going to be some famous do-gooder, I was going to be—well, *me*, and we would be the sexiest couple at every holiday gathering." His arm went limp, though he kept a firm grip on the neck of the bottle. "Then it all went to hell after you died. Or, 'scuse me, after we were told you'd died."

"Sorry." Vax didn't know what else to say. Apologizing for the things he didn't remember seemed to be the best he could do.

Zai sniffed, and wiped roughly at his eyes, to Vax's alarm.

"God, what happened to you?" Zai whispered.

Vax's throat closed up. "I don't...I don't know. If I did, I would tell you."

Zai gave a bitter laugh. "And so, here we are. I've got a target on my back for being a lowly journalist, and you're a risen-from-the-dead *assassin*, for fuck's sake. God, Ethan, where did we go wrong?"

Ethan. The name sent a strange thrill through him. Not one of recognition, no; it still felt like a stranger's name, not a name that belonged to him, but...it felt like someone he *wanted* to be. Someone more than just an assassin; someone with good memories; someone who had been loved.

He slowly put a hand on Zai's arm. Zai looked at him, his eyes glassy with unshed tears.

"I fucked up," Vax whispered. "I don't even know what I did, but I fucked up really bad somewhere along the way, and—I'm so sorry, Zai. I'm so sorry."

Zai blinked. He looked as though he were on the verge of shattering. Years of grief swam in his eyes, eyes like a desolate November midnight, and in that moment, all Vax wanted was to take that sorrow away from him.

Vax leaned forward and kissed him, lightly, briefly. Zai didn't draw away, but he didn't respond, either.

"This..." Zai swallowed. "This was a mistake."

Vax's insides twisted, folding into knots. "Why?"

"Because..." Zai glanced at him and then looked away, but not before Vax could see how much pain his expression held. "Because every time I look at you, all I can see is that Ethan isn't there. I see his face, I hear his voice, but it's not *him*. And that hurts more than anything in the world."

Vax's breath hitched. "I...I could be him. I could try."

Slowly, Zai shook his head. "No, we should...just leave it."

Zai got up from the couch. Vax stayed sitting there, his chest so tight he could barely breathe.

"I don't mean to hurt you," he whispered. "I'm sorry."

Zai turned back and gave him a long, uncomprehending stare.

"Let's just...forget any of this ever happened, okay?" he finally said. "Once we're done taking down Cyrex, we can...go our separate ways. I go back to my job, and you can...go back to...whatever."

Vax felt as if Zai had hit him in the solar plexus. *No*, he thought, *no, I don't want to. I don't know who I am, and you're the only thing that makes any sense. Please don't leave me. Don't leave me alone. Please...*

"Okay," was all he said, in a whisper.

Chapter Nine

A COFFIN RESTED in front of him.

Hesitantly, Vax approached it and opened the lid. He stumbled back when he saw the dead person inside. The corpse's face...it was *his* face.

What...?

"Oh, Vax." He heard Atali's voice. Where had he come from? "You actually thought you were Ethan Tromer? You're not. He's dead."

"No," Vax said, his voice shaking. "No, that can't be."

"It is. And you killed him."

Confused, Vax looked at his hands. They were slick with crimson blood, the metallic scent so thick he could almost taste it.

"Silly Vax. You're an assassin—that's all you are, all you've ever been, and all you ever will be. I should know. I created you."

A cold shudder went through him. "'Created'...? No...I...I'm a human being. You didn't *create* me."

A light switched on, blinding him with the sudden glare. When his vision finally adjusted, Atali's face swam into view in front of him.

"On the contrary. I did, and you are my property."

Out of nowhere, a knife appeared in Atali's hand, and Atali stabbed him. All the air left Vax's lungs. The knife carved a line across his stomach, and Vax cried out in pain. Then, Atali grabbed hold of the cut edge of skin and tore it off, exposing metal and circuitry underneath. Vax stared blankly at it.

"You're not Ethan Tromer. You're not even a person. You're just a machine with delusions of personhood. And sadly, you're defective." Atali tossed the knife away and moved closer to him. "Though at least certain...*essential* parts still work..."

"No," Vax choked. "No—stop it—*no!*"

Vax clawed out of sleep with a muffled shout. He sat up in the darkness, gasping for breath as he leaned against the back of the couch, gripping the frame as though he would collapse without it. His other hand went to his abdomen for a moment before he realized that was stupid. He'd nearly bled to death days before. Androids with advanced enough AI to mimic real human behavior didn't exist, and even if they did, they couldn't bleed. He could still feel the scar from his bullet wound, and he fingered it through the fabric of his shirt.

Just a dream, he told himself as his breathing slowly evened out. *Just a dream...you're okay...you're okay...*

He took the handgun lying on the coffee table, double-checking to confirm it was loaded. He went to the door, making sure it was still locked. He walked around the entire room, checking to see that no one was hiding in some shadowy corner. Then he went back to the couch, drawing the blanket back over his knees, but he was too jittery and unsettled to go back to sleep.

If he wasn't Ethan Tromer, then who was he?

If he wasn't Ethan Tromer, why did he have a shred of memory about someone who wanted to marry him?

But if he was Ethan Tromer, why had Zai rejected the idea so definitively?

He rested his head against the back of the couch. There was an awful, numb hollow in the center of his chest. He felt as lost as he had when he'd first woken up with no memories and couldn't recognize his own reflection in the mirror. Occasionally he dozed off into a half-asleep state, but he always startled awake again when disturbing images or voices came back to him.

Ethan Tromer's dead...you're not him...you're not him...

In the morning, Zai dropped his tablet onto the kitchen table and fell into a chair. Deep shadows underlined his eyes; clearly he hadn't slept well, either. The memory of last night formed a tangled ache in Vax's throat. He tried to swallow it back down. He didn't want to talk, didn't want to break the tenuous silence between them, but he had to.

"There's something...something you need to know," he forced himself to say.

Zai jerked, turning his bruise-tired gaze to him. He looked like he was a breath away from saying that whatever Vax wanted to tell him, he didn't want to hear it.

"At the lab," Vax went on, unsteadily, "on one of the computers, I found files with pictures of...the nine people."

Zai blinked, the fatigue fading from his expression. "What? Really?"

Vax nodded once. *And I was there, too. I'm part of it...whatever it is.* But that part remained wedged in his throat; he couldn't say the words aloud. The last thing he wanted was for Zai to look at him as though he were some kind of...science fair project on display.

"That's it. That's the proof I need," Zai muttered to himself. He turned to Vax with a new light in his eyes. "What else did the files say? Anything about what Cyrex was doing with them or what happened to them?"

"I...didn't exactly have time to look through them before security found me," Vax said. He reached into his pocket and withdrew the drive from Integrity. "I started to download the files, but the download was interrupted. I don't know how much the drive picked up."

"Let me see." Zai took the drive from him and plugged it into his tablet. He scanned the screen. "Hmm...there are some medical charts here for about half of the nine, and...some video files that are completely corrupted." He slumped over the table. "Damn it."

Vax bit his lip, hesitating, and then said, "I don't know what the point of the project was, but...B4 is a bioaug testing lab, so maybe that's what Cyrex was doing with them."

"Right...you said that's where you got your bioaugs from." Zai frowned deeply. "I don't get it. They were testing bioaugs on human subjects...and then selling them to assassins? Why?"

"No one sold me anything," Vax said.

Zai turned his frown to him. "You're telling me they gave you the bioaugs for free?"

Vax knew, at this point, he should probably spell it out for Zai, but he couldn't quite bring himself to. "Not...for free, exactly. It's a bioaug testing lab," he repeated.

He watched Zai's face as the pieces slowly fell into place for him.

"You..." Zai's expression was dismayed. "You let them *experiment* on you?"

"I...I had to. I owed him a debt," Vax said in a detached voice.

"A debt?" Zai repeated. "To who?"

"Atali Norman."

Zai's brow furrowed. "So you owed Norman some money, and he...what, told you he wanted your body as payment instead of cash?"

Vax blanched at Zai's choice of words. "Not money. I owed him my *life*. Without him, I'd be dead."

"Dead?" Zai echoed.

Vax looked down. "I...I told you about the injury that left me with amnesia. It...nearly killed me. He paid for the procedures necessary to save my life." Atali had shoved that fact in his face God knew how many times over the years. As if the patchwork of scars on his body didn't remind him every day.

"And that justifies what he did *how*?" The vehemence in Zai's voice startled him. "Number one, debt bondage is illegal. Number two, it doesn't matter *what* you owe him, he doesn't get to—to do whatever he goddamn *wants* to you."

Vax tasted something sour at the back of his mouth; an absurd, broken, humorless laugh burst out of him. "Too late, I guess."

Zai gave him a weird, uncomprehending look.

"Why do you even care?" Vax asked. "You hate me because of the things I've done."

You hate me so much, you don't want to believe I'm Ethan Tromer.

"Two wrongs don't make a right," said Zai. "We're going to get proof of what Cyrex has been doing, and—"

He stopped short. Vax looked at him; Zai was giving him a wide-eyed stare.

"You're part of the project, along with the other nine people," he breathed.

Vax dropped his gaze. That much should've been obvious to Zai by now.

"Wait...you *knew*." Zai's voice was sharp with accusation. "You *knew* about Cyrex's project, about the other nine—"

"No, I *didn't*," said Vax. "I only found out two days ago. When I was looking through the files on the lab computer. I had no idea about those nine people—I didn't know I was part of some larger project with them."

Zai's eyes narrowed. "How is that possible?"

"Oh, I don't know...maybe because no one *told me* anything?"

Zai still looked skeptical. "But you have to at least know what the project is for, right?"

"No, I don't." He was sick of being asked questions he had no answers for—and the one thing he was certain of, Zai didn't believe him.

"You just said Cyrex experimented on you—"

"For their bioaug prototypes. But I don't think there was any pattern or overarching goal to the tests. If that's all their secret project is, it's hardly worth killing anyone over, isn't it?"

"Covering up human experimentation is." Zai's mouth pressed into a grim line. "You know that's a criminal offense, punishable by both fines and jail time? Not to mention public evisceration by the media once they get wind of it."

Vax's frown deepened. Was it possible? The super-secret project...was only to get illegal human test subjects for random prototypes?

Zai seemed to hesitate. "Did it hurt?" he asked, in a quiet voice.

That question took Vax so completely by surprise, he had no idea how to answer for a moment. "I...um...I guess...some of the side effects...weren't great."

"What kinds of side effects?"

He was beginning to have flashbacks to the tests they did with the hearing augments, when his hearing sensitivity was cranked up so high, he couldn't sleep and couldn't step out of his apartment without being overwhelmed to the point of pain. And the pain inhibitors...his heart began to pound in his chest as he remembered his terror at being permanently outfitted with them. There was a reason inability to feel pain was considered a dangerous medical disorder—not that anyone cared about his opinion.

"Migraines. Seizures. Sensory problems. Temporary paralysis. Stuff like that," he said, his voice dull, not in the mood to elaborate. His biggest fear had been death or permanent debilitation, and he'd counted himself lucky that neither had happened to him.

It was silent for a long time.

"We're going to get Cyrex for this," said Zai. "If things were that bad for you, I can't imagine what happened to the others. The world needs to know what happened—to them, and to you."

Vax's heart sank at those words.

"You...want to write about me?"

"Of course." Zai's eyebrows drew together in mild puzzlement, as though the answer were obvious. "Those nine people are most likely dead. You're the only living witness."

Well, him and Jane, but obviously Jane wasn't going to sit for an interview.

"Right," he said, emotionlessly. "And you'll end up with an article that's guaranteed millions of views. Everyone loves a story about graphic human experimentation, right? Too bad you didn't realize I was that useful sooner—it would've saved you time and trouble."

Zai looked taken aback. "I—that's not why I'm doing this—"

"If you're going to *use me*, at least be honest," Vax ground out.

"Use—? It's not like that—"

"Don't *lie* to me." Because he was tired of being lied to. First Atali, now Zai. He didn't care that that was Zai's ulterior motive—well, he did, but that was his own fault for hoping for something more. He just wanted honesty.

"I'm not lying to you." Zai spread his hands. "What Cyrex has done, the lives they've ruined..." Vax could feel Zai's eyes on him, but when he looked at him, Zai glanced away. "People deserve to know that this—this isn't something you can do and get away with, or else they'll just keep going, and it'll get worse. More people will get hurt. They have to face justice for what they've done—at least in the minds of the public. *That's* why I'm doing this. But I'm not—I don't want you to feel like you're going to be some kind of tragic clickbait—"

"Don't pretend you care about me except as a means to an end." All the stresses and crushed hopes from yesterday bubbled to the surface in a tide of resentment. "Not after you've spent all this time talking about how much you hate me. You—you can talk people into hanging on to your every word. And I'm *sick* of being manipulated and jerked around."

"I'm not...I'm not trying to manipulate you," Zai said quietly.

Vax watched him, trying to decide whether to believe him or not.

Zai rubbed his forehead, and then he sighed. "Look...if you truly don't want to tell me anything, I can't *force* you to talk. I haven't forgiven you for the things you've done, but that doesn't mean I can't feel bad about the way Cyrex treated you. I just want to help," he said. "Honestly."

So he was worthy as an object of sympathy only because Cyrex mistreated him. Depressingly, that was better than nothing—it was either this, or go back to suspicious mistrust because he was an assassin. Zai had made it clear that he would never see Vax as anything more than that.

"Do you know the scientists who work in B4?" Zai asked, in a soft voice.

Vax exhaled, his shoulders sagging. "I'll give you the names I know."

Zai passed him the tablet, and Vax began typing. *Dr. Amanda Fields. Dr. Anila Kaur. Dr. Adam Green.* He paused after writing *Dr. Irene Tran.*

"This is a guess," he said, slowly, "but Dr. Tran might be the best person to speak to."

"Why's that?"

"She seemed...nice. Then again, I can't judge people for shit, so you can take that with a grain of salt."

Zai was looking at him. Vax glanced back at him, irritated. "What?"

He shook his head. "Nothing. I'll try contacting Dr. Tran."

Zai typed a message into his tablet and sent it off. The thought of waiting at the table with Zai for a response felt unbearable, so Vax retreated to the couch, pretending to be intently focused on the news.

A few minutes later, Zai's tablet rang. Vax glanced up. A video screen appeared in the air with a face Vax knew well—an East Asian woman in her thirties. *That was fast.*

"Hello?" she said.

"Dr. Tran? My name is Zai Lumero. I write for the *Daily Voice.* You work in Cyrex's north lab, on level B4, correct?"

"That's correct..."

"So, what is your research focused on?"

"Animal testing," she said after a pause. "We test bioaugment prototypes on mice and rabbits, that sort of thing."

"Is that so," said Zai, slowly. "That's funny, because I'm investigating what seems to be a project that involved testing bioaugs on *human* subjects."

Dr. Tran wasn't quite so good of a liar; she flinched at Zai's words. "I don't know what you've heard, but human experimentation is illegal—"

"According to the ARC, every ethical code that governs scientific research, and the criminal code," Zai finished for her. He leaned forward over the table. "But that's really hard, isn't it? The ARC's stringent procedures result in *decades* before bioaug prototypes can even be used in human trials, let alone gain approval for sale to the general public. That's a lot of wasted time that could be spent helping people instead."

Vax still had no idea how Zai could say all of this with a completely serious face and tone, as though he sincerely believed what he was saying. It was hypnotizing to watch. Dr. Tran was quiet, though, her gaze downturned.

"So what's a few casualties along the way?" Zai continued, his voice deceptively soft. "Especially when they're people who won't be missed?"

Dr. Tran sucked in a breath. "It's not—it's not like that."

"Then please, tell me, what's it like?"

She rubbed her hands across her face. Dark smudges underlined her eyes.

"None of us...all of us looked the other way. We didn't question where the subjects—where the *people* came from. We should have. I think, deep down, none of us wanted to know. We weren't even supposed to talk to them, beyond what was necessary for the experiments." She exhaled, shakily. "I'm not supposed to be telling you any of this. Technically, I'm violating my NDA."

"And, technically, experimenting on people without the express authority of the ARC is illegal," said Zai, mildly. "What prompted your change of heart, Dr. Tran?"

She hesitated. "I guess...I saw too many things. Eventually, I couldn't pretend not to see the truth anymore. Subject Ten—" She winced. "Sorry, he told me his name was Vax—what happened to him was..." She shook her head. "No matter how many times I was told he'd volunteered for everything, it didn't feel right to act like we could do all the things we did. He was so young," she said, her voice fading.

Vax felt the weight of Zai's gaze on him in that moment. He kept his eyes fixed on the table.

"I'm not...trying to excuse my guilt," she went on, after a pause, her voice uneven. "There were things I could've done, but I didn't, because I was too scared to say anything."

"Well, it's not too late," said Zai. "If you'd be willing to go on record, and if you have, maybe, some lab records that could confirm Cyrex's illegal activities, you can still do the right thing."

"I can do better than that," she said. "I have *all* the lab records, plus emails and other things. I've slowly collected them over the past year."

"Really?" Vax didn't miss the note of interest in Zai's voice.

"Not...that I had the greatest motives for copying them." She sighed. "At first, it was for insurance—I thought I was going to be fired at one point, so I thought I could bring this stuff to my next job."

"So you're not actually a believer in NDAs," said Zai, dryly.

Dr. Tran coughed in a way that might've been an aborted laugh. "Anyway, it's all on a physical drive—I was afraid it'd be easier to hack into if I put it in a cloud. I can give it to you."

"Sure. Send me your address, and I'll be right there. Thank you so much, Dr. Tran."

"Just...please bring justice to those people," she said quietly.

DR. IRENE TRAN lived on the east side of the city, in one of the nicer condominiums surrounded by greenery. The idea of seeing her outside of the lab felt strange to Vax. In a way, he supposed he hadn't quite thought of the doctors as people, either.

They climbed the stairs to the second floor and Zai pressed the doorbell beside her door. But Vax thought he heard a strange noise coming from the other side.

"Wait," he whispered to Zai, pulling him back from the door.

"What?"

It was probably nothing. But a week of being shot at had aggravated his paranoid streak, and he wasn't taking chances. For all he knew, this was another setup, and Dr. Tran had said what she had to lure them here.

He pushed Zai to the side, so when the door opened slightly, he was the only one visible. He saw Dr. Tran through the fraction of space, though her eyes widened when she saw him.

"Oh! I—I didn't expect to see you here."

Something in her voice and expression heightened his feeling that something was wrong.

"Hello, Dr. Tran. Is everything okay?" Behind his back, he made a *stay back* gesture at Zai with his hands.

"Y-yes, everything's fine." It wasn't like her to stutter. "But I'm kind of, ah, busy right now, so you'd better—"

She abruptly paused, and then said, in a different tone, "I mean—come in. Please, come in."

Vax's heart sank. Had they walked into yet another ambush?

He held his hand up behind his back, praying Zai would get the hint and not try to come in as he entered the condo. The door closed, and he inhaled sharply.

Standing behind Dr. Tran, with a gun pointed at her head, was Jane Shaw. Subject Eleven.

She raised an eyebrow. "You're still alive."

"Yeah," he managed to say. "Sorry to disappoint."

Dr. Tran looked distressed. "Vax, I'm so sorry, I swear I didn't mean to—"

"Quiet." Jane pressed the gun harder against her head, and she flinched. Keeping her eyes on Vax, Jane said, "This goes one of two ways. You tell Lumero to come in—and don't pretend he's not outside, I heard two sets of footsteps in the hall—and I'll let the doctor here go. Or, you can act like you have no idea what I'm talking about, and Dr. Tran will start getting bullets. It's your call."

"How stupid do you think I am?" Vax retorted. "You're not going to let her go. All three of us are dead either way."

Jane didn't blink. "*You* might stay alive. But how fast they die is up to you."

Vax gritted his teeth. After her showing by the river, he didn't doubt she was serious. "Okay. Fine. Just...can we talk, first?"

"Talk?" she repeated. "About what?"

This was his one chance. He took a deep breath. "We're part of some kind of secret project Cyrex has been working on."

"I know."

Vax blinked, disoriented. "You...know?"

"You are VAX Ten. I am VAX Eleven. I am your replacement." She narrowed her eyes. "Now tell me where Lumero is before someone gets hurt."

"VAX Eleven"? Replacement?

"I'm not *'Ten,'*" Vax sputtered. "And you're not 'Eleven.' This project—it's bigger than the two of us. People have *died*—"

"Lumero, or the doctor is about to lose her kneecap."

It was no use. Just as it had been no use when Zai had tried to talk to him, that night when Vax had tried to kill him.

"Okay, okay. Just...hold on a moment." He inched back toward the door, even as his mind spun with possible exit strategies. He could draw his gun—but the question was whether Jane—Eleven—would start shooting before he could. He was at a disadvantage, and she knew it. Could he tackle her and get her away from Dr. Tran? Risky, again.

Or...

He opened the door. Zai was nowhere to be seen.

For some reason, his absence was a punch to Vax's gut, even though he knew it was the smart thing to do. *Get the hell out and let the assassin deal with it.* A nagging voice in the back of his head reminded him that it wasn't Zai's style to run from danger, but...maybe Zai had finally developed some common sense.

Vax closed the door. "Problem," he said, trying to keep his voice calm. "Lumero left."

Eleven swore. "Then get him back. Now."

I don't take orders from you, Vax thought. Aloud, he said, "I can *try,* but—"

Eleven abruptly swung the gun toward him. "He cares for you, doesn't he? If he doesn't come, *you're* the one who's dead."

Vax stared at the gun pointed at his head.

And then he started to laugh.

It was a broken, hysterical laugh that welled up in his throat and couldn't be choked back down. *Cares? As if.*

"What?" Eleven demanded. "Why are you laughing?"

He didn't answer. Instead, he lunged for the gun.

He shoved it aside before it went off, his momentum sending them both crashing against a table. *Pain inhibitors. Have to neutralize her fast.* He grabbed her gun arm. Slammed it against the table edge. The bone snapped.

Eleven didn't flinch. She slammed her head into Vax's.

Pain exploded across his forehead. He swore, staggering back. Eleven collided with him, knocking him to the ground. He barely rolled out of the way before her boot came down hard on the ground, where his gut would've been. Then her other foot kicked him in the spine.

Vax choked. Suddenly, the world spun dizzily around him, and he couldn't move.

He heard her footsteps as she went to retrieve her gun with her good arm. "I don't know what Mr. Norman sees in you," she said, through her teeth, "but—"

Abruptly, she stopped, the gun falling from her hand as her eyes rolled up into her head. She crumpled to the ground.

Zai stood behind her, the neural disruptor in his hand.

"Sorry I'm late," he said.

Vax almost choked out another laugh at that, except just then a surge of pain went through his spine and he blacked out.

CONSCIOUSNESS CAME BACK to him. He was lying on a bed—God, it was so much more comfortable than the couch he'd been squeezed onto for the past week—and his spinal bioaug throbbed, pulsing with a dull, rhythmic ache.

Carefully, he sat up. At that moment, the door opened. Vax squinted. It was Dr. Tran, standing in the doorway.

"Hi," she said. "How are you feeling?"

"I'm..." Vax clenched and unclenched his fingers. "Okay...I think. What happened?"

"Well, your spinal augment wasn't designed to withstand a lot of force." Dr. Tran sounded apologetic. "I checked it, but it doesn't look like it was damaged. It probably just needed to recalibrate on its own."

"Ah." Right; he vaguely remembered her telling him that some time ago.

"I thought you'd died," she said quietly. "That's what Mr. Norman said."

He almost laughed at that, but his chest seized up and it came out as a wheeze instead. "I guess he failed to add that he was the one who tried to have me killed."

Dr. Tran shuddered. "So...you and Eleven...is this what you do?"

He looked at her for a moment before he remembered that she only knew him as a test subject. He didn't quite know how to respond. *Yeah, you've been doing my medical checkups for these past four years without knowing that Atali sent me to kill people for money. Crazy, huh?*

"It's just..." She sighed and shook her head. "Sometimes I still can't believe how much I never knew."

You're not the only one.

Vax tried to stand, and Dr. Tran went to his side, steadying him.

"If you're dizzy, you should rest some more."

"I'm okay. Is Zai—uh, Zai Lumero—"

"He's in the kitchen."

She helped him out of the bedroom. Zai was leaning against the kitchen counter. His dark eyes snapped to Vax's face, and he straightened. "You're okay?"

Vax shrugged. "Thanks to you," he admitted. "By the way, how did you...?"

"I went next door, convinced them to let me in, and jumped onto Dr. Tran's balcony."

Vax blinked. "You did *what*?" He wished he could've seen that.

"The balconies weren't that far apart," was all Zai said, as though jumping balconies was something he did all the time.

Vax decided to take his word for it. He surveyed the living room with an upended table and things scattered everywhere. "Um...sorry about the mess."

Dr. Tran waved a hand. "You saved my life, so...don't worry."

Eleven was nowhere to be seen. "Where's..."

Dr. Tran and Zai glanced at each other. "We figured the hospital was the best place to drop her off," said Zai. "You know, because of the broken arm."

Vax would've felt bad if not for the fact that she'd shot him in the abdomen a few days ago. He frowned. "Isn't she going to escape as soon as she heals?"

Dr. Tran coughed. "Well...I also filed a police report, so that should tie her up for a bit. All I said was that she'd ambushed me in my home," she added before Vax could ask.

"Oh. But, uh...At—some people at Cyrex aren't going to be happy about that."

"If they haven't officially fired me by now, they will soon." Dr. Tran reached into her pocket and pulled out a microdrive. "I guess I wasn't as sneaky as I thought I was— someone must've realized I'd been quietly making copies of the project files. Eleven came to destroy my copies, and to get rid of you," she said to Zai. "I don't know if she had bugged my tablet or what. Anyway, you'll find all the information you need here, and some other things from an accountant."

"Wait," said Zai. "You knew Celia Duquette?"

Dr. Tran nodded. "She came to me at some point, trying to ask about what was going on in B4. Her ideas weren't quite right, but she knew Cyrex was covering up something big."

Zai took the drive from her. "I can't thank you enough," he said. "You might want to get out of town for a little while..."

"Yeah, I was planning to. Good luck," she said. Turning to Vax, she added, "And...I'm sorry. For everything."

Vax wasn't sure how to reply to that. Technically, she'd been complicit in all the tests and experiments. And yet, she'd been the only person in the lab who'd ever asked for his name.

"Stay safe," was all he said, inclining his head.

Chapter Ten

WHEN THEY GOT back, Zai immediately sat on the couch and inserted the drive into his tablet. His eyes widened as he looked at the screen, and he let out a low whistle.

"Wow...she hit the jackpot. There's a *lot* of stuff here." He pursed his lips. "A bunch of email conversations with Atali Norman, too. Hmm...'Virtual Asset Experimental Project. Project V.A....' Shouldn't that be an 'E'? Why is it an..."

Zai's voice trailed off. Vax realized Zai was staring at him.

"What?" Vax asked, lost.

"V-A-X," Zai said, sounding unsettled. "It's not a name. It's an acronym. The title of the project."

"Oh," was all he could say.

Your name is Vax.

Suddenly, everything seemed like a sick joke to him.

"Um..." Looking uncomfortable, Zai turned back to the tablet. "Let's see what else is here. 'Disposal protocol'? Is that..."

He stopped again. "What?" Vax asked.

"My God." Zai's voice was strained. "Those nine people... they weren't just killed. Their bodies were completely dissolved."

Vax wished he could say he was surprised, but he wasn't. That sounded exactly like an idea Atali would have.

Zai cleared his throat. "There are also a lot of video files." Vax moved behind him, studying the list of files on the screen. "Let's see..." Zai selected one at random and pressed play.

Wait.

The video showed one of the rooms in B4, and inside the room was—

That's me, Vax thought, a cold lump forming in his stomach. He didn't know they recorded everything. He had no idea...

The video showed him strapped to a medical chair, wearing a mouth guard, with electrodes attached to his head. Vax jerked his gaze away from the screen, but he couldn't block out the sound of his own muffled cry of pain coming from the tablet speakers, nor the sound of Zai's sharply inhaled breath. Dr. Fields's voice intoned, "The pain inhibitor augments are still not optimally effective—"

"Stop it," Vax whispered hoarsely.

"What?" Zai said, in a faint voice, as though he hadn't processed what Vax said.

"I said stop it—turn it off!"

Zai hit the pause button. Vax backed away from the video, feeling oddly light-headed. He didn't...he didn't know they'd recorded the experiments.

He didn't know.

"Are you...okay?" Zai asked, uncertainly.

No. No, I'm not okay. Living through it had been bad enough. But knowing someone else could watch him go through it again was a whole new level of disturbing.

Vax searched for his voice and forced himself to speak. "Don't...watch the videos. Please."

"Okay," said Zai. "We'll look at something else."

Vax exhaled, a little surprised Zai had listened to him.

Zai's brow furrowed. "Hold on...there are some audio files here."

Vax shook his head to himself, trying to clear the thoughts crowding his head. "Audio files?" he echoed.

"Yeah. The file names are numbers—no, wait, they look like dates. Same month—January, four years ago, but different days." Zai's frown deepened. "Not too long after that factory explosion, in fact."

That was also the time of Vax's first memories. "Maybe there's something incriminating about the explosion?"

"Maybe." Zai pressed the play button. Atali's voice came from the speakers.

"Hello, Ethan. How are you feeling?"

The recording abruptly paused. Vax glanced at Zai, whose face had frozen into a stunned mask. Zai rewound the file and played it again. Atali Norman's voice repeated, *"Hello, Ethan. How are you feeling?"*

Ethan.

"What..." Zai's face had an ashen pallor. "What is this?"

"I don't know," Vax answered truthfully, even though his heart was beating rapidly. "I've never heard it before."

After a tense, drawn-out pause, Zai resumed playing the file.

"Better, thank you." That was his voice. Vax's...Ethan's voice. But Vax didn't remember any of this...

"You remember the terms of our agreement? What you agreed to, in exchange for your care?"

A pause. *"Yes, I...I do."*

"Good. That's good."

"Mr. Norman, does my...does my family know I'm okay? The people I love? Do they know?"

Vax bit down hard on his lip and clenched his shaking hands. *No. No, no, no.*

"Yes, of course," Atali said, in a soothing voice. *"I've contacted them. They know."*

"Oh, good. Thank you." Another short pause. *"When...when can I see them?"*

Atali hesitated for a moment. *"Soon,"* he said, his voice still calm. *"Very soon. I promise. As soon as the next round of surgery is done."*

"Okay. Thank you, Mr. Norman. I can't thank you enough."

Vax wanted to scream. *No!*

"You're welcome, Ethan. Now, rest."

When the audio file ended, Vax buried his face in his hands, taking deep, harsh, shuddering breaths. This wasn't what he remembered.

THE FIRST THING he could remember was waking up.

There was a dull ache pulsating throughout his body. In his eyes. And his head...hurt. It felt so heavy. Everything looked fuzzy at first, but after a few minutes, the details began to sharpen. He tried to focus through the insistent pain in his skull.

It looked like he was in some sort of hospital room. He was lying on a bed, wearing a hospital gown.

Where was he? How did he get here?

He...couldn't remember.

He couldn't remember *anything*.

Not what had happened to him, not where he came from, not even his own *name*.

What...?

Just then, the door opened, and a tall, pale, blond-haired man walked in.

"Hello there. Glad to see you're doing better," the man said with a smile. The man was looking at him as though they knew each other, but he didn't remember the man at all.

"Do I...know you?" he asked. His voice sounded rusty and unfamiliar to his own ears, like the voice of a stranger. That thought scared him, and he fought not to panic.

The blond man appeared puzzled. "Yes, we've met. You don't remember?"

He swallowed hard, feeling as though something jagged and painful was stuck in his throat. "No, I...I don't... remember..."

"Oh dear." The blond man sighed. "You've been severely injured. You've also sustained head trauma, and... as a result, you've been having memory issues."

"Memory issues?" he echoed.

"Yes."

The sense of panic was growing stronger. "Is it permanent?"

"The doctors placed a neural implant to try to undo the damage. They said your ability to encode new memories should be stable now, but as for your old memories..." The man shrugged. "It's too early to know for sure at this point."

"I..." His breath hitched, and his voice came out frail and plaintive. "I don't...do you...know my name?"

The man paused for a moment. "Your name is Vax."

"Vax?" he repeated. "Just...Vax?"

"It's the only name you've ever given me."

He—Vax—mulled that over. It was better than nothing.

"How...how do I know you?"

"My name is Atali Norman. I'm the CEO of Cyrex Corporation. You've done contract work for me in the past."

"Oh," was all Vax could say. Obviously, he couldn't remember what kind of work he'd done for Cyrex.

"You don't remember our agreement?"

"What...agreement?"

"Well...your injuries were very severe. Nearly fatal. You didn't have enough insurance to cover the cost of the reconstructive surgery necessary to save your life, so I offered to pay—but in return, you'll have to work exclusively for me to repay that debt."

"Oh..." It was clearly too late for him to back out of the agreement, even if he remembered it. "I...see..."

"In any case, I hope you have a speedy recovery, Vax. I'll have work for you soon, once you've gotten back on your feet."

Atali began to leave.

"Wait," Vax said, in a surge of desperation. "Do you know if I...have any family? Any friends? Anyone who can...who can help me?"

Atali paused.

"No, I...I'm afraid I never knew much about your personal life. You've never mentioned having any family. As for friends...you were in the hospital for days, and no one came for you."

"I...I see," Vax whispered, his voice shaking. "Thank you."

When Atali left, Vax stared at his hands. He turned the palms up, as though maybe the answers were written there, in the unfamiliar lines and calluses.

Who am I?

He repeated the question aloud. "Who am I?" His voice still sounded unfamiliar and strange to him, and that felt so wrong.

Everything felt so wrong.

VAX PACED BACK and forth, almost gnawing his lip bloody.

No. It didn't make *sense*.

If he'd lost his memories due to a head injury, as Atali had told him, then why was there a recording of him talking to Atali and sounding completely normal? Atali told him it was because of the same injury he needed multiple surgeries for saving his life, he told him—

He fucking lied.

Vax leaned his palms and forehead against the wall, breathing hard. Atali fucking *lied to him.*

Which meant...

His memory loss hadn't been accidental at all.

It had been *planned*.

He reached up and ran his fingers along the surgical scar on the side of his head, underneath his hair. A growing sense of horror filled him. *What did he do to me?*

"You..."

Vax jerked and turned. Zai was staring at him as though he were looking at a ghost.

"Ethan?" Zai whispered.

Vax wasn't as shocked as Zai was, but he still twitched at the name. So many emotions swirled in Zai's expression—doubt, grief, fear, confusion.

He didn't know what to say.

Zai stood and slowly came over to him. Zai raised a trembling hand and touched his face, and Vax—Ethan—whatever the fuck his name was—instinctively flinched.

Let's just forget any of this ever happened.

All I can see is that Ethan isn't there.

He hadn't forgotten Zai's words, and remembering them hurt all over again.

He walked past Zai, but the apartment was too damn *small* and there was nowhere for him to hide. He made his way to the kitchen and opened a cabinet, pretending he was intently reading the labels of the packaged food inside, because they were so damn fascinating.

Zai didn't say anything. Maybe he was in shock. That was fine with Vax. Shocked silence was better than...literally anything else.

"How?" Zai finally asked, sounding choked.

How...what? How had he survived? How had he become a killer?

How could he possibly be Ethan Tromer?

Vax closed the cabinet door and just shook his head, his hands clenching. All this time—all these years—he'd mourned the cosmic misfortune that had left him with amnesia, and the fact that there was nothing he could do about it.

But all this time, it had been a lie.

And all this time, Atali had known the truth.

"You killed people," Zai said, his voice still shell-shocked.

Thanks, I had no idea, Vax wanted to say. But the pure betrayal in Zai's voice killed his sarcasm. Accusation, heavy with disappointment, as though Vax had personally let him down.

But it's not fair. I didn't know.

Zai held his hands up. "I can't—amnesia or no amnesia, you'd *never*—I just don't get it. Your memories of your life are gone, but you still know things. Facts. How could your entire sense of morality have shifted? Everything you once believed in—"

"I *don't know*." Desperate anger flared up inside him, but he was too exhausted for it to take hold. "I—I didn't know who or what I was. You have to believe me," and he sounded like he was pleading.

"But you honestly believed Atali Norman when he said you were an assassin? Just like that?"

"I didn't have a *choice*," Vax said, in a hoarse voice. "I owed him, and I didn't know he was lying. I didn't think he had any reason to."

He remembered when Atali informed him he was an assassin. He remembered the initial feeling of shock and disoriented confusion that went through him. *I kill people for a living?* It didn't feel familiar or right, but then again, nothing did. Not even his own face or voice.

Atali had handed him an unloaded gun, asked him to take it apart and put it back together. He did, without difficulty, and he recognized the model as well. He knew how to aim and fire and load it. That had convinced him at the time. Maybe he should have thought about alternative explanations, but...Atali had saved his life, and how was he supposed to have known Atali had an ulterior motive? And he had been desperate, so desperate, for something to hold on to.

Zai shook his head, eyes narrowed. "I saw you. Even killing enemy combatants in the middle of war tore you apart. That was who you were. If you managed to throw that all away..."

Then...what? He wasn't actually Ethan Tromer?

He couldn't do this. Couldn't stand there and keep listening to Zai tell him, to his face, that he was *wrong*.

"The last four years of my life have been completely *fucked up*." His voice cracked. "I don't—I don't even understand what the fuck *happened* to me. Zai—"

He didn't move, but Zai stepped away from him. As though just his voice, his plea, were tainted.

"I can't—" Zai wasn't looking at him. "I need—"

Silence clotted the air between them, thick and heavy, as Vax waited for him to finish his sentence.

"You know that night you were waiting for me in my apartment?" Zai said, in a scratchy voice.

Vax froze, as though all his muscles had been pulled taut at the same time.

"You almost killed me," Zai went on, nearly whispering. "You *would've* killed me."

"But I didn't *know*," Vax said helplessly. His voice was shaking. "I didn't—I never would've—"

"I need to think," said Zai. "I just—need to think."

Without another word, he turned away and retreated to the bedroom.

Vax didn't know how long he stood there, staring at the closed door. He didn't know what to think, or how to feel. Did he really believe that, in the face of clear proof, Zai would accept everything and forgive him? Maybe he did. Maybe he wanted an easy answer for once in his damned life.

He went back to the couch and sat down, staring at the tablet Zai had left on the coffee table. The only thing he knew for sure was that everything Atali had said to him was a lie.

But why?

His head hurt from trying, and failing, to make any sense of it. Why all the lies? Why the procedure he couldn't remember—and sure as hell would not have consented to—that turned him into an amnesiac? Was it just because Atali *could*?

That idea didn't even surprise him, and that was what scared him the most.

He buried his head in his hands, trying to breathe. Every time. Every single goddamn time he thought he'd understood Atali well enough to predict what he would or wouldn't do, he was proved wrong. Why couldn't he ever learn that Atali was nothing but a sadistic bastard who didn't play by any rules when trying to make his life as miserable as possible? Or that apparently someone out there had designated him as the universe's punching bag?

He didn't want to think anymore. The tablet screen showed the list of audio files, including the several other ones that had the same file name format. Syncing his ear node to the tablet, Vax pressed the play button and listened.

HE COULDN'T SLEEP after listening to those recordings.

He stayed awake all night, sitting on the couch with his knees hugged to his chest and the scratchy blanket wrapped around him, staring hollowly at the wall. Once in a while he'd nod off, only to start awake again after being haunted by images of fiery explosions and buzz saws trying to cut his skull open. Not memories, just ghastly pictures drawn by his mind in an attempt to fill the blanks in his memory with something.

And every time he fell halfway asleep, a voice echoed in his mind, *It's your fault...it's all your fault.*

In the morning, he staggered to the kitchen to look for something to eat. When he heard the bedroom door open, he turned around. Sleepless shadows hung beneath Zai's red-rimmed eyes, and seeing him made Vax's heart constrict. Wordlessly, Zai picked up the tablet from the coffee table, walked to the kitchen, and sat at the table with his tablet in front of him, his stare never leaving Vax.

"The people you've assassinated," he said, his voice blunt and cold. "Start talking."

Vax flinched. He leaned back against the counter and took a slow, deep breath.

"How many?" Zai demanded.

"Five."

Zai went on, "Did you ever stop to think that they had families? People who cared about them? Or did they not matter because you didn't know who they were?"

He hadn't *let* himself think of their families or who they were. But saying that aloud would only confirm Zai's worst opinions of him.

"What were their names?" Zai asked, relentless.

Vax closed his eyes. "Joseph Lowell. Jerome Adams and Ann Jameson." He paused. "Paul Emerson. John Richter."

"Wait," said Zai. "Jerome Adams and Ann Jameson? The two notorious augment traffickers? That was *you*?"

Vax nodded without feeling.

Zai's eyes narrowed. "Why?"

"I don't know. Trafficked augments were giving Cyrex a bad name?" That was his guess, in any case.

Zai still looked a bit unnerved. He typed into his tablet, frowning. "Joseph Lowell...not the murderer who was released on early parole?"

Vax shrugged.

"Why him?" Zai sounded baffled.

"I never asked." Although, now that he thought about it, maybe it had been meant to be a test run of some sort. That was a disturbing thought.

Zai's frown deepened. "What about the last two?"

"They were...both ex-Cyrex employees." Paul Emerson...that was a name that would haunt him forever. John Richter, on the other hand, didn't haunt him at all. Not after what Vax saw him do to a sex worker while he was surveilling him. Given his own profession, he rarely felt like he was in a position to judge his targets, but that had been an exception.

Zai seemed to mull over the information. "Just because some of your targets were criminals doesn't make their deaths okay."

Vax blinked at him. "I...know that?"

Was that what Zai believed—that he thought he had some kind of moral high ground? The idea had never crossed his mind. Besides, it wasn't like Vax had chosen his targets.

"Did you ever feel guilty?" Zai asked.

His voice was quiet, but the question felt weighted, like a test Vax was sure he would fail. He ran through some possible answers in his mind, and discarded them all.

"Say something," Zai demanded.

"It doesn't matter." Vax's voice came out scratchy, monotone. "Guilt isn't a defense. Nothing is."

"I know that," Zai said, his jaw clenched. "But I'd like an answer anyway."

Vax shifted on his feet. "I don't know. Maybe...sometimes," he finally said. "Not...always."

After another long pause, Zai said, "So. Let me get this straight. You murdered five people after you lost your memories—"

"I didn't lose my memories," Vax cut in. "That recording that you heard—it's proof that Atali *lied*. I didn't get any kind of head trauma."

Zai was staring blankly at him. "Excuse me?"

Vax gritted his teeth. "I have a neural implant, remember? I always thought—he told me it was to try to undo some of the damage from the head trauma I sustained. But if he was lying about the head injury, then the only possible reason I have a neural implant—"

"Hold on a second," Zai interrupted. He closed his eyes briefly and took a deep breath, massaging his forehead.

"You're saying that Atali Norman—put a neural implant in your brain that—gave you amnesia?"

Vax nodded.

Zai looked at his tablet, frowning deeply. "And then he told you that you were an assassin, and you believed him, and you killed five people for him."

"Basically," said Vax, his throat tight.

Zai raised his head again. "And he also tested experimental bioaug prototypes on you."

Vax shrugged in assent.

Zai leaned back in his chair, silent for a long while. The silence grew so long Vax thought maybe the conversation was done, and he went to grab a frozen breakfast bar from the fridge and defrost it in the microwave. Sitting at the table with Zai seemed too awkward, so he stayed standing, leaning against the kitchen counter as he ate, quietly.

He heard a chair scrape against the floor, and he turned to see Zai walking toward him. Vax tensed, but Zai merely made his way to the wall opposite Vax and stayed there, standing, watching him with an unreadable expression. Vax looked away, unable to keep staring into Zai's intense dark eyes.

He wondered, for a second, if Zai would grab his chin and force him to look up. Instead, Zai spoke.

"You *died*, Ethan," he said.

The name sent a strange jolt through Vax's artificial spine. It still didn't entirely feel like it belonged to him, like a coat in the wrong size. He shifted uncomfortably, unsure if he was supposed to respond.

"I—I went to your *funeral*, I—"

Zai abruptly trailed off, as though he didn't know what he was trying to say.

Funeral. What a strange idea—that there had been people who'd mourned him.

"Was it nice?" he asked absently, wistfully.

Zai gave him a blank, bewildered stare.

"Y...yeah...I guess."

Another long moment of silence passed.

"You died," Zai repeated, but all the force of his earlier hostility was gone.

"I'm sorry," was all Vax could say.

Zai reached toward him, but stopped midway, his hand hovering in the air. Vax watched his hand, not knowing what he was about to do. Then, he continued, slowly, until his fingertips were lightly touching Vax's arm. Like the way he'd touched Vax's face the night before—as though to make sure he was real.

"You died, except you didn't, and you became an assassin," said Zai. "And you don't remember anything."

Vax shook his head, his chest tightening.

Zai let his hand drop. "I...I guess it was stupid of me to think you would still remember the most important things," he said, his voice hoarse. "That...you would remember *me*."

Confused guilt coiled in Vax's throat. "I'm sorry," he said, again.

"Stop," said Zai, and the brusqueness of his voice made Vax flinch. "Stop apologizing, just *stop*—"

He abruptly paused, as though he'd run into a wall. Vax stood there, his back pressed against the counter, with no idea of what he was supposed to do or say. He was tired of arguing. Maybe this was his fault—no, of course it was, he was the one who fucked everything up—but he couldn't travel back in time to undo it all now. And he'd try to make up for it all if he could. He just didn't know how. The space between them felt heavy, like a cloud filled with unspoken words that was about to burst.

Zai dragged his hands over his face. He sighed, and the tension in the room broke, dissipating.

"Sorry," Zai said, his voice quiet.

Vax started and looked at him, wondering if he'd misheard.

"All of this...it's a lot to take in." Zai dropped his gaze. "I...shouldn't have gotten so angry. I just...don't know what to think."

Yeah, me neither. "Join the club," Vax offered.

Zai stared at him for a moment.

"Your neural implant," Zai finally said. "Do you think... it affected your brain in other ways? Like...brainwashing, or something?"

Vax felt his eyebrows knit. "Brainwashing?" he echoed. "I don't *feel* brainwashed..."

"Well, of course you wouldn't. That would defeat the purpose."

The tone of Zai's voice, and the way Zai was looking at him, made him feel deeply uncomfortable. As though he'd suddenly become a problem Zai was trying to solve.

"I thought we agreed that the brainwashing stuff was false. Also...how is something like that even scientifically possible?" It seemed too neurologically complicated.

"I mean, I've never heard of using a neural implant to induce amnesia before," said Zai. "So maybe other things are possible, too. And maybe Jane had to say that to keep it consistent with what I already knew."

Vax remained quiet, thinking. *Brainwashing? Really?* He instinctively recoiled from the idea. The thought that he somehow hadn't been in control of his actions these past four years was terrifying. Although...at the same time, there was an allure to it, as well. If he'd been brainwashed, he wasn't responsible for everything that happened. It wasn't his fault.

Yeah, right, a voice in the back of his head sneered. *That's bullshit, and you know it. You always had a choice. You just kept making the wrong decisions, over and over again.*

"I...I don't know," he mumbled. "If I've been... *brainwashed*, then I shouldn't have been able to ditch Atali after he tried to have me killed, right?"

"Maybe you broke free of it," Zai suggested.

Vax shook his head. "No, I...I don't think so."

Zai didn't respond to that. Silence once more settled between them, like an uninvited ghostly houseguest.

"I guess I..." Zai swallowed. "I haven't been fair. To you."

Vax couldn't understand this sudden one-eighty-degree turnabout. "You're okay with me, just like that? You spent all this time talking about how I'm a horrible person who did horrible things, and now...it doesn't matter anymore? Because of who I *used* to be?" His voice turned flat, dull. "What happened to 'Ethan never would've become an assassin'? And 'Ethan isn't there'?"

Zai dropped his gaze. For a moment, he simply stood there, breathing in and out.

"I...I didn't know all the facts," he said. "I didn't know everything that had happened. You didn't have a choice. Norman *forced* you—"

"But he didn't. Not...really." Vax's hands clenched, his voice sticking in his throat. "I could've—walked away, I could've—"

He couldn't speak. Those words chased each other in his head, around and around in circles, illuminating a truth that he didn't want to face.

I could've walked away.

So why didn't he? Why did he keep going?

It's all my fault.

"You thought you owed him," Zai said, his voice firm. "Besides, he could've killed you if you didn't do what he said. Like he tried to do last week."

"I didn't even *know* he'd put that tracker on me. I *could've* tried to run from him if I wanted to, I...just..."

Didn't know. Didn't have a single fucking clue as to why he stayed and endured everything, no matter how unbearable it was. Because of a misplaced sense of duty? Or was it because Atali seemed to be the only person who knew him? *Except that turned out to be a lie, didn't it?*

He thought back to the recordings he'd listened to. The not-so-miraculous story of how Ethan Tromer survived dying in the war...only to end up in a whole different hell.

"I fucked up," he said, his voice heavy and miserable. "It's all my fault."

"That's not true—"

"You didn't listen to those other recordings. You don't know how he—" *Shit.* "How *I*—ended up here. Alive, not dead."

Zai's eyes widened slightly. "You...you know?"

Vax kept his gaze lowered. "Atali asked about what happened. It must've been from when..." He swallowed hard. "When I...still remembered."

"So...what happened?" Zai asked, breathless.

"There was a bombing, right?" Vax began. "The one you thought I died in. I...I was at the edge of the blast radius. It was pure, dumb luck. Everyone else in my squad was resting, but I wanted to be alone for a few minutes to think, and then...the bomb fell. I was the only survivor."

Vax remembered the way he'd broken down then, in the audio recording.

"I'm...not exactly sure what happened next. It sounds like I had a mental breakdown, or something." His voice sounded horribly clinical, detached. "Apparently I was already feeling guilty because of the things I did and saw, and after that bomb fell...I couldn't go on anymore. So I deserted. I was trying to get to the coast and get on a ship headed back to the States."

Zai was quiet for a moment. "But...that doesn't explain how you ended up with Cyrex."

Vax exhaled shakily. "You remember the factory? The one that exploded, four years ago?"

"Yeah...?"

"I was there. I was in a car, driving past, when the factory exploded." Vax's shoulders hunched. "I saw it. And then..."

"Then?" Zai prompted, when he faltered.

"I went inside the factory." He released a shuddering breath. "And then there was a second explosion, and I...I got caught in it."

There was no sound, except their out-of-sync breathing.

"That's how I ended up almost dead in that hospital, where Atali found me. And then he—he must've used saving my life as an excuse to put in the neural implant." His throat seized up, making it hard for him to talk, to breathe. "Don't you get it? I...I *fucked up*. I don't know *what* I was thinking—that I could *help*? That I could—*do something*? If I hadn't gone in there like a fucking *idiot*, I wouldn't have—none of this would've happened, and—I—it's all my fault."

"It's *not*."

Zai's eyes were narrowed, his voice feverish with suppressed anger.

"It's not your fault. Atali Norman *chose* to—to remove your memories with a bioaug, to lie to you, to *experiment* on you, for God's sake. You didn't *ask* for any of that."

Vax exhaled slowly and didn't respond. He heard Zai's words, knew they made some sort of logical sense, but he couldn't quite believe them.

In a quieter voice, Zai asked, "You...you really did remember...when I said I wanted to marry you?"

Vax glanced at him. The hope in Zai's eyes was too much to bear.

"Don't, um..." He stared down at his hands. "Don't...get your hopes up. It was...only a small thing. Barely a memory. I don't...remember the context, or where or when or why, let alone anything else."

"But...you still remembered." Zai drew closer to him. "You remembered *me*."

"I...I'm sorry," Vax said, wincing. "But I don't. I was—just *guessing* you were the one who said that. It was a shot in the dark. I didn't...remember *you*."

Closer. "Then why did you kiss me?"

Because you remembered was Zai's unspoken answer, except...it wasn't true. Vax *wished* it were true, but it wasn't. The truth was, he did it because he wanted to know what it would feel like. To have someone care about him that much out of something as pure as love, not because he was merely useful, not because he was a convenient body to be used and abused. He wanted that, desperately.

And Zai...Zai was *nice*. He cared about people. Tried to do the right thing with a stubborn, unyielding determination. Even tried to save his life, after all their disagreements. He had no idea what Zai was like before, or why or how he'd fallen in love with Zai the first time. All he knew was that he wanted Zai now to like him, as impossible and utterly stupid as that sounded.

"I don't remember," Vax forced himself to say. "It's been four years, and still nothing. I'm sorry."

"Well...maybe...I could help. Maybe all you need is something to remind you."

A hiss of breath whistled through his teeth. "Don't you think that if something familiar could jog my memory, I wouldn't have tried to shoot you in the head?"

Zai flinched.

"Sorry," Vax mumbled.

"No, it's...it's okay. You didn't know."

The problem was, he *still* didn't know.

"Do you think..." Zai cleared his throat. "If you lost your memories because of the neural implant...wouldn't it be possible to get them back?"

Vax exhaled slowly. The idea did occur to him—a frail ray of hope he was almost too terrified to nurture. "I've...thought about that. But unless I rob a bank, there's no way I could pay for something like that," he said bitterly.

"What, Norman didn't pay you the big bucks for assassinating people?" Zai asked, sardonically.

Vax shook his head. "Only enough to pay the rent, eat, and have a tiny bit left for emergencies." Or the luxury of being able to visit the aquarium once in a while.

"So you're saying that not only did Norman force you to be his personal assassin and lab rat, he also paid you way less than any real assassin would charge?" Zai's lips pressed into a thin line. "That's cold."

Honestly, he'd never thought about it before. Maybe that should've been a clue that he'd never been in this business to begin with.

"And the lack of a right to healthcare strikes again," Zai muttered. He fell silent for a moment, and then looked at Vax again with guarded hope. "But the implant was placed without your knowledge. There has to be a way to get it removed without having to pay thousands of dollars."

Vax's fingers fidgeted. "Are you sure that's really how it works?"

"It's worth a try, isn't it? If you could get your memories back?"

"Well...even if you're right, how the hell am I supposed to explain how the implant got in my brain, and—aren't they going to ask for an ID or something?"

"I..." Zai hesitated. "I know someone who might be able to help. Someone who can keep a secret."

Vax looked at him. "Your sister? The doctor?"

"She's a resident neurosurgeon." Zai returned his gaze. "If she doesn't know someone who can help you, I don't know who else can."

VAX WAITED NERVOUSLY, his fingers twisting around each other in his lap, as Zai called his sister on his tablet. Zai was seated opposite him at the table, so the camera would pick up his face only.

A video screen appeared in the air, showing the face of a young woman with shoulder-length black hair. At a glance, she and Zai were obviously siblings, though her skin was a lighter shade of tan.

"Hey, Miki," said Zai.

She raised an eyebrow. "You're not dead. That's a good sign. Now, can you tell me where you've been?"

"In a second. Are you somewhere private? Somewhere no one else can hear you?"

"Yeah, yeah. I'm off-shift and at my apartment, and my roommate's out. So?"

Zai's eyes met Vax's, and he gestured for him to come over. Vax made his way around the table until Miki could see him.

"Uh, hello..." Miki did a double take. "You look a lot like—"

"Mik, this is Ethan," said Zai.

Miki stared at him. "You'd better start at the beginning."

Zai stuck to a bare-bones explanation of how Vax—Ethan had survived. Vax noted that Zai didn't describe the way they'd reunited. Zai spent most of his time explaining the situation with Vax's neural.

"Huh," was all Miki said once Zai finished. She was frowning. "Never heard of a neural being used to suppress memories. That sounds like dangerous technology."

"So we need to remove the neural," said Zai. "Do you know someone trustworthy who can do it?"

"Yeah, of course, but...there's going to be a problem with the cost."

Vax's tentative hope withered.

Zai frowned. "How much is it going to be?"

Miki shifted back and forth. At least she looked no happier than Vax felt. "Well...neurosurgical procedures are expensive..."

"So?"

She hesitated before finally answering. "Somewhere in the neighborhood of a hundred thousand dollars."

That was more money than Vax had ever seen in his life.

"But—I didn't even *want* this implant," he burst out. "It was put in without my consent. Isn't there any other way...?"

"I'm sorry," said Miki, softly. "I didn't make the rules."

"Miki," said Zai.

They exchanged a glance, and Vax wondered if they had some sort of sibling telepathy, because Miki's brow wrinkled. "I don't think that's going to work."

Zai turned to Vax, who was confused. "Sorry, can you give us a minute?" he said. The video screen disappeared, and Zai tapped his ear node. "I can convince them."

Vax could only hear one side of the conversation, which meant he had no idea what Zai was talking about.

"Yeah, I know, but I also haven't asked them for anything in three years. Don't worry; I know what to say. Want to bet on that? How about five hundred bucks? No? Fine." He paused, his brow suddenly furrowing. "*Yes*, of course I am. Uh-huh. I'll call you when it's done. Okay. Bye."

Vax cleared his throat once Zai had tapped his node again to end the call. "Um...what was that about?"

Zai turned to him. "I can pay for the procedure."

Vax started and stared at him. "What?"

"Worst-case scenario, I'll just have to spend a few years paying off the debt to my parents." Zai shrugged. "Which isn't terrible."

"Zai—no, I can't ask you to—"

"It's the only way," Zai interrupted him quietly. "Unless you get a job tomorrow with amazing health insurance—and even then, it might still take *years* for you save enough money for the operation."

Vax swallowed hard. "I—I don't want to be in your debt."

Without warning, Zai gave a sad laugh.

"You said something similar when I offered to pay your exemption fee, so you wouldn't have to be drafted into the war." Zai shook his head. "It was your decision, I know, but when I thought about how you wouldn't have died—almost died—if I'd just paid the damn fee—" He cut himself off and sighed. "Listen, I know you've always...felt weird about the fact that I could just—throw money at a problem and make it disappear. Because I had the good luck to be born into a rich family, and whatever."

Not that Vax could remember ever saying or thinking that.

"But—with everything being as screwed-up as it is, since people in this damn country don't think health care should be a universal right—" Zai's jaw clenched. "There's just—no other way. Unless you want that thing Atali Norman stuck in your brain to stay there for who knows how many more years."

Vax looked down. No, he didn't.

"It's...too much money. I can't pay you back," he said.

"You don't have to. I mean, unless you really, *really* want to, in which case—we can discuss it later. But this is the only way you might be able to get your memories back."

He couldn't argue against that.

"Thank you," he whispered, feeling how inadequate those words were to convey his gratitude.

FOR THE FIRST time in a long time, Vax felt cautiously optimistic.

His pessimistic instincts still whispered to him that maybe something would go horribly wrong during the surgery and he'd bleed out on the operating table. Or maybe Atali would find him in the hospital, somehow. Or...something else.

But even those fears couldn't crush the fragile hope that fluttered in his chest. The neural implant was what was suppressing his memories. If he could get it out, then he could finally fill all the holes in his brain that had haunted him for years.

He could finally remember who he was.

It wouldn't change everything that had happened during the past four years—the things he'd done, the things that had been done to him—but as long as he got his memories back, he could deal with all of that later. The weight of loss that had sat on his shoulders for so long finally lifted at the thought that everything he'd ever wanted was within reach: family. Happy memories. Even...a relationship.

The waiting period was excruciating, though. He had to visit the hospital twice, first for the brain scans, and second, a week later, for the actual surgery. Though the neurosurgeon, Dr. Murithi, seemed nice, Vax still had some deep, instinctive dislike of hospitals, and he couldn't decide whether it was because of the sterile white lights, the idea of being poked and prodded by strangers, or the unpleasant memory of waking up in a hospital room and realizing all his memories were gone.

Between visits, Zai was busy writing his article, while Vax had nothing to do except surf the internet and pace restlessly around the room. It was strange, not having to worry about their current or impending safety risks for a change, and Vax found himself still wired with nervous energy. According to Cyrex's files, Eleven was the last augmented assassin they had, but Atali was still out there, scheming. The thought that Cyrex couldn't have the city's hospitals monitored kept Vax from panicking outright, but his initial excitement kept fluctuating with anxiety until the day finally came.

"Nervous?" Zai asked him, after the doctor had called him in and he'd changed into a hospital gown. He felt too exposed, wearing only the thin paper garment, and he kept fidgeting with it.

"I don't like hospitals," he muttered.

Zai put a reassuring hand on his arm. "Don't worry. Everything will be fine."

Vax tried to take a deep breath. "Yeah, well...the last time I was in a hospital, things didn't go so well."

Zai winced. "It's different this time."

"I know, I just...I guess I'm going to wake up feeling like a completely different person. And I'm...a little anxious about that," he confessed.

"One thing at a time," said Zai. "When you get your memories back...we'll figure it out."

"Yeah." Vax closed his eyes for a brief moment, before opening them again. "See you on the other side?"

Zai gave him a smile. "Yeah. See you."

The anesthesiologist came in, and Zai left. She instructed Vax to lie down and relax. He winced as he felt the needle puncture his skin.

The anesthesia began to pull him under, a leaden weight suffusing his body. For a split second, cold panic took over, and he tried to fight the anesthesia, struggling to stay awake, but he couldn't move. He couldn't *move*. The harder he fought, the more consciousness slipped away from him.

No, wait.

I'm scared.

Help me—

Then, there was nothing but darkness.

Part III

Searching for Ethan Tromer

Chapter Eleven

"HELLO? HELLO, CAN you hear me?"

He gasped for breath, his eyes flying open.

"Whoa, whoa, take it easy. You've just had a surgery."

His muscles tensed for a second before he remembered. Right. The surgery to remove the implant in his brain.

Miki Zhao Lumero tried to give him a reassuring smile. "Can you tell me your name?"

"Va—" He cringed. "Sorry...it's...um...Ethan Tromer."

Maybe the anesthetic was still wearing off, but he had to drag the name out of his throat. It felt wrong—the syllables felt clunky in his mouth, all awkward edges, and they didn't sound right when he spoke them aloud.

As though the name still didn't belong to him.

"Can you tell me where you were born?"

He tried to think. He came up blank.

"I...don't..." He clenched the bed sheet in his hands.

"Hey, uh...don't worry. You just woke up. It might take some time for things to come back to you." Miki tapped something on her tablet. "Can you tell me the first thing you remember?"

"The first thing?" he echoed. "I...remember...waking up in a hospital room. Not this one, but like it. That was four years ago. Before that, it's only...a few bits and pieces."

"What kinds of bits and pieces?"

Still only the one fragment of a memory, no clearer than before. But he didn't want to describe it. Even if Miki was Zai's sister, it felt too...private.

"Voices. Impressions. But...nothing I can make sense of."

"Okay." She gave his shoulder a gentle pat. "That's all for now. Dr. Murithi will be in soon to check that everything looks okay, and we'll have to run some more tests later, but for now, get some rest."

"Is Zai..." He swallowed. "Is he...?"

"He's outside, waiting. Would you like to see him?"

Vax looked down at his hands and nodded once.

"All right."

Miki left. A minute later, Zai came in.

"Hey." Zai gave him a tentative smile as he sat next to the bed. "How are you feeling?"

A lump throbbed in his throat. "I, um...I still don't remember..."

"It's okay. Miki told me. There's no rush."

He closed his eyes. "But I thought—I thought I'd wake up and feel like *myself* again—"

He choked up, unable to admit he could barely even refer to himself by his own name. *Ethan Tromer.*

"Hey." He felt the warm, light pressure of Zai's hand slipping over his own. "Sometimes things just...take time, you know? The implant's gone. Things will come back to you. We just have to be patient."

Vax sighed and nodded wearily. He really wished he had woken up with all the gaps instantly filled in. The waiting period was going to be agony, but there was nothing anyone could do. *I just have to wait. Everything will come back to me now that the neural's out. It's going to be fine,* he told himself.

When he'd recovered enough to be able to stand and walk around, Miki brought him to another room and ran him through a battery of tests. How well could he remember famous figures and world events, how was his motor control, how was his visual memory, whether he could remember any more autobiographical information. He did fine on everything except remembering his own past—it was still almost entirely blank. Nothing new had come to him since the implant had been removed.

"Is it supposed to take me this long to remember anything?" he asked Miki anxiously.

"Well...honestly, I'm not sure. Retrograde amnesia is generally really rare to begin with. When people get it through a TBI—traumatic brain injury—they usually do end up remembering everything except, possibly, what happened right before the injury, but...your case is unusual. We'll probably have to keep monitoring to see what happens." She touched his shoulder. "Sorry. I wish I could give you a better answer."

"No, it's—it's okay," he said, lowering his gaze. "I understand."

Miki scrolled through something on her tablet. "Why don't you come back in...one week, and we'll see how you're doing, all right? And in the meantime, if you experience any pain or weird side effects, please don't hesitate to call."

"All right. Thank you," he said.

ZAI DIDN'T SAY much as they rode the sky rail back to the safe house—probably because they were still trying to avoid attention. But when they got back and closed the door, Vax realized he didn't know what to say to him. It felt...awkward between them. He wasn't the person he was supposed to be yet, but with the truth hanging on his shoulders, he had no idea how he should act around Zai.

"There's...something I have to tell you," Zai said suddenly.

Vax looked at him, frowning slightly at the trepidation in Zai's voice. "What?"

Zai wrung his hands. "I...I should have told you sooner. No—I should have asked your permission. I'm sorry for going behind your back."

Vax couldn't take the suspense anymore. "Just tell me what you're talking about."

Zai took a breath. "I...lifted some fingerprints from a glass you touched—this was two weeks ago—and I asked a friend who works in forensics to discreetly compare them to the prints on file from when you were drafted." Zai raised his eyes to meet Vax's gaze. "It was a match, so...that's the final confirmation that puts any remaining doubt to rest."

"Good to know," said Vax. Not that there had been much doubt in his mind, after all the other evidence, but it was nice to know he wasn't a long-lost twin or secret, scientifically improbable clone.

Another moment of silence passed. Zai picked up his tablet from the table and fiddled with it for a second.

"Here." Zai handed him the tablet. "Do you recognize this picture?"

It was...a picture of *him*. Except he had a shaggy head of hair, thick-rimmed glasses, and a wide smile on his face.

Zai was in the picture, too. They were sitting at some sort of restaurant, eating noodles. He didn't recognize the restaurant, and he had no idea when or why the picture was taken.

"No, I...I don't remember..."

"That's okay," Zai said softly. "This was our favorite ramen restaurant near campus. We used to come here all the time on special occasions."

He took another long look at the picture. Nothing looked familiar. He didn't have a clue as to what he might have ordered there or what it tasted like.

Zai changed to a different picture. "How about this one?"

Him again, standing over what looked like a half-dissected pig, making a face at the camera.

Vax shook his head, his throat tightening.

"Biology lab," Zai said, still sounding unworried. "That's how we met—we were in the same introductory biology class."

Zai scrolled through more pictures. Vax couldn't recognize anything—least of all the smiling, carefree version of himself—and a dull, throbbing pressure built at the base of his throat every time he said "no" or "I don't remember," until he couldn't take it anymore.

"I—" He stood abruptly. "I can't do this."

He walked into the kitchen but, at a loss for what to do, ended up leaning against the refrigerator, staring at the ground.

Zai's footsteps followed him. "Sorry. I just thought—I'm sorry."

"Could you...tell me, instead?" he asked. Listening was easier than having to face the gaping holes in his head.

Zai paused. "What do you want to know?"

Everything, Vax thought, even though he knew how ridiculous that sounded.

"You said we met in biology class in college?"

"Yeah." Zai ran his fingers along the countertop. "In freshman year. We were lab partners. After the first day of class...I asked you out. You said yes. That's how it started."

"That's...simple," Vax commented.

"Well...there was a bit more to it than that, but..." Zai's eyes met his, and then drifted away. "I'll tell you some other time."

That was slightly odd. But, after pondering for a moment, Vax decided to let it go for now. He went on, "When was I drafted?"

"Junior year," Zai answered quietly. "You left after the end of the fall semester."

Vax did some quick math. They would've been together for two and a half years at that point. "So...did you graduate by the time...um, you heard I was dead?"

"Not quite. That was right before my last semester." Zai rubbed the back of his neck. "Actually...I had to take that semester off. I ended up graduating in the fall."

"Oh." Vax tried to imagine what kind of shape Zai must have been in, if he had to take a semester off. It wasn't a pretty picture. He swallowed and asked, "Was I really such a saintly, selfless, perfect goody-two-shoes?"

Zai looked at him with a startled expression.

"I read my, um, obituary—" That had to be one of the most screwed-up sentences in the history of spoken language. "—and it all sounded so hard to believe. No one's that nice, not without some kind of ulterior motive," he said bitterly.

"Well..." Zai looked a bit lost and uncharacteristically discomfited. "It...wasn't an act or anything. You didn't have an ulterior motive. You just...had a strong sense of fairness and compassion, and I think...helping people made you feel useful."

That didn't help very much.

"You mentioned...I wanted to go to law school?"

"You wanted to use your education to give back to society. That's why you wanted to go into public interest law. You told me that public service was a tradition in your family."

Vax couldn't imagine having that kind of aspiration now. But then again, he supposed he just wasn't the same person without his memories.

"That was my goal in life?" Asking that out loud sounded so weird. "Public service?"

"That, and living a quiet, happy life, with friends and family," said Zai.

So much for that. What he wouldn't give to go back to a normal life, with normal hopes and dreams.

He became aware of Zai moving closer to him, and he grew tense, even though he wasn't sure why part of him wanted to flee. What was wrong with him? He wanted this, didn't he? And he shared a history with Zai, even if he couldn't remember it yet. It wasn't like...

Zai's fingers brushed against the side of his neck. Wired up as he was, he recoiled before he could think about what was going on, remembering a different kind of touch, and the brief flash of hurt he saw in Zai's expression made him feel guilty.

"I'm sorry," he stammered. "I'm—"

"No, no, I'm the one who should be sorry," Zai said quickly. "We should...take it slow."

The awkwardness that settled between them was unbearable. Vax crossed his arms and looked to the side. "How's your article going?"

Zai seemed a little startled. "Uh...well, I'm done."

"Oh...you are?"

"Yeah." Zai tapped his tablet and then held it out to him. "You can read it if you want."

Vax took the tablet and skimmed the document on the screen. Murder of at least nine individuals in the course of illegal experimentation without informed consent, according to a former Cyrex employee. Plus a pretty extensive discussion on the vulnerability of homeless persons whose lives weren't valued by society.

There was no mention of him in the article, and he released a breath before turning to Zai. "You're really okay with leaving me out of this?"

"Of course," said Zai. "I mean, doing unethical experiments on people that led to death is one thing. Wiping people's memories is another. This is only the first article in what I'm sure will be a major exposé into Cyrex's secret, off-the-books project." Zai met his gaze. "But I promise I won't reveal your identity if you don't want me to."

After a pause, Vax nodded. "So...is it live?"

"Not yet. I'm going to do one last round of proofreading tomorrow, and then send it to my editor." Zai smiled crookedly. "Trust me, if it were live already, everyone would know."

Vax blew out a breath. So close, and yet...not there yet.

"Hey." Zai touched his arm, and he tried not to startle. "It's almost over."

Almost. But the closer they got, the uneasier he felt. He was almost convinced Atali had some sort of backup plan that he was waiting until the very last moment to spring on them. After all, he had to be desperate by now. Vax had escaped him, and Eleven was out of commission. He knew that Zai was about to blow Cyrex apart. There was no way Atali would sit there and gracefully accept defeat.

"It's too easy," he said.

"Too easy?" Zai echoed, with a disbelieving laugh. "Both of us nearly died several times over. How is it *too easy*?"

Vax shook his head. "You don't—you don't know Atali. He doesn't like loose ends." He bit his lip. "It just feels like he has to have something else planned."

"Like what?" Zai said, unconcerned. "Killing all of us off with his own private army? He's not a dictator. He can't just snap his fingers and do anything he wants."

"He has enough money and power to get pretty damn close," Vax muttered.

"You always were a worrier. Listen, you've just lived through a long nightmare. But things are going to be okay now. Let me take care of whatever curveball Atali Norman wants to throw. Just...trust me. It's going to be okay."

He wanted to believe Zai, but he couldn't. The tight knot of fear in his chest wouldn't relax. He was afraid Atali would retaliate; he was afraid that even after his memories came back, he still wouldn't be the same Ethan Tromer he used to be.

"Trust me," Zai repeated.

Vax closed his eyes. Maybe he could. For just this moment, maybe he could believe he was Ethan Tromer, and everything was going to be okay.

Chapter Twelve

DID YOU REALLY think you could get away from me?

Vax was shoved against the wall. The back of his head collided with the plaster, painfully jarring his skull. There was a hand around his throat, crushing his windpipe. He couldn't breathe.

I own your life. You belong to me.

No, he tried to scream, but his voice wasn't working, and he couldn't move. *Let go of me! No!*

"Ethan! *Ethan!*"

Who the hell is Ethan? Just leave me alone! Leave me alone!

The nightmare receded slowly from him, like water reluctantly sliding away from the shore, the terror still lingering. At first he was aware only of the sound of his breaths, harsh and panting. Then, as the world came into focus, he realized Zai was underneath him, pinned to the coffee table, and he was pulling weakly at Vax's arm jammed against his throat.

Horror hit him like a thunderclap. He yanked his arm back, scrambling away until he collided with the far armrest of the couch and sank down, trying to shrink against it. Zai slumped to the floor, taking deep, gasping breaths as he massaged his throat.

"I'm—I'm so sorry," Vax said, in a small, shaking voice. "I didn't mean...I'm so sorry."

Zai drew slow breaths. Vax waited, his chest tight, still partly frozen by the remains of his nightmare, what he had done, and fear of how Zai would react.

Finally, Zai raised his head. His voice was slightly hoarse, but strangely, he didn't look that upset. "It's not your fault. I should've known."

Vax blinked. His heart stopped—and then resumed at triple speed. *Known? Known...what? He can't know...he can't possibly know...*

"What—what do you mean, you should've known?" he croaked.

"That you have PTSD."

No. A new wave of terror constricted him. *How did he figure it out?* He frantically racked his memory, trying to figure out what gave him away.

"How...how do you know it's PTSD?" he managed to ask.

"I did a lot of reading when you were still on your tour," Zai said. "You seemed like you weren't doing so well with the war, so I thought it was a possibility." He gave Vax a wan smile. "Guess that research paid off."

Vax's lungs finally started working again. *Oh.* Zai believed he had PTSD from the war. Hell, maybe that wasn't completely wrong, either; he'd had trouble sleeping and strange reactions to certain things for as long as he could remember. They'd just gotten worse...after.

Vax lowered his gaze. He realized he'd wrapped his arms tightly around himself, gripping the fabric of his sleeves with trembling fists. "I...I almost killed you," he mumbled. "Again."

"You didn't mean it. I was the one who should've known better than to try and shake you out of your nightmare. And you can get help when this is all over."

The remnants of the nightmare were still fresh and raw in his mind, and when Zai tried to touch his shoulder, he recoiled.

"I'm sorry—" The distress in Zai's voice made Vax wince.

"I just—need to be alone right now," he said hoarsely. "Please."

"Okay." Zai sounded sad, but he stood up from the couch and crossed over to the bedroom door. He paused for a second. "Good night," he said quietly, and shut the door behind him.

Vax let out a shaky breath and slumped forward, hanging his head. God, he hoped getting his memories back would—fix this, make things better, *something* so he wouldn't have to feel as freakish and fucked-up as he did at that moment.

He hoped so.

HE WAS RELUCTANT to face Zai the next morning, but Zai acted as though nothing had happened the night before. That was reassuring, he supposed.

He heard the faint, telltale buzz of Zai's node. Zai answered.

"Hey, Ashleigh, I was just about to email you—" He broke off. A crease appeared between his eyebrows. "Slow down, *what* happened to the *Voice*?"

Vax watched with concern as Zai listened in silence, his frown deepening.

"All right," Zai finally said, in a shaken voice. That didn't bode well at all. "Thanks for telling me. Let me know ASAP if anything changes."

He ended the call and grabbed his tablet, typing rapidly. "What happened?" Vax asked.

Zai turned the tablet around to show him the screen. "*This* happened," he said, grimly.

The internet address was set to the *Daily Voice*'s home page, but instead of displaying news, the page was totally black with large white capitalized letters splashed across: THE DAILY VOICE LIES.

Zai rubbed his forehead. "The *Voice*'s had to deal with some serious hacking attempts before, from people who don't like the fact that it's an independent news site, but this attack is unprecedented."

Vax stared at the hacked home page. A chill slowly spread throughout his body, leaving him numb with cold.

"They don't know who did it yet," Zai went on, "but they're working to—"

"It's Atali," Vax heard himself say. His voice sounded distant. "He did this."

Zai stopped. "How do you know? There isn't a name or a calling card left behind..."

"That's the point. Hackers always claim credit for what they're doing, right? Unless they're being paid not to. Besides, he's used hackers before, remember?"

Zai didn't argue against that.

"It's a message," Vax said. "If he can't kill you to stop you from telling the truth, he'll at least take away your microphone to try to silence you."

"That's ridiculous," said Zai. "The digital space is free—he can't *own* it. And there's nothing he could do to stop me from publishing with another website, or even on my own blog if I have to."

Vax raised his head and met Zai's gaze. "Would you?"

Zai's jaw tightened. "It...wouldn't be ideal," he admitted. "No corporate-funded news site would break something like this. Among the independent news sites, the *Daily Voice* has a lot of internet reach. If I posted something on my blog—well, first I'd have to create one, and second, it could take a long time before it goes viral, given how much digital noise there is on the internet. But for God's sake, I can't just stand by and do *nothing* while Atali Norman tries to control the internet. Who knows, he might even be trying to destroy the evidence of Project VAX as we speak."

That was the problem. It wouldn't take long at all to scrub Cyrex's servers of all the files. The uneasiness Vax had felt the day before solidified into a lump of despair in the pit of his stomach. He knew Atali wouldn't give up. He *knew* it. Even if this wasn't checkmate—even if it could be reversed—Atali was buying time to continue their cat-and-mouse chase, and there was nothing either of them could do.

Nothing, except...

Eleven had said she'd been ordered to take Vax alive if possible. He'd tried to avoid thinking about that, because there was only one real reason he could come up with as for why Atali still wanted him breathing, even though he'd broken all the rules—even though Atali had been fine with murdering nine other people before him—and that reason made him sick.

Vax had to be out of his mind if he was considering *that*. Besides, he couldn't be certain that it would work—Atali had already proven that he was perfectly fine with ordering Vax's death. But what other choice was there? What else could he do?

"I...have an idea," he said, slowly, dragging the words out from his throat.

Zai glanced at him. "What's that?"

"There are two things Atali wants." Vax moved past Zai without meeting his eyes. "He wants your story to go away for good, and..." He swallowed hard, his mouth dry. "He wants me."

"Yeah...he wants to *kill* you. Remember how this whole thing got started?"

How could I forget?

"Trust me, he'd rather keep me alive if he can. Besides," he added, before Zai could protest, "I might be able to convince him to undo the damage. I...think I can get him to listen to me."

Now he could feel the full weight of Zai's baffled, disbelieving stare.

"Ethan," Zai said, sounding cautious, "is this some kind of Stockholm Syndrome thing?"

Vax whirled around. "No, Zai," he snapped. "I don't have fucking *Stockholm Syndrome*—"

He realized Zai had recoiled and backed away from the force of his anger, and he struggled to bring himself under control. *He doesn't know. He can't know. I can't let him know.*

"I'd rather jump off a roof than have to face him again," he said, keeping his voice level. "But the *Daily Voice*...means a lot to people. To you. And the world deserves to know what happened to those nine other test subjects. So I'll do it, if that's what it takes."

Zai still looked uncertain. "How do you know for sure that he'll listen to you?"

It was a gamble, and he knew it. But it was the only card he had.

"Just...trust me," he said, hoping he sounded more confident than he felt.

"All right," Zai said, at last. "What's your plan?"

"It's pretty simple," said Vax. He reached for his gun.

VAX STOOD IN front of Cyrex's building, staring up at the windows lit brightly against the night sky.

It was probably just as well that he hadn't given himself a lot of time to think too hard about his plan beforehand. Dread churned in the pit of his stomach, a leaden, nauseous anxiety. Paranoid, pessimistic thoughts kept worming their way into his head: this was never going to work, Atali was never going to believe him, he was signing his own death warrant.

But he had to do this. Besides…no matter how afraid he was, he still wanted a chance to face Atali one more time. To ask him *why*.

He swallowed hard and walked toward the entrance.

He half expected to be stopped as soon as he walked through the lobby, but nothing happened. He swiped through security without a problem. He wasn't sure whether it was reassuring or even more worrying.

He took the elevator up, as he had so many times before. He walked to the door to Atali's office, as though he were there to make a normal report or receive another assignment. The only difference was that the office was dark; Atali wasn't in.

Vax vaguely wondered for a moment if Atali were on vacation somewhere in the middle of the Caribbean Sea with his wife. In which case, his plan was somewhat screwed. Swallowing again, he tapped the button on his node.

"Hold line one. Call Atali Norman," he said, trying to keep his voice steady enough for the node to recognize the name.

The line rang. Once. Twice.

"Hello, Vax. It's been a while."

Atali spoke as warmly as though they were old friends who had fallen out of touch, not as someone who'd ordered an assassin to kill Vax, and not as someone who had wiped Vax's memories and then lied to him about it. His tone left Vax speechless for a second.

"Uh..." He cleared his throat. *Stay on track.* "You've tried really hard to kill me these past two weeks."

"Capture," Atali corrected. "It was never my desire to kill you."

Vax steeled himself and went on. "I know you were upset that I screwed up with Lumero, sir." The word "sir" felt like slime on his tongue. "But...I did finish the assignment. And I have access to the backup copies of his research. So...could you maybe stop sending people to kill or capture me?"

The line was silent for a long while.

"Are you saying you killed Lumero?" said Atali, softly.

"Yes, sir."

"Where are you now?"

"Right outside your office."

"Well, I'm in the middle of dinner with my wife right now, so sit tight for a few minutes. I'll be right over." Atali ended the call.

Almost an hour passed before he arrived, during which time Vax nearly broke the buttons on his jacket while fiddling with them to try to stave off the crushing boredom, picked his already blunt fingernails to the quick, and contemplated the morbidly creative things he'd never get to do to Atali for defining "a few minutes" as "whenever the hell I feel like it."

At some point, he began to wonder if Atali was gathering a group of security guards or police officers, which revived his almost-numbed anxiety. But when the elevator door finally opened, Atali stepped out alone. He didn't say anything—not to explain his lateness, and certainly not to apologize. He opened his office door, and Vax followed him inside.

Vax's entire body tensed. He hated this office. In any other context, it would've been a nice place—spacious with a comfy sofa, shiny white tile floor, panorama screens on the walls, a couple of potted plants, and a great view of the city—but Vax had had too many bad memories from the place to admire it anymore. Every atom of his being rebelled against being back there, face-to-face with Atali again. But he had to. He couldn't let Atali guess the truth.

"What did you do with the gun?" Atali asked in a pleasant tone.

"It's in my pocket, sir."

Atali's eyes went to his pockets, not betraying any surprise. "You didn't get rid of it?"

Vax tried to keep his expression blank. "I wasn't sure whether or not you'd bring a squad of security guards to tranq me, so I kept it."

"So little trust? I'm hurt."

Trust? That's rich, coming from the guy who hid my real name and identity from me and fucking lied to my face about who I was, for starters.

"You were the one who tried to have me killed," Vax pointed out, focusing on keeping his voice deadpan. "I've been feeling a little on edge. Sir."

"Hmm. I guess that's understandable." Atali raised his palms. "Believe me, I didn't *want* you dead. Eleven was just meant to be your replacement. Like a superior machine model or computer software version."

Incredulous fury surged through him. *I am not a fucking machine model!*

Atali shrugged. "Clearly our calculations were wrong, because you managed to beat her. I can't say I'm completely displeased." He gave Vax a smile that seemed oddly...proud. Like a mad scientist regarding his first invention. "You always were my favorite."

Revulsion and terror crawled down Vax's artificial spine. *No, no, no, don't go there.*

"I have to say, I'm curious. How did you get Lumero to give you access to his backup copies?"

Vax forced himself to maintain eye contact with Atali, as unpleasant as it felt. "It...wasn't easy, sir. It took a while to figure out how to convince him to tell me, but...I finally managed it."

"Then what happened?"

"Then I shot him, sir. In the back of the head."

Atali studied him. "Are you saying you deceived him all this time? I didn't think you had it in you."

He was walking along a razor's edge, and he knew it.

"Well...not exactly, sir. At first, I thought...maybe I *should* help him. You tried to have me killed," he repeated.

"Trust me, it wasn't personal."

Vax vividly and uncomfortably remembered saying those exact same words to Zai during their first meeting.

Atali went on. "So when you broke into the north building, you were genuinely trying to help him?"

"Yes, sir."

"What changed your mind? I thought you would've formed an attachment to Zai Lumero and wanted to help him in his little crusade."

"Why, because of our past history?"

Atali shrugged a little.

"Did you know?" He kept his voice utterly blank. "When you sent me to kill him?"

"Of course I did. Not that it was supposed to matter, until you screwed everything up. After all, you had no idea."

That knowledge sank like a stone in Vax's mind, coming to rest along everything else he knew about Atali.

"But...you were afraid that I'd find out," Vax said slowly. He focused hard on what he was saying, on slotting the puzzle pieces together. "That's why you initially ordered Eleven to kill me. Wasn't it?"

"I wasn't sure how you'd react," said Atali. "Since you've been somewhat—excuse my saying so—emotionally unstable at times."

After everything you did, I wonder why.

"So?" Atali said. "No rekindling of lost love?"

"He hated me." Vax's voice remained robotic. The lie came easily this time, perhaps too easily. "Because I wasn't the same person he remembered."

"And then?"

Vax let his gaze drop.

"I...there was no point in being around someone who hated me that much. I thought..." Even though he'd scripted his answer beforehand, it still felt so hard to say the words aloud. "Maybe, if I finished my original assignment..."

"That I'd forgive you?"

Vax forced himself to nod, scalding humiliation crawling up his throat. A long, tense, drawn-out moment passed.

He's not going to buy it, Vax thought, his palms slick with cold sweat. He was sure that Atali was seeing right through his pitiful attempt at deception, and he knew Zai was alive and listening to the conversation as they spoke through the open channel in Vax's node.

Instead, Atali said, in a voice that was almost amused, "You always come back, don't you?"

A knife-sharp pang of shame went through him, but he couldn't protest. He bit his tongue and stayed silent.

"So. Where are the backup copies?"

Trying not to feel too relieved—*It's not over yet*—Vax gave him the address and password to Zai's cloud drive. Atali accessed it on his tablet, scanned the screen for a second, and then tapped the screen. To delete the files, Vax assumed.

"Sir," he said, "will the *Daily Voice* remain down forever?"

Atali tilted his head. "I don't know what you mean."

"You financed those hackers, didn't you?"

Atali shrugged.

"Did my desperation seem that obvious? Of course, I didn't know you were still trying to complete your assignment." He paused briefly to tap rapidly onto the tablet. "I suppose there would be some satisfaction in letting them report Zai Lumero's death."

Zai spoke suddenly into Vax's ear, from his node. "Is he calling off the hackers?"

I don't know, Vax thought, silently. But he didn't dare say anything aloud.

When Atali finished, he put the tablet down and held his hand out, speaking as though he were trying to calm a wary animal. "Give me the gun, Vax."

Vax tried not to flinch at the name. *You liar. You* know *what my fucking name is. You've known it all these years.*

He lowered his gaze. "I...could I ask some questions, sir?"

"Sure." Atali answered in an indulgent tone, as though he were doing Vax a favor.

Vax inhaled deeply. This was it. His last chance to ask Atali the questions that had been eating at him all this time—but he had to stay focused. He couldn't betray himself.

"The neural implant in my brain...did that have any effect other than making me unable to remember anything about myself? Did it...um...brainwash me, or anything?"

Atali burst out laughing at that. Vax stared at him.

"Brainwash? If only. If anyone understood the human brain well enough to be able to induce brainwashing using a neural implant, that person would win a Nobel Prize. And tons of money from government and military contracts."

So no, then.

"Why did you take away my memories?" Vax went on.

He expected some cackling, sadistic response, but instead, Atali shrugged. "They weren't important."

Vax blinked, disarmed. "Excuse me?"

"Ethan Tromer was a mediocre person." Vax's skin crawled at Atali's use of past tense. "Just one soldier among thousands, who was left for dead by the army. There was nothing of value about him or his memories."

How about my family? Vax wanted to spit at him. *The person I used to be? Whatever hopes and aspirations I used to have? The future I planned on having? It was my life.* Mine. *You had* no right *to take it from me.*

"Did the other nine people before me...have their memories taken away, too?" he forced himself to say.

"Not exactly. The purpose of Project VAX was to find ways to instill obedience in people. But we found that brainwashing wasn't quite possible with neural augmentation, and psychological conditioning took too much time." Atali glanced at him. "Take away someone's memories, though, and they become very receptive to suggestion."

Vax fought to keep any trace of anger or distress from his expression, though his stomach turned.

"The first nine were...unfortunate casualties of science. The brain is a delicate organ, you know. One wrong step, and you could cause a coma or brain death. But you, Vax...you were the culmination of years of research. The first functional prototype." He spoke with a note of pride, as though "prototype" were a compliment and not a name for an object instead of a person.

"What happened to them?" Vax asked.

"They were failures. They had to be disposed of."

Just as I *had to be disposed of once you no longer had a use for me.*

"You...gave me other augments, sir. Were they also part of the project?"

"Not initially. But who was I to turn down an opportunity to test more prototypes?"

Translation: *Since you were here, I decided I might as well use you as a lab rat. It's not like you would have gone to the authorities to protest.*

"Did you wake up one day and decide you wanted to create obedient...assassins? Sir."

"We were working on a different project, but the opportunity was simply too good to pass up."

"What kind of project was that?"

"One funded by a generous sponsor," said Atali.

Vax frowned. "Who?"

Atali only smiled. "Someone you won't have to concern yourself with."

Vax silently cursed.

"It's back online," Zai breathed.

"The gun, Vax," Atali said at the same time.

Slowly, his eyes never leaving Atali, he withdrew his gun, removed the magazine, emptied the chamber, and handed it to him, handle first.

Atali took it. "The magazine, too, Vax."

"Why? Are you planning to shoot me?"

Atali laughed, but the smile didn't reach his eyes. "You know me better than that."

No. I don't. I really don't.

It was a control thing, he knew that, forcing him to literally put his life in Atali's hands. Just as how Atali had always forced him to do things he didn't want to do, over and over again. Wordlessly, Vax handed it to him.

Zai whispered, in a rush, "It's live—it's live! Social media feeds should be exploding in a few minutes..."

"Now." Atali tilted his head, regarding him. "What to do with you?"

No.

Every muscle went taut in Vax's body. He couldn't have disguised his reaction even if he'd tried. He saw that Atali saw it, an eyebrow arching with amusement. *Fuck, where are the feeds?*

"Relax," said Atali. "I wouldn't want you to hurt yourself."

No.

Vax thought about killing him if Atali touched him. No—he *knew* he was going to kill him if he did. Even if it was only a mind game to provoke a reaction from him. *No more. Never again..*

Atali leaned toward him. Vax's fingers clenched tightly into fists.

And just at that moment, a startled expression crossed Atali's face, followed quickly by an annoyed one as he put a finger to his ear, turning aside.

"Now is really not a good time—"

He broke off, falling silent. Vax waited, not daring to breathe, the moment stretching into an agonized eternity.

"I'll deal with it," Atali finally said. He paused. "I'll *deal* with it," he repeated, his mouth tightening. "Don't worry. Keep me updated."

He ended the call by tapping his node and looked at Vax. Vax searched his face for a reaction, but found nothing.

"You lied." Atali didn't sound angry or even shocked; his voice remained disarmingly mild.

"Yeah. I lied." Vax narrowed his eyes. He could let the anger seep through now, the cold fury that had been seething under his skin. "What, you didn't think I had it in me?"

He saw Atali's hand move, and though he knew the gun was unloaded, he grabbed for it, not wanting to leave him with a single weapon—

He glimpsed the taser in Atali's other hand too late.

Everything went white, blinding white, the electric current ripping a scream of pain from him. He dropped, and the ground hit him like a wall of concrete.

"What's going on?" Zai yelled faintly in his ear. "Ethan! What's going on?!"

Atali kicked him in the stomach, viciously, and he curled up, trying to protect himself.

"It didn't have to end this way," Atali said, sounding disappointed, like a parent let down by a child. He kneeled on the ground next to Vax, and his voice was closer than Vax wanted it to be.

Vax unclenched his jaw long enough to speak. "After everything you did? And what you did to *me*? Did you really think I was going to let you get away with all of that?"

Atali raised an eyebrow. "You're so ungrateful, Vax. You would have died in that hospital if I hadn't come along. You were a nobody, unidentifiable because you were officially a dead man, with no insurance to cover the expensive medical procedures that were necessary to put you back together. I raised you from the dead and made you into something so much better."

"Some*thing*," Vax echoed bitterly. "Because it never occurred to you that I might be a fucking *human being*?"

Atali grabbed his chin and jerked it up. Cold terror suddenly washed through him.

"Oh, I *know* you're human," Atali murmured. "All those nights together...how could I not?"

Shit. Shit shit shit.

Zai must have heard that.

Vax didn't want to think about what Zai must be thinking.

He shook his head violently, trying to dislodge Atali's hand. *"Don't touch me."*

Atali's thumb dug deeper, the thumbnail biting a painful crescent into his chin. Then, Atali finally released him—only to reach into his pocket, pull out the gun and the magazine, and begin loading it.

"Wait," Vax rasped, trying to push himself up from the ground with shaking arms. "You're not going to kill me. If you do, the world will know."

"Know what? That I killed an assassin in self-defense?"

"Zai knows," said Vax. "He knows I'm here. He has the evidence of what you've done. How do you think that will look, if I disappear tonight after I told him I was coming to talk to you? Or is getting rid of me worth going to jail?"

He wasn't going to care about his face being broadcast to the media if he was dead. He could hear Zai's harsh, unsteady breathing in his ear. Atali had the coldest expression Vax had ever seen, as though he wanted to personally dismember him, and for a long moment, he wondered if he'd gambled wrong. If Atali truly was willing to kill him rather than let him gain control, this one time.

Or...Vax's stomach dropped. Maybe he wouldn't go for killing. Maybe he'd go for worse.

Then Vax heard the faint sound of Atali's node buzzing with an incoming call.

He lunged for the gun, banking on Atali's momentary distraction. It worked. He knocked Atali to the ground, wrestling the gun from his hands, and rolled away until he got to his feet, gun pointed at Atali.

For the first time in four years, he saw fear flash across Atali's face.

Vax paused. *You could pull the trigger*, an ugly, angry voice whispered in the back of his head. It was as much as Atali deserved, after everything he'd done to him. The years of lying, experimentation, an unwanted neural implant, nightmares for the rest of his life...Vax could finally even the scales and make sure Atali could never hurt him ever again. His finger twitched, itching to pull.

But...Zai believed in bringing Atali to justice the right way. The person Vax used to be would've believed in bringing Atali to justice the right way. So Vax swallowed hard, buried that voice in the back of his mind, and kept his finger off the trigger. He wouldn't stoop to Atali's level. He could be better than that.

"Here's what's going to happen," he said, trying to keep his voice calm. "You're going to answer that call and *not* page security, while I walk out of here unharmed. And then you and I are never going to see each other again."

Atali said nothing, but his eyes were full of venom. Slowly, Vax backed to the door, opened it, and slipped out. It was all he could do not to sprint down the stairs and out of the building. He switched the gun's safety back on, tucked it away, and managed to take the elevator down and leave the building without drawing any attention to himself.

He didn't dare breathe until he'd walked a block away and then broke into a run, running as fast as he could from Cyrex. He didn't stop until he realized Zai was trying to speak over the wind roaring in his ears.

Vax slowed to a walk.

"What?" he said, breathing hard.

"You did it," Zai said breathlessly.

Vax wished he could feel the same sense of triumphant satisfaction as Zai did, but all he could feel was numb shock, instead. That they'd actually done it—they'd taken Atali down. It was hard to believe, after all this time.

Now, if only he could get his memories back.

Chapter Thirteen

VAX VENTURED OUTSIDE the next morning, on a mission to get some "real" food for himself and Zai, only to find himself faced with news stories about Cyrex plastered on screens every few feet.

"Cyrex accused of conducting illegal human experimentation."

"Is this the end for the bioaug titan?"

"Did Cyrex CEO Atali Norman really participate in experimental murder?"

Reading the headlines and trending social media hashtags was entertaining, and quite satisfying, but there were more pictures of Atali's face plastered on the screens than usual, and Vax hurried along, not wanting to dwell on what had hopefully been the last time he'd ever see or speak to Atali Norman again.

By the time he got back, he found Zai at the table, speaking rapidly to whoever had called him on his node as he simultaneously typed on his tablet. Zai barely got a second to breathe—he answered calls and emails all day, and for the next several days after. Vax followed the news with some interest, particularly the news of an impending shareholder lawsuit.

Mostly, though, he scrolled through more of Zai's pictures of them, trying desperately to see if one of them would jog his memory. A week had passed since the surgery, and he still didn't remember anything. Not even a vague sense of déjà vu. He battled against panicked pessimism, clinging to his thread of hope. *I'm sure everything's fine. I'm sure it's just taking a while and there's a perfectly reasonable medical explanation for that.*

Vax felt bad about Zai coming with him to his follow-up appointment at the hospital, but Zai assured him it was no big deal.

"Honestly, I'm relieved not to have to take calls for an hour or two," he said. "It's gotten to the point at which I'm basically saying the same thing over and over."

Miki frowned slightly when he told her nothing had come back. She suggested they do an MRI. "You know, just to make sure nothing serious is going on."

"Do you think there's something serious?" he asked.

"Well, it doesn't hurt to check."

After the scan had finished, Vax changed out of his hospital gown and waited in the room along with Zai. It was quiet for a moment before Zai started talking.

"Things've been pretty crazy, huh? We haven't gotten a chance to talk since you spoke to Norman."

Vax shrugged. "Like you said, things have been pretty hectic."

Zai seemed to hesitate for a long moment.

"So...I have to ask..."

Shit. Here it comes. His stomach twisted into painful knots. He waited for the question with dread, the one thing he'd hoped Zai would never find out.

"You were...Norman's lover?"

Vax jerked. That wasn't what he'd expected. "*What*?"

"I mean, not that I'm mad or anything." Although Zai still sounded tense. "You didn't have your memory, so—"

"No, it wasn't like that—"

"Though I'm kind of surprised by what he said, since before, you were never really into—"

"It *wasn't fucking like that*, Zai!" Vax snarled.

Zai blinked.

Vax tried to breathe. Inhale. Exhale.

"I..." Vax looked away, eyes shut, swallowing hard. "I never wanted to—I never *wanted* it—I—"

"Wait." Zai's voice was strained. "Are you saying...?"

Vax fisted the fabric of his cargo pants with painfully clenched hands. He shouldn't have said anything. He should've lied. What if Zai didn't believe him? Or what if Zai couldn't look at him anymore without disgust in his eyes?

"I didn't—I hated it, but I couldn't stop him—I couldn't—"

"Ethan...my God, Ethan..."

Vax flinched away from Zai's touch, from the horror in his voice.

"It sounds so fucking stupid when I say it out loud, like—why didn't I fight him? Fuck, why didn't I *kill* him? I don't know. I was so fucked up, I didn't—didn't fucking *know*. All I could do was get stone-drunk after each time and try to forget."

At first, he'd thought the world of Atali Norman. He'd believed he was a kind, generous man for having saved his life. That was before he learned Atali was a manipulator, before he saw how easily Atali could go from charming to cruel. Maybe that was why he never saw it coming, why even afterward, he couldn't untangle the confused feelings of betrayal and gratitude and the sense of debt that broke any idea of resistance. Or maybe he was just stupid and gullible and easy to manipulate and too cowardly to fight back.

He stared at the linoleum floor, his heart beating out the long seconds like a ticking clock. Every word he'd uttered echoed in his head, turning inward and digging into him like knives.

After an eternity, Zai touched his shoulder. "Ethan—"

"I didn't want to tell you any of this, okay?" Vax tore the words out from his throat. Rage pulsed through his veins, and he didn't even know who he was angry at—Atali, Zai, or himself. "I didn't—want you to know. I didn't want you to know what I—what I *let him* do to me. For *years*." He let out a bitter, angry, broken laugh. "I mean, how much *more* of a disappointment can I be, right?"

Zai sounded frozen. "You didn't—you didn't ask for this—"

"Yeah, well, it doesn't matter, does it?" Vax couldn't look at him. "It doesn't fucking matter—what I asked for, what I wanted or didn't want."

He wanted to leave, wanted some excuse—any excuse—not to have to see the expression on Zai's face, but he couldn't. The walls were closing in around him, making the room smaller and smaller until there was only him and Zai and the awful *thing* that, after four years, he still couldn't face.

"I..." Zai sounded choked. "All this time...you were carrying this around, and I had no idea—"

"I *don't want to talk about it, Zai.*"

Mercifully, Zai was quiet after that, leaving Vax to his thoughts. Or attempts to avoid thinking. He tried so hard to avoid thinking. Thinking about it meant getting dragged back into that black, swampy quicksand of ugly questions and self-hatred.

The door opened. He was thankful for the distraction at first, but as soon as he saw Miki's face, he knew something had gone wrong.

"What is it?" he asked, his voice coming out sharp.

Her eyes flicked between them. "You might want to sit down—"

"Just tell me," he said.

She took a deep breath and brought up some brain images on the wall.

"Initially, we thought the implant had just been suppressing activity in your brain that correlated with retrieval of long-term episodic memories. It...turns out there wasn't just suppression." She swallowed. "The implant caused lesions. Permanent damage."

"Wait...what are you saying?" asked Zai.

Miki turned to Vax. "I'm sorry. I'm...afraid your memories may never return."

For a long moment, Vax didn't say anything. It felt as though the world had stopped turning, and Miki's words ricocheted in his head until they became meaningless noise.

"Isn't there anything...?" Zai's voice faltered.

No. There wasn't. Neurons didn't grow back. Anyone with a rudimentary knowledge of biology knew that.

Miki slowly shook her head.

A hollow space grew inside of him, like a parasitic seedling that was swallowing everything up with a blooming void. He'd been so stupid. So fucking *stupid*. Thinking— *believing*—he could get back what he'd lost. That all the missing puzzle pieces would magically fall into place, and he'd wake up and be—whole. Normal.

He moved toward the door slowly, as though he were swimming through water. Distantly, he heard Zai call his name—the name that was supposed to belong to him—but he didn't turn back. Couldn't.

Seeing the disappointment reflected in Zai's expression would kill him.

YOUR MEMORIES WILL never return.

He was sitting—he didn't even know where he was sitting. In some hallway in the hospital, with doctors and nurses walking back and forth, the background noise registering as only a dull buzz to him. All he could hear were those words, over and over, playing on a loop in his head.

Will never return.

Never return.

Never.

"Ethan."

Vax jumped. Zai was standing in front of him, a worried expression on his face.

"Are you...okay?"

He looked down.

"No," he said, his voice hoarse. No, he wasn't fucking *okay.*

Zai sat down next to him. "I'm sorry."

A choked, strangled laugh welled up in Vax's throat.

"*You're* sorry? For what?"

"I'm sorry that—it didn't work—"

"No," Vax cut him off. "No, Zai, *you* don't get to be sorry. *I'm* the one who's sorry. Sorry I can't make things right. Sorry I can't remember who I used to be. Sorry all I've been is just one long fucking *heartbreak.*"

Zai flinched. Right. Because *Ethan* wasn't supposed to swear. Yet another reminder that he was so far from the person he was supposed to be.

"Ethan—" Zai put a hand on his arm, and Vax fought the urge to recoil from the sudden contact. "Look, I know everything seems bleak right now, but there's still hope—"

"How? There's no *fixing* me, Zai. I'm literally *brain-damaged.*" He stared at the ground. "I'm not that—kind and forgiving person you fell in love with. I don't know him, and

I'm never going to remember how to be him. I'm the assassin you hated. I'm not the one you want."

"Don't say that." Zai's voice shook, and Vax loathed himself so much for being the cause. "It's not...it's not true—"

"Isn't it?" He narrowed his eyes. "Just answer one question, Zai. If I'd turned out not to be Ethan, would you have cared about me at all?"

Zai winced. That was all the answer he needed.

"That's what I thought."

And suddenly, it hit him—a wave of bone-shattering grief, so thick it filled his lungs and almost made him choke. Zai didn't love him, just the memory of who he used to be, and no matter what Vax did, he couldn't compete. Couldn't be that person. Too much had happened; he'd lost too many pieces of himself.

Vax got up and started to leave.

"Where—where are you going?"

He cringed at the obvious distress in Zai's voice.

"It's over, okay?" His voice broke, and he blinked hard at the ground. "Scratch that—it was over four years ago. You're in love with a memory, and that memory is dead."

He walked away. Part of him prayed Zai would call after him, telling him that he was wrong, *No, it's not like that.*

But Zai didn't say a thing.

And Vax left the hospital alone, biting down on his lip hard enough to draw blood so he wouldn't sob.

THE ONE GOOD thing left was that Vax could finally return to his apartment.

On the way back, Vax stopped by a liquor store to buy some whiskey. He hadn't dared to make any e-payments until now, in case Atali could track the transactions, but he figured he was in the clear now.

Except when he tried to check out using his pod, the app informed him, "Payment invalid: bank account no longer exists."

Vax stared at the screen. He hit the "Retry" button several times, making sure he entered the right PIN. The app only informed him of the same thing each time, in stark text: "Payment invalid: bank account no longer exists."

So. He was now penniless, no doubt thanks to Atali.

He still had some cash, but since that was now the limit of his money, he decided to keep it, in case he needed it for something else. When he got to his apartment, he noted, almost without surprise, a microcamera placed on the door. Probably set there by Atali, or someone under him, to monitor if he'd return. If so, he doubted anyone was still monitoring it now, after everything that had happened. He pried it off and crushed it under his heel before unlocking the door.

When Vax stepped inside, an empty unit greeted him.

He stared blankly at the furniture-less space until slow realization wound its way through his haze of dull surprise. Of course Atali had removed everything, probably destroyed all his personal items, to erase any trace of his existence.

He'd never had much stuff. No decorations, no pictures, no personal touches; just the plainest and cheapest furniture available. Thinking back, he realized none of it probably belonged to him in the first place—Atali had set everything up and lied to him about it. Still, he'd grown used to thinking of the apartment and everything inside it as *his*, as the only things that belonged to him, and seeing it all stripped away made his chest hurt with a slow, pulsing ache. He wanted to be angry, but after everything else that had happened, he just felt numb.

Still dazed, he walked around to see if there was anything left behind. A shirt, a pack of tooth tabs, anything. Nope; the entire apartment had been stripped clean. He returned to the main room and sat in the middle of the floor, feeling the emptiness surround him like a thick, heavy shroud.

It was an almost hilariously on-point metaphor for his life—a home that had had everything taken out of it, and there was nothing left inside.

The silence grew oppressive. He needed a distraction, something that would keep his mind off—Zai, everything. He took the pod out from his pocket—his only possession left, other than his gun and his wallet—setting it to a news channel. He regretted being sober now, and he vaguely wondered how much cheap whiskey he could buy with fifty dollars cash.

"—amidst the controversy, Cyrex Corp CEO Atali Norman has recently resigned, pending an investigation into the allegations raised—"

Atali's face flashed on the screen. Vax couldn't take this right now; he tapped the screen to switch the channel.

"—still questions as to how a noted philanthropist such as Atali Norman could have allegedly sponsored unapproved human trials—"

Pressure was building at the back of Vax's head. He tried changing the channel yet again.

"—longtime acquaintance and former classmate expressed shock and disbelief that Atali Norman could have been involved in such a crime—"

No matter what he did, Vax *still* couldn't escape from him. His face was everywhere, taunting him. As Vax stared at the picture of him on the screen, his hands clenched into fists.

Everything was that bastard's fault.

Everything wrong in Vax's life—his lost memories, being turned into an assassin, enduring years of pain, becoming a person Zai hated—was all because of Atali.

Vax had nothing left—nothing, except pure, bitter, white-hot hatred. He'd lost too much. Endured too much. The only thing left for him now was revenge.

Turning off the news, Vax pulled up Atali's address.

FOUR YEARS, AND this was the first time he'd seen Atali's house—a massive mansion in the suburbs outside Orphis City proper. If he'd been a little less resentful, he might've been jealous of the huge backyard with an elegant patio and swimming pool. Getting into the house wouldn't be easy, but Vax's anger had sharpened into a relentless patience, and he'd get his revenge or die trying.

After all, it wasn't as though he had anything left to lose.

He did have one stroke of good luck: a few days of surveillance led to the conclusion that Atali's wife and children were all currently out of the house. An email to Atali's wife's office at Revogen Pharmaceuticals confirmed that she, at least, was elsewhere in the country on a business trip, and she wouldn't be back for another week. Those were three fewer complications to worry about. He wasn't sure if the kids were coming back sooner, though, which mean he had to move fast.

His surveillance also confirmed that Atali had an advanced home security system, complete with glass breaks and motion detectors. The motion detectors weren't on during the day, but the door alarms were.

Vax fantasized about bringing a hand drill or a hammer, but given his lack of funds, he only had enough cash to pay for zip ties, a taser, a new lock decryptor, and a circuit disruptor, plus a small black duffel bag to hold everything. He still had his handgun and knife, and those would have to be enough.

He took the sky rail to the suburbs and spent a while observing Atali's house some more before making a move. Atali was currently on the second floor, studying his tablet screen.

Don't move. Just stay right there.

He inserted the lock decryptor into the patio door. When it was done, he aimed the disruptor at the wall where the alarm system was and pressed the activation button. Then he slowly eased the patio door open.

Not a single sound.

Carefully, quietly, he slid inside and shut the door.

Vax had no idea how well sound carried in this mansion. Just in case, he removed his shoes and carried them in his hand as he crept through the house. Elegant, and doubtless expensive, furniture decorated the rooms. Canvases of modern art—actual physical canvases—that featured strokes and splashes of color arranged in abstract patterns adorned the walls, and Vax had to admit, grudgingly, that Atali had good taste. That thought only made him hate him more.

He tried to keep himself on task, but photographs of Atali's family—featuring Atali, his wife, daughter, and son, all smiling—kept catching his eye. There were also e-cards pinned to the wallscreens, with digital drawings and messages like "Happy Father's Day" and "Happy Birthday, Daddy." Vax didn't know how to feel—whether he was furious at all these signs of Atali's apparently happy family life, or whether he was just cynically glad Atali treated his children better than he'd treated Vax.

He silently ascended the stairs to the second floor. Atali was still sitting in the study, with his back to Vax, watching something intently on his tablet. Slowly, Vax set his shoes down, withdrew his taser and gun, and then held them out in front of him. He crept forward.

Atali didn't move. The faint sound of tinny voices came from his ear nodes.

Vax lunged forward, slamming the taser into Atali's neck.

Atali convulsed before crumpling to the ground, his tablet clattering to the floor with him. Vax stood there, breathing hard. Tasering Atali had given him a rush, leaving him giddy and light-headed, and he wanted to do it again.

Reluctantly, he put the taser away, as well as the gun, and slipped his shoes back on. No way was Vax going to carry him, so he settled for dragging him across the room and down the stairs to the basement, hoping Atali would get bruises from bumping down the steps.

Then there was the question of where to put him. Atali's basement was too damn *comfortable*, what with the elegant tile and lights everywhere, and a wine cellar whose contents Vax was pretty sure cost more than the monthly income combined of the poorest quarter of Orphis City's population. In the end, Vax ended up dragging him to the room with the water heater, which was the only all-concrete, somewhat depressing-looking room. He grabbed a chair from another room and heaved Atali onto it, binding his wrists and ankles with zip ties.

When he was done, Vax backhanded him across the face. "*Wake up!*"

Atali groaned, stirring. He opened his eyes and blinked. "Vax. Why am I not surprised?"

"Because who else have you completely fucked over?"

"Many people, actually. When I first started at Cyrex—"

Vax punched him in the face. Sharp pain echoed through his knuckles, but he didn't care; punching Atali gave him a vicious kind of catharsis. He shoved Atali backward, letting him crash to the ground, and pressed his boot against Atali's neck, slowly cutting off his airflow.

"Is this why you did it?" he spat. "Because you liked the rush of power that came with hurting someone while they're helpless in front of you?" He drove his foot down harder, and Atali choked. "How does it feel, being on the receiving end? Painful? *Degrading?*"

Atali looked at him, his eyes almost bugging out.

"I—have—a family," he gasped.

Vax stared at him, rage and disgust curling in his gut. He took his boot off and righted Atali's chair—only to punch him in the face again. Blood began to trickle from Atali's nose.

"So did I," Vax hissed, "but you didn't give a fuck about that, did you?"

Vax took his gun from the duffel bag and deliberately flicked the safety off; Atali's eyes darted to it.

"A vigilante-style execution? You're playing the part of the assassin till the bitter end, I see."

Vax pointed the gun between Atali's eyes. "You *made* me this. Now you can reap what you've sown."

"Is that really what you think?" Atali shook his head. "Vax, Vax—"

"Don't. Fucking. *Call me that.*"

"*I* wasn't the one who made you a killer, you know," Atali went on, as though he hadn't heard him. "You can thank your army training for that. All I did was put a gun in your hand and point you to the targets. You took care of the rest yourself."

"Shut up. Shut the fuck—*you lied to me.*"

This was not how he wanted it to go. His emotions were spiraling out of control, taking him from righteous fury to unhinged, betrayed anguish. He could tell Atali had noticed, and something in Atali's eyes shifted with that knowledge. But now that he'd started, he couldn't stop.

"You told me you didn't know who I was. You told me I'd lost my memories because of a head injury, when the truth was you'd erased everything yourself. And then you told me that I was a career assassin, that killing people was the only thing I was good for. But everything—*all of it was a lie.*"

Atali still looked calm. *Why does he look so fucking calm?*

"Oh, please. If you didn't like what I told you, you could've run away. But you didn't. Instead, you came crawling back."

Vax blanched, as though Atali had stabbed him in the gut.

"You...you would've found me anyway," he said, fighting to regain his balance. "Since you'd tagged me with a fucking GPS tracker and a *camera.*"

"But that's not what happened." Atali smiled, and Vax wanted nothing more than to beat that nauseating smile into a bloody pulp. "You came back on your own."

Vax remembered. He remembered packing up in the aftermath of that job, staring at a strip of bright sunlight outlined against his motel bed, and suddenly realizing he could *leave.* And he remembered, with equal clarity, sitting on a park bench a week later, watching some mallard ducks swim across the river and not knowing what to do. Trying to start a normal life had made him feel even more anxious and broken than he had before. He talked himself into feeling guilty and afraid enough to go back.

"You would've hunted me down," Vax repeated, half to himself, "if you thought I would actually escape."

"You didn't know that. And the fact that you didn't even try—"

"Just shut up already!"

Vax jammed the gun against Atali's gut. Atali grimaced.

"Have you ever been shot before?" Vax asked. "Because I'm more than happy to introduce you to *that* world of pain. A bullet to your gut, and you can be here for days, slowly bleeding out, unable to do a damn thing about the agony, until you're begging me to blow your brains out." He traced the gun up to Atali's forehead and pressed it hard enough to tilt Atali's head back. "But I'm not going to make it that quick. Oh, no. I've got a knife, after all. I'll make you *intimately* acquainted with what a stab wound feels like."

Atali's mouth twisted into a crooked, humorless smile. "You've thought this out."

"Yes, I have."

"What was it you said, after the Emerson job?" Atali mused. "'I'm not going to torture people. I'm not a fucking monster'?"

Vax blinked.

Inhaled.

Took a step back.

Realized his hand was shaking.

No, he wasn't—and yet, when he looked at Atali, all he could think about was how much he wanted to kill him. How much he wanted to hurt him and make him suffer.

He wanted it so badly.

What did that make him, then? A fucking *monster*?

"No," he said, hoarsely. And then, in a louder voice, "*No.* I'm not—I'm not a monster. *You're* the monster."

"So if it's revenge, it doesn't count? Come on, at least be honest with yourself. At least admit that, after all that whining about the fact that I 'made' you into something you weren't, you've decided you don't care anymore."

"Shut up," Vax said again, but his voice cracked. "Don't talk like you know what I care about—because of you, there's *nothing left*—"

Nothing. He couldn't be Ethan Tromer, no matter what he did, no matter how hard he tried. Ethan wasn't a killer. Ethan wasn't a *torturer*. He couldn't be Ethan, because Ethan was a good person, and whatever Vax was, he was not that.

"Nothing?" Atali echoed. "Or nothing except the satisfaction of hurting someone while they're helpless in front of you?"

Vax recoiled. "I—I'm *nothing* like you—"

"But you're enjoying this, aren't you, Ethan?"

Ethan. Atali pronounced the name mockingly, like a slap to the face. Vax stared at him.

"Don't feel bad," said Atali. "If I were in your position, I'd do exactly the same thing."

Vax's stomach churned with horrified revulsion, sour bile flooding his tongue.

No. We're nothing alike! He deserves *this!* Except Atali kept watching him with those cold, glittering eyes, as if to say, *Don't fool yourself. You and me, we're the same. We're both monsters. You can't deny it.*

It wasn't supposed to be like this.

Vax lowered his gun. Flicked the safety back on. He carried it to his duffel bag, dropped it inside, and zipped the bag back up.

"Leaving already?" Atali asked.

"Shut up." He slung the bag over his shoulder and headed toward the door. "If you're lucky, someone will find you. If not, I don't fucking care."

"And where are you going?" Atali's voice held an edge of cold amusement. "Back to the arms of your lover?"

Vax froze with his hand on the doorknob. Agonizing grief welled up in his throat, choking him.

"Now that you've been reunited, I'm sure he's forgiven you for all you've done. Does he whisper into your ear every night that he still loves you?"

He had to get out of there.

Vax shut the door behind him, barely restraining the urge to slam it. He left Atali's house the way he came, and once he was far enough away, he broke into a run and didn't stop until he dashed into the open doors of a train waiting at the station to take him the hell out of there.

ON THE WAY back, Vax returned the contents of his duffel bag, except for his gun, and used the crumpled bills he received to buy two bottles of whiskey. When he returned to his apartment, he sat on the floor with his back to the wall and popped the top off one of the bottles, tipping a quarter of its contents down his throat. He wanted to forget. God, he wanted so badly to forget. All of it. Everything.

The fact that there was still a seething part of him that wanted Atali hurt and maimed and dead.

The fact that his life was so *fucked up.*

The fact that he was just a shadow, a mockery of Ethan Tromer. Ethan was kind and forgiving and flinched from violence; he had a family and an adoring lover and bright plans for the future.

Vax...Vax was nothing but a killer and a torturer, a mess of pain and rage and self-loathing. He was nothing but nightmares and the blood on his hands. He'd broken free of Cyrex's grasp, he'd tried to get his revenge and failed, and now suddenly he didn't know what to do with himself anymore, and wasn't that so fucking pathetic? That he was so fucked up, he didn't know what to do if he *wasn't* running around killing people?

He curled up in a ball on the hard, cold, laminated wood floor, nursing the bottle of whiskey. Not enough; it was never enough. Someone needed to give him a goddamn lobotomy. Or just blow his brains out. *Anything* to make him forget what a fucking mess he was.

Anything.

God, please...

He didn't even know who he was praying to. No one was listening.

It was just him, and he was alone.

A FAINT BUZZING noise woke him from drunken unconsciousness. He groaned, automatically reaching for his ears to turn his nodes off, thinking vaguely that the buzzing sounded more distant than usual. Then he realized that he wasn't wearing his nodes—he'd taken them off a few days ago, while focusing on his revenge plan.

He unzipped his jacket pocket to turn off the buzzing, but then hesitated. Who was calling him, anyway? Atali? The thought made him feel ill. Or...the police? Even worse. But he was so far gone that his apathy turned back into morbid curiosity. Let someone find him. Maybe they could end the misery for him.

He put a node in his ear, pressed his finger to the button, and answered hoarsely, "Hello?"

He heard a sharp intake of breath on the other side, and then—

"I've been trying to get a hold of you for days." It was Zai, his voice sharp with worry. "You never answered, I had no idea where to find you—"

"I'm at my apartment." He didn't want to explain what he'd done. Not now, not to Zai. The thought made him feel worse than he already did. "What do you want?"

"There's something I need to talk to you about."

He closed his eyes and massaged the bridge of his nose, but all he drew in his mind was a blank. "Okay. Talk."

"Not...over the phone. In person. I'll come by, if you can text me the address. I mean, if that's all right."

"Okay."

"Okay. See you in a bit."

The call ended, and after sending his address, Vax rubbed a hand over his face. There was a heavy, sinking feeling in his chest. Whatever Zai wanted to tell him, it couldn't be good. Because nothing good ever happened to him. It might as well be one of the goddamned laws of physics.

He grabbed the other bottle of whiskey. He was more than three-quarters of the way through it by the time his door beeped. He answered it, and Zai stepped in.

"This...is where you live?" Zai asked, taking in the empty apartment with an expression that was part confusion, part disbelief.

"I'm pretty sure Atali had it cleared out," Vax said, in a detached voice. "And probably set fire to all my stuff."

Zai's gaze then went to the whiskey bottle in his hand, and he did another double take. He opened his mouth, but, after a pause, closed it again. Vax couldn't understand his reaction until he remembered what Zai had said about him before. *Didn't swear, didn't drink, didn't party.*

Too late to fix that now.

Zai gave him a strangely searching look, but he didn't say anything more. Vax didn't say anything, either. He wasn't sure there *was* anything else for him to say.

"Something weird happened today," Zai finally said, as Vax returned to where he'd been sitting on the floor. "The police found Atali Norman tied up and a bit injured in the basement of his own house. He told them he didn't know who took him, just some guy with a black mask on."

Damn, that was fast. Vax was disappointed Atali hadn't been there longer, thirsty and starving, panicking as he waited for someone to find him. Should he have been relieved Atali didn't reveal his identity to the police? Then again, any inquiry about him would lead straight back to Cyrex.

"You wouldn't happen to know anything about that, would you?" Zai asked carefully.

Vax swallowed another mouthful of whiskey. Well, Zai already knew everything there was to know about him and then some; why not add yet another reason he was so fucked up that Zai should clearly stay the fuck away from him?

"What do you think? Yes, I knocked him out and dragged him there and tried to torture him."

Zai was quiet for a minute. "You didn't get far with the 'torture' part."

Vax examined the whiskey bottle. He didn't want to see what expression Zai had on his face at that moment. Didn't want to see if he could disappoint Zai even more than he already had, if Zai's broken heart could be ground into pieces like glass dust.

"There was...one person I'd tortured, because Atali told me to, and afterward I felt sick and disgusted with myself and had nightmares for months. I told him I wouldn't do it again, even if he would kill me. I told him I wasn't a fucking monster." A harsh, bitter, broken laugh tore out of him. "Well that's a great big fucking lie, isn't it? Of course I'm a monster, and he proved it. I've never—almost never—wanted anything as much as I wanted to hurt him and watch him die."

There was a long pause.

"Why did you stop?" Zai asked.

"I..." He rubbed his forehead. "I don't know. I guess I...didn't want to give him the satisfaction of knowing he was right about me. Even if he was. I mean, why do you care? Either way, I'm just..."

So fucked up. I'm so fucked up, I want you to stay even though I'm a monster and a killer and a torturer, and you should stay the fuck away from me, because no person in their right mind would ever want to be near me, and because I've hurt you enough.

Zai didn't say anything. Vax waited to hear his receding footsteps, to hear the door slam shut behind him as he walked away.

Instead, Zai came over and sat down on the floor next to him.

"I was worried, earlier, when I couldn't reach you," Zai said, in a quiet voice. "I thought...something had happened."

"I didn't know you cared."

Zai inhaled sharply, as though he were stung. *Fuck.* Vax didn't mean it that way. But that was all he was good for, wasn't it? Hurting people.

"Sorry, I—that came out wrong," he muttered.

"I guess I deserved that," Zai said slowly. "After our last conversation."

Which Vax was in no mood to rehash.

"Look...you were right," Zai said.

Vax frowned. "About what?"

Zai dropped his gaze, taking a deep breath. "I—all I wanted was the person I knew back. The perfect image of you I'd preserved in my memory. I got excited because I thought...you could still be that person, and things could go back to the way they were. But—that wasn't fair to you. You didn't ask for the things that happened—"

No, he couldn't handle Zai apologizing. *Zai* wasn't the one who had done anything wrong.

"Yeah, things change," Vax said flatly. "And that kills relationships all the time. You know what also kills relationships? When someone gets fucking *amnesia* and then becomes a murderer and a torturer. Who in their right mind would want to stay with a person like that?"

Zai exhaled, his shoulders slumping.

"Someone...someone who cared? At least...as a friend?"

Vax stared blankly at him. "Out of pity? Because I don't want your pity, Zai. You were more than willing to crucify me for what I did before you found out—who I was. Now you're—your feelings are making you justify what happened so that I can be innocent—so I can be that good person you remembered—but I'm *not*." And suddenly he was too exhausted to be angry anymore. "You're just deluding yourself."

"I—" Zai started, and stopped. Then he started again. "I'm not here to ask you to be someone you don't feel like you are anymore. I never had the right to ask you for that. I just...wanted to make sure you were okay," he finished.

"I'm fine. As you can see."

Zai glanced at him, but didn't reply to that. A long silence filled the room, but Zai still didn't leave. Finally, Zai released a slow breath and rubbed his face.

"I called the federal district attorney's office and they actually talked to me, if you can believe that."

Changing the topic? Sure, Vax could handle changing the topic. Anything to avoid talking about torture or dead relationships.

"The government is launching an investigation into Norman and Cyrex for instigating the deaths of the nine people, Celia Duquette, and possibly others," Zai went on quietly. "And then, most likely, a lawsuit. If everything goes well, he could go away for life."

Vax finished the last dregs of his whiskey.

"That's great, I'm sure. Too bad it's too fucking late for me."

Zai inhaled. "Ethan—"

"*Don't.*" He meant to put anger into his voice, but it came out sounding tired and broken instead. He stared into his empty whiskey bottle. "Let's not keep pretending I'm Ethan Tromer, or that there's any bit of him that's left in me. He died a long time ago, alone and in pain, when they made me into—into *this*. And I can't bring him back." His voice cracked. "No matter how badly I want to, I can't—I can't bring him back."

Ethan Tromer was dead. He was Vax, and he was no one.

Zai touched his shoulder. It almost burned his skin.

"There's no point," he went on, his voice dead-sounding. "There's no fucking point in me being alive anymore. Maybe there never was. I should have...I should have died when you thought I did. Then at least your perfect memory of him could've remained intact."

Zai didn't say a word; he gently pulled Vax into a hug.

Vax froze, at first. He'd—never been hugged before, not that he could remember. Something inside him snapped, and he sagged against Zai's shoulder, crying. He cried for Ethan Tromer, who was a good person and never, never wanted any of this to happen. He cried for the love Zai lost, and all that he had suffered. He cried for himself, a lost soul who didn't know who he was or what he was supposed to do with himself anymore.

"Ethan—"

Vax shuddered. "Don't...don't call me that," he mumbled. "I'm not him, and I never can be."

"I'm not going to call you by what they branded you with when they turned you into their *possession*," Zai murmured. "They stole your memories. They stole your life. They stole your *name*. You deserve to have it back."

"No, no, I don't—"

"It's not your fault, okay?" Zai's breath hitched. "None of this is your fault. It's the fault of those who turn people into *things* that can be used and disposed of when they're no longer needed. That's what the draft did—why are we even fighting the war? Who the fuck actually *knows*? And that's what Cyrex did—seeing people as just tools, and profits. You opened my eyes to all of this, and it's why I've been working to expose corruption. Illegal wages. Substandard working conditions. Dangerous new augmentations. Every time I thought I'd seen it all, I'd learn about something worse." Zai swallowed. "But people—people aren't *things*. Every person deserves dignity, and humanity. And so do you. I know they've taken a lot from you. I can't imagine how hard that must be. But it's not too late. It's never too late to try to rebuild. Ethan."

Vax—Ethan?—shivered.

"I don't...I don't understand," he whispered. "Why did you come back?"

Zai was quiet for a while.

"Because, once upon a time, I was a spoiled, selfish kid," he finally said. "And I saw you—the shy geek in my class who was always willing to help anyone who needed a hand—as just an easy conquest, someone I could manipulate into falling for me, all because I was bored. You found out the truth, later, after *I* was the one who had fallen for *you*, and we had a terrible argument, and you stomped off, and I was so scared that I had lost you. I saw, for the first time, what a horrible person I was. And I thought that, if you left me, I deserved it."

He took a deep breath.

"But you came back. I didn't understand why. You said—for all the things I'd done and all the mistakes I'd made, you didn't think I was a bad person. And you believed in second chances." Zai drew back and gave him a faint smile. "I took that to heart, you know? I believe in second chances. Everyone deserves a second chance—including you, Ethan."

Zai hugged him again. Ethan hugged him back. He was crying again, but it didn't hurt so much anymore.

It wasn't so painful anymore, because he wasn't alone.

Chapter Fourteen

HE WOKE UP slowly, in an unfamiliar bed with an absurdly soft comforter wrapped around him. He sat up in a surge of panic before he remembered where he was and how he'd gotten there.

He was in Zai's apartment, wearing a T-shirt and sweatpants Zai had lent him. Zai had invited him there last night, refusing to leave him in the empty apartment, and had also insisted, over his objections, that he take the bed.

Muted sounds came from the kitchen. Sighing and rubbing his eyes, he got out of bed and went to see what was going on.

Zai was standing in front of the stove with a frying pan. He turned around. "Morning, Ethan. Egg omelet?"

Ethan blinked. "You're...cooking?"

"Don't look so surprised," Zai said smugly. "I'm a man of many talents."

"I can see that."

Zai poured a bowl of raw eggs into the pan and leaned back against the counter, looking at him.

"So...how do you feel?" he asked, softly.

Ethan remembered what a complete wreck he'd been the night before, and he tried not to cringe in embarrassment. Even though Zai hadn't shown any judgment so far, only sympathy, Ethan found his eyes drawn to the animated fish on the walls rather than Zai's face. The wallscreens had been set to a calming underwater coral reef scene.

"I don't know," Ethan finally said, after a long pause. "Just...tired?"

Zai passed him a mug. It was full of coffee.

"Not...the kind of tired that can be fixed by coffee. But thanks." He took a sip.

"How are you dealing with...everything?" Zai asked.

"I...I don't know," Ethan confessed to his mug. "I haven't really...I guess I don't know what I'm supposed to do. Just...remembering my own name...kind of feels like a struggle, never mind...anything else." He grimaced. "Sounds pretty fucking pathetic, doesn't it?"

"No, it's...it's understandable. And you don't have to know what to do. You've...been through a lot." Zai paused, and then asked, quietly, "I have to ask...do you still think there's no point for you to be alive?"

Ethan blinked and looked at him for a long moment. "I'm...not sure," he finally said. "But I don't *think* I'll shoot myself in the head in the foreseeable future."

Zai exhaled and gave him a small smile. "Hey, that's...that's a start."

He turned back to the stove, using a spatula to fold the omelet in half. He then lifted the omelet onto a plate and handed it to Ethan.

"Breakfast is served. Yours, at least."

Ethan took the plate hesitantly. "You didn't...you didn't have to."

"Hey, when's the last time you had a home-cooked meal?"

Ethan's mouth tilted into something that might have resembled a smile. "Well...I appreciate it, thanks."

He went to the kitchen table with the omelet and coffee and started eating. Zai joined him a few minutes later.

"So, um...have you thought at all about...seeing your family again?" Zai asked gingerly. "I mean...no pressure, either way."

Ethan swallowed a mouthful of egg and blinked at his plate. The idea *had* crossed his mind. But...

"I don't know," he said, slowly, heavily. "Maybe they're...better off not knowing about me."

"Why do you say that?"

Ethan ran his fingers back and forth along the smooth table surface, tracing nervous patterns. "I don't want to have to explain to them that I'm alive, except I don't remember them, and also I killed people and might be put away for life for that."

Zai was silent for a moment. "Is that...what you think is going to happen?"

"Don't you agree?"

Zai shook his head. "Norman erased your memories, told you that you were indebted to him, and lied to you. You didn't do this of your own free will."

Ethan hesitated, but then replied, "No one's going to buy that. Like you said before, I still knew things. I knew what I was doing was wrong."

Zai was frowning, as though he wanted to argue, but he didn't say anything. Probably because there was no real counterargument.

"What about everything Norman did that was wrong?" Zai asked, instead. "You have plenty of charges to press against him, civil *and* criminal. Fraud, assault and battery for sticking bioaugs into you without your consent..." Zai met his gaze. "Rape."

Ethan flinched.

"What he did to you—"

"I know what he did. I remember all of it."

Zai was quiet.

"But I also know how this works." His voice came out bitter. "There's no hard evidence of anything"—because unfortunately Atali hadn't been stupid enough to take trophy pictures or videos—"and the last thing I'd ever want would be for his lawyer to deny it all and spin some story about how I was a crazy stalker and I was *asking for it*—"

"Ethan..."

"I can't go through that." Ethan realized his hands were shaking. "There's no way, there's no *fucking* way he'd let himself go down for a rape charge. If he did, he'd set me on fire so he could watch me go down in flames with him."

Not to mention that there was no outcome that would completely satisfy him. What he wanted was to turn back the clock and erase everything that had happened, but that was impossible.

Zai's knuckles had paled. "It's not fair, letting him get away with everything he did to you."

"Things aren't always fair," Ethan said to the table. That might as well have been the title of his depressing autobiography.

A heavy silence fell over them for a long while before Zai said, "We'll...we'll figure it out. I promise, Ethan. We'll figure something out."

He doubted that was a promise Zai could fulfill, but he appreciated the gesture, at least.

"Thanks," he murmured.

"Of course."

"I mean..." Ethan gestured vaguely. "Thanks for... breakfast. The clothes. Letting me stay here for the night."

"Hey, if I'd left you to sleep on the floor of that empty apartment, I wouldn't have been able to sleep myself."

"You didn't have to give me your bed."

Zai shrugged. "Seriously, it's not a big deal. The couch is pretty comfortable."

"All of this, though...it really means a lot," said Ethan.

Zai was quiet for a minute.

"You know, I..." He faltered and cleared his throat. "I spent a lot of time thinking about...some of the things I did and said. I...screwed up pretty badly."

God, were they really going to go through this *again*?

"For fuck's sake, Zai, you don't have to apologize, okay?" Ethan pushed the remaining scraps of egg around on his plate with his fork. "You weren't *obligated*"—*to still love me*—"to do—whatever it is you thought you were supposed to do, just because we were...together in the past. You'd grieved and found closure, and then I came in and wrecked it all. You were upset, and disappointed. Your feelings *matter*."

"No, Ethan, listen. I *pushed you away*. You were...God, you were alone and hurt and confused as hell, and I couldn't even *look* at you. Because..."

His voice trailed off, and he didn't finish his sentence. Ethan glanced at him. "Because what?"

Zai closed his eyes. The words came out unevenly, as though they were hard for him to admit aloud. "Because I preferred you to be dead than alive and...that different from how you were before."

Ethan didn't know how to respond. Should he have felt...sad? Offended? Angry?

Zai's hands clenched into fists on the table. "And that was...it was so wrong of me, on so many levels. It was so unbelievably *selfish*." He turned his palms up. "It's not about—whether I feel 'obligated' to feel the same way as I did before. If we're talking about caring about you as a friend, or hell, even *basic human decency*, I failed miserably. Refusing to see what was right in front of me until I couldn't ignore it any longer. I built you up into this flawless image, and I had no right to use that image—of what I *wanted* you to be—to hurt you the way I did."

Ethan blinked.

"So just...let me apologize, okay?" Zai sounded tired, as though the outburst had exhausted him. "You have a right to be angry with me. If you want to yell, or anything...please, go right ahead."

Ethan shifted in his seat. "I, um...I get what you're saying, but...I'm not mad at you, Zai. Maybe I was, at some point. But not right now."

It was hard for him to feel angry at the person who'd offered him a bed and food when he'd been on the verge of suicide.

Zai dragged his hands over his face, sighing. "I...you don't remember this, but I promised you once that I'd always be on your side. And I broke that promise pretty spectacularly."

A promise. A promise that Ethan had no memory of, now.

"Can I ask you something?" Ethan said after a moment of silence.

"Sure."

"When..." He swallowed hard. Maybe he shouldn't ask, but... "When did you say you wanted to marry me? Just...out of curiosity."

"Oh. That was during junior year, before you were drafted. I sort of blurted it out one morning." Zai's mouth slanted into a nostalgic half smile. "I hadn't really meant to say it out loud. You asked me if I was serious, and I said I didn't joke about commitment. Which is true."

Ethan was quiet. Listening to Zai reminisce was starting to make his chest ache. It was a reminder of a time and place he could never go back to, and the things he used to have that were now lost forever.

"I thought you had to work today," he said, casting around for a less painful topic.

Zai shrugged. "I can work from home, you know," he said. "One of the perks of writing for a living."

"But you usually don't," said Ethan.

Zai opened his mouth, looking a little surprised, and then seemed to change his mind and closed it again.

"No," he admitted, "but after spending a month in hiding, I'm kind of in the mood to enjoy my own apartment for a while."

Not that Ethan could blame him, but he couldn't help wondering if that was Zai's only reason. "Isn't there a lot of news to cover about what's going on with Cyrex?"

"Some of the other writers have got that covered, and besides, there hasn't been too much since the criminal investigation started. It's all been kept pretty hush-hush."

Ethan absorbed that, fiddling with the handle of his fork. "How long do you think the investigation will last?"

"No idea...I mean, these things can take months. And if a lawsuit goes ahead, and they have more discovery? Then we're talking *years*."

Ethan felt the weight of Zai's eyes on him, and he had a feeling he knew what Zai was about to say.

"I don't want to say this, but...it's only going to be a matter of time before someone finds out," said Zai, in a low voice. "About you."

Ethan kept his eyes fixed on the light glinting off his metal fork. "I know."

The more he thought about it, the more he found himself drifting farther and farther away from the fragile oasis of peace and calm he'd been enjoying. There would be a public trial, his face and history splashed all over the news, and then a lifetime of imprisonment to look forward to.

"It's going to be okay," Zai said.

Ethan looked up at him, not understanding how Zai could sound so determined. "No, it's not," he said, in a quiet, tired voice.

Months. Years. How long would he have to spend, with the doom of discovery looming over his head? He would never be able to move on—if there was even anything left for him to move on to.

"Maybe I should confess," he said.

Zai's fingers clenched and flexed against the table. "Are...are you sure?"

"It's the right thing to do, isn't it? Besides, I can at least take Atali down with me," he said, in a dull voice.

Zai was silent for a long while. "Why don't you...think about it for a bit," he said. "It's been a rough couple of days."

So Ethan thought about it.

He thought about it for most of the day, while obsessively checking the news for any updates on the Cyrex investigation. There wasn't any new information, but what Ethan found instead was a new set of hashtags: #DownWithTheConspiracy and, to his shock, #IBelieveAtali. The most reblogged posts included:

"I don't think it's Atali's fault. Maybe VP Lydia Alejandro convinced him to do everything."

"Totally a smear campaign by @MeridianInc to beat Cyrex. @Zaixzl your bias is showing. #Bringbackethicsinjournalism"

"Atali donates to Orphis's animal shelters every year. There's no way a guy that nice did human experiments!"

He knew he should stop reading, but he couldn't help it, even as a pressure built in his throat and behind his eyes until he was on the verge of hurling the tablet across the room. He finally punched the button to power off and tossed it at the couch cushion, glaring at it.

"What's wrong?" Zai asked from the table, sounding concerned.

It took Ethan a long while to find his voice. "I guess I shouldn't be surprised that people don't believe Atali actually did what he did." His tone was flat and bitter. "Because he's such a *nice guy* who donates to animal shelters."

Zai exhaled. "You read the hashtags?"

"They're hard to miss."

"Well, for your sanity's sake, I'd suggest trying to ignore them."

Ethan twisted to face him. "But this is what *real people* are saying. There are people out there who actually think that Atali is *innocent*."

"Yeah..." Zai's gaze dropped for a moment. "Sometimes it's hard for people to let go of the figures they've built into heroes. They'd rather ignore the evidence than face the truth."

For a second, Ethan had a sinking feeling that Zai wasn't just talking about the people on the internet anymore.

"The point being," Zai quickly went on, "idolizing people like that is unhealthy. In any case, there's always a vocal minority of skeptics and haters on the internet. And yeah, they suck, but they'll always remain just that: a minority."

"How do you know?" Ethan insisted. "They could convince others…maybe even convince someone who's in a position to do something. Or question your credibility to try to make people think you made things up. Hell, some people are already trying to do that."

"You mean the people convinced I'm running a pro-Meridian agenda?" To Ethan's bewilderment, Zai laughed. "It's hilarious that everyone's forgotten about the article that my parents still haven't forgiven me for, even though it's literally on the first page of results if you search my name on the internet."

Ethan frowned at him. "You're not worried or upset at all?"

"It's an occupational hazard—comes with the territory. You should've seen some of the nastier comments I got on my article about Meridian when I was first starting out. Besides, the facts are on our side," Zai said confidently. "The trolls and conspiracy theorists will yell until they're tired and eventually move on to something else."

Ethan wished he was nearly as convinced. He kept thinking about what to do while he was unable to sleep at night, and he was still thinking about it the next day. By that point, he was mostly thinking in circles, bouncing back and forth between two equally bad options, disagreeing with himself on which one was marginally less bad than the other.

The next evening, while they were eating takeout for dinner, he said, "I really think I should go to the police and confess."

Zai's easy smile faded, and his knuckles paled around his fork. "What happened to wanting to keep out of the public eye?"

Ethan released a breath. "I mean...you're right. No matter how careful Atali was, someone's going to find out eventually. There are the lab videos, for starters, and anyone who gets a hold of those can see my face." He bit his lip. "I don't want to live under a cloud of suspense forever, dreading the day someone knocks on the door to ask me what happened."

Zai was strangely quiet for a while. "Do you think there's any concrete proof tying you or Norman to the murders? Besides your confessing the truth."

Ethan glanced at him, confused. "I...I don't know. I tried to be careful about not leaving fingerprints or DNA evidence behind..." He winced. "Why are you asking? A confession is enough, isn't it?"

Zai fiddled with his plastic fork. "Just wondering what the odds are of no one discovering what you did if you don't confess."

Ethan stared. "Did...did you really just say that? *You*?"

Zai's mouth flattened into a thin line. "I mean, do you really think I'd be comfortable with telling you to hand yourself over to the government so you can spend the rest of your life in a cell? Because I'm not. To be completely honest, I'd rather hope no one finds out."

"But that's...that's not *right*."

"*None* of this is right, Ethan," Zai said, with sudden vehemence. "What happened to you wasn't right. For God's sake, you've lost twenty-five years of your life. *Twenty-five years*. I don't see how it's any more *right* for you to lose the *rest* of your life in prison."

Ethan looked down. His fists clenched. "Maybe...maybe it's what I deserve."

"*No*." The intensity in Zai's voice made him start. "No. I can't believe that. You didn't have a choice."

"Of course I had a *choice*," Ethan ground out. "I could've *chosen* not to do what he told me to, I could've chosen to run—"

"Yeah, but what kind of choice was that? He performed unwanted *brain surgery* on you and lied to you and, as you said, you had no choice but to believe him. For God's *sake*, Ethan—he spent four years *torturing you*."

The words rang with barely suppressed anger. Ethan flinched.

"The legal system," Zai went on, in a more controlled voice, "isn't equipped to deal with this kind of situation. I asked one of my cousins, who's a lawyer, about your case—as a hypothetical, obviously. She said, if you're *lucky*, you might get less than a life sentence, but it would be just about impossible to avoid a first-degree murder charge entirely." He shook his head. "I know the law is the law. But like I said, I can't stand to think that this is the universe's idea of fairness. Sometimes...sometimes, there are no right answers."

"You don't get to decide that," Ethan murmured. "That's not how justice works."

Zai exhaled, slowly. When he spoke again, he sounded tired. "Look, I'm not going to stop you from confessing if it's what you want to do. I just...really don't believe jail is going to help you. At all."

Ethan was almost certain he wouldn't survive life in prison. He wasn't even sure he could survive a trial.

"Maybe not," he said. "But...staying silent and letting this loom over the rest of my life—I'd never be able to move on."

Zai's shoulders sagged, but he nodded. "I...I understand."

Ethan thought about his life—all four years that he could remember of it. He thought of everything he'd lost, the lies that had been told to him, and the things he'd done. If there was a single thing he was glad for, it was that he'd spent time with someone who'd seen him as a person.

"Thank you," he said.

Zai's eyes flickered with surprise. "For what?"

"For..." He searched for the right words. "Not abandoning me, I guess."

Zai glanced away for a moment before he looked back at him again and said, "Whatever happens...I'm on your side, Ethan."

Are you sure you want to be? Ethan was tempted to ask. But he didn't. At this point, he was too tired not to accept small kindnesses, even if he felt like he didn't deserve them.

"Thanks," he said again, in a whisper.

HE COULDN'T SLEEP at all, restless thoughts running in his head like a tireless hamster running nonstop in a wheel, so Ethan eventually got up at some freakish hour in the morning and slunk out of the bedroom. He made coffee, sat at the kitchen table, and, not wanting to be left alone with his anxiety, began mindlessly playing solitaire on his pod. He was still there by the time the sun rose and Zai got up.

"Hey." Zai rubbed his hands over his face and blinked at him. "How long have you been up?"

"I couldn't sleep," Ethan admitted, closing his game.

"At all?"

Ethan shrugged.

Zai went to the counter and poured himself a mug of coffee. "I'm surprised you're still coherent. Food?"

"Don't think I can keep anything down right now."

"Maybe you could bring something with you. It would suck if you fainted in the middle of giving your confession."

Ethan's mouth twitched in spite of himself. "Yeah, that would be bad."

The doorbell suddenly beeped, making him start.

Zai frowned.

"Wrong delivery?" he said, as he went to answer. He scrutinized the monitor beside the door for a moment before unlocking the door and peeking outside. "Can I help you?"

"Zai Lumero?" A woman's voice answered him.

"Yes?"

"My name is Tana Brasher, from the U.S. Army Bioaugmentation Research Division. We've been looking for Private Ethan Tromer."

Ethan froze.

From his position in the kitchen, he was fairly sure he wasn't visible to anyone standing outside. Zai shifted a little, as though trying to further screen him from view. Ethan's eyes darted around the kitchen, looking for a weapon. Steak knife? Coffee pot?

"Ethan?" Zai repeated, with what would've sounded like genuine surprise. "But...he's dead."

"Let's not play this game, Mr. Lumero. You and I both know he survived his presumed death and was the subject of experimentation by Cyrex's special projects arm."

A long pause followed, as though Zai were weighing his options. Ethan realized he wasn't breathing and forced himself to inhale, slowly.

"Fine," said Zai, dropping his act. "Why are you looking for him?"

"We need to speak to both of you," she said.

"About what?" Zai pressed. "Whatever it is, you can tell me right here."

"I'm afraid I can't do that. This location isn't secure. Either you cooperate with us, or we will enter your apartment to make sure he isn't here."

"Don't you need a warrant or something to do that?" Now Zai sounded annoyed.

Ethan heard a sigh. "Mr. Lumero, the bioaugments implanted in Private Tromer were funded using government grant money and are therefore government property. Now, will you cooperate?"

Zai hesitated, but he was clearly trapped. Ethan moved to the counter, grabbing the steak knife. Finally, Zai opened the door wider and stepped aside. Tana Brasher's eyes met Ethan's.

"Good morning, Private Tromer," she said. "There's no need for the knife; no one will harm you as long as you come along without a fuss."

He wasn't sure he believed that, but he saw the armed security guard standing beside her, and there wasn't much he could do against a gun. Slowly, he set the knife back down on the counter, forcing his shaking fingers to unclench from the handle.

"Good," she said. "Please follow us."

TANA BRASHER AND the guard escorted them to a black car with tinted windows, which didn't do much for Ethan's peace of mind. The longer the trip was to their unknown destination, the more uneasy and anxious he became.

USABARD...what did they want with him? What did they want to do to him? *More* experiments? Was he doomed to be locked up as a lab rat again? Or were they being abducted? Because Zai knew too much, and Ethan was a murderer? Were they about to end up as two bodies in an unmarked grave?

"Hey." A light touch on his arm made him flinch before he realized Zai was trying to reassure him. "It's going to be okay."

He swallowed hard, keeping his eyes on the floor. Even if he wanted to, he couldn't speak past the fear tangled in his throat.

The slow-burning terror worsened as the car pulled up to what looked like a side entrance to an unfamiliar building. Ethan had no idea where they were. Tana Brasher swiped a key at the electronic lock; it beeped, and she opened the door, gesturing for them to enter. Inside was a narrow hallway with unadorned white walls, gray linoleum tile on the floor, and fluorescent lights that drilled a low, incessant buzz in Ethan's ears. Tana led them to another door that opened into a gray-walled, windowless room with a table and several chairs. The security guard remained outside.

At this point, Ethan was so wired with adrenaline that he was ready to fight—or flee—at the smallest sign of danger. He caught Zai giving him concerned looks, but Zai didn't say anything as he sat down. So did Tana Brasher, sweeping some of her braids off her shoulder as she settled into her chair. Ethan was the last one left standing.

Tana gestured at the chair. "Please, Private. Sit."

Ethan didn't want to sit.

"I'm sure it's not a problem if he listens while standing," said Zai mildly.

Tana gave him a long look. "All right, then."

Zai leaned against the table. "We've gone along quietly with everything up to this point. Now seriously, what is all of this about?" His eyes narrowed. "And how long have you known about Ethan? If you've been keeping quiet about this for *years*—"

"Calm down," said Tana, looking unimpressed. "We only found out a few days ago, after running facial recognition through some of Cyrex's lab videos. We've been working around the clock to find him ever since."

"What do you want with him?" Zai demanded. "He has rights, just like any other citizen. You can't lock him up without a trial or make him disappear or whatever else you're thinking."

Tana gazed at Zai coolly. Ethan had to admit, she had nerves of steel. She reached into her pocket and held out a chip that looked identical to the one that had been removed from Ethan's brain.

"How did you get that?" Zai asked, sharply. "Is that from...?"

"Sergeant Sabela Barros." Tana glanced at Ethan. "I believe she has you to thank for her broken arm."

So that's what Eleven's name was.

"How did you find her?" Zai asked.

"A certain Dr. Irene Tran volunteered her knowledge once we started tracking down the employees who'd worked in B4. She's been quite helpful." Tana tucked the chip back away. "It's simple. Imagine what would happen if people knew this kind of technology was out there, and what it could be used for. Imagine if criminal kingpins were inspired to go around—" Her eyes went to Ethan. "—doing the same thing to other people as Atali Norman did to Private Tromer and Sergeant Barros."

Ethan blanched.

Zai frowned. "So you want to keep this detail out of the spotlight and not give the wrong people any ideas."

"That's correct."

"But you can't keep a lid on this forever," Zai went on. "If Norman figured it out, other people are eventually going to do the same."

"I know. But even a few years' head start on trying to come up with scientific countermeasures and a legal framework for punishment and deterrence would help. The last thing anyone wants is for multiple human rights violations of this kind all over the world." She leaned back. "It's a simple deal. You two will agree not to tell the media—or anyone else—about Atali Norman's neural implant. For the greater good."

"The greater good," Zai echoed. "Also for your own interests, right? Because I guess it won't look too good if people knew the military had been funding a project that experimented on former American soldiers, does it?"

The last piece fell into place. Atali's mysterious sponsor.

Tana gave him another cool look. "While it's true that this project began as a matter of military interest, we never knew Cyrex had been experimenting on live people. And we had no interest in amnesia-inducing neural implants."

"Uh-huh." Zai's eyes were narrowed. "Why do I find that hard to believe?"

"Believe what you want, Mr. Lumero. All we ask is that the two of you also agree not to reveal the military's role in funding Cyrex's 'research.'"

"You're asking me to hide the truth," Zai spat. "That's against my ethical duty to the public."

"Technically, you've already been hiding the truth," she said, mildly. "You've had plenty of chances to report Private Tromer to the police as a criminal, but you haven't."

Ethan almost jumped.

Zai's expression changed. "How do you know he's committed any crimes?"

"It's difficult to imagine what else neural implants that cause memory loss would be used for. Besides, it's one of a handful of reasons that would explain why he's been avoiding public attention since your article came out."

Ethan winced. She had a point.

Tana went on. "In exchange for your cooperation, we will offer full immunity for any crimes Private Tromer may have committed while suffering from amnesia."

Ethan's jaw went slack.

"In addition, we could arrange for Private Tromer to enter witness protection, so as to avoid—"

"No!" Ethan burst out.

Tana and Zai turned to look at him, and Ethan cringed at his outburst. But...witness protection? He'd have to change his name, and he couldn't bear that. Not after he'd gone through so much to regain it in the first place. And he didn't want to move away from Orphis City, either.

"Sorry. I just...I don't want to have to change my name," he mumbled.

She shrugged. "As you wish."

"Full immunity?" Zai repeated. "There aren't any loopholes?"

Tana placed a tablet on the table. "The full terms are here. Feel free to read them as carefully as you want. Trust me, this is a mutually beneficial agreement, Mr. Lumero."

"Yeah, except for the part where I have to hide the truth."

She spread her hands. "Why are you making us the bad guys here, Mr. Lumero? We all know that what Cyrex did to your friend was a travesty, but the law won't recognize it. Unless you're willing to chance a jury trial."

Zai exhaled, slowly.

"So? What will it be?"

Zai smoldered at her. He scrutinized the tablet, scrolling through the pages for a few long minutes.

"Fine," he said, through clenched teeth. "Give me the stylus."

"Zai—"

"I'll sign it," he said, with a tone of finality. "But on one condition. If I find out the government has weaponized these implants for their own purposes? I'm coming back for you."

"Your condition is noted."

"I want it in writing."

The stare-off between them that followed was so intense Ethan had to look away, even though he wasn't part of it.

"Fine," Tana Brasher said in a clipped tone. She took the tablet back from Zai, typed into it for a few minutes, and then handed it back to him. She turned to Ethan. "And you, Private?"

Well, he was the one who had nothing to lose. Wordlessly, Ethan took the tablet and stylus after Zai had finished, only to pause. "Uh..."

"Is there a problem?" Tana asked.

"I—" Ethan's face burned with humiliation. "I don't—remember how to sign my name."

"Just make your best effort."

He did, scrawling something in ridiculously ugly cursive, and then handed the tablet back to her. She took it and shook his hand with a firm grip, her eyes fixed on his face.

"Welcome back to life, Private Tromer," she said.

Chapter Fifteen

THE LACK OF sleep finally caught up with Ethan once they'd been dropped off back at Zai's apartment, along with an adrenaline crash, and he practically passed out for the rest of the day. When he woke up the next morning, he found himself staring blankly out Zai's window at the city, as though he'd never seen it before. Every detail, every way the sunlight glinted off the glass windows, every flashing screen—it all felt new and strange and incomprehensible to him.

Welcome back to life, Private Tromer.

For so long, he *hadn't* had a life—at least, not one that truly belonged to him. Even after Atali had been exposed, he'd still waited for the day the truth would come out and he'd be sent to jail for the rest of his meaningless existence.

But now...he was free. Free to do anything he wanted. Free to *live*.

The problem was, he didn't know how. Didn't have a clue as to what to do. All the choices in front of him didn't make him feel happy or empowered; instead, he felt scared to death. If he was a dead man who had been dug up from the grave and offered a second chance to live, all he wanted to do was crawl back into the coffin.

Something is seriously fucking wrong with you.

He buried his head in his hands and let out a slow, shaky breath. *Tell me something I* don't *know.*

When he raised his head again, his gaze fell to the picture frame standing on the nightstand next to the bed. It was the same picture he'd avoided looking at the first time he'd visited Zai's apartment, and somehow he'd still missed looking at it until now. He picked the frame up to look at it more closely.

The picture was of Zai...and him. Judging by his appearance, they were still in college—he still had the glasses and the shaggy hair. But what struck Ethan most was the way they were both smiling widely in that picture, as though they were about to burst out laughing at some inside joke. He realized Zai must have seen this picture every time he went to bed and woke up in the morning.

Unsure how he felt about that, Ethan set the picture aside and got out of bed.

Zai was stirring on the couch as Ethan stepped out of the bedroom.

"Morning," he yawned, stretching his arms over his head as he sat up. "When I die, I want 'Was blackmailed by the government' carved on my tombstone."

"Not something more cheerful?" Ethan asked.

Zai ran a hand through his rumpled hair. He had a pretty terrible case of bed head, with black tufts sticking up all over the place. It was kind of cute.

And that was a thought Ethan definitely did *not* need to have.

"They can't sue me or throw me in jail if I'm dead," Zai grumbled. "If they think I'm never going to tell anyone, even if it's on my deathbed, they're delusional."

A sudden stab of anxiety went through him.

"Do you regret signing it?" he asked.

"Huh? Oh, no." Zai scowled. "I just hate that they made me choose."

Ethan wasn't sure what to think about that.

Zai got up from the couch and went to the kitchen. "Anyway, what d'you want to eat? There's plenty of cereal, some bread in the freezer..."

"Why do you have that picture of us next to your bed?" Ethan asked, before he could think.

Zai looked at him, eyebrows raised in surprise.

"It's the only picture you have in the entire apartment," Ethan went on. "You don't have any pictures of your family or friends or...anyone else."

Zai glanced around the apartment, as though he'd only just noticed what Ethan was talking about. "Well, you might've noticed that I'm not big on interior decoration in general."

Ethan frowned at his light tone. "It's literally the last thing you see before you sleep and the first thing you see when you wake up in the morning. Was it—was it that hard to let go?"

He didn't mean it, but that question came out sounding like an accusation. *Why didn't you let go? You would've been—happier—*

"That...wasn't exactly it." Zai exhaled, slowly. "Sometimes...I had a really hard time getting out of bed in the morning. Or justifying to myself why I did what I did...what was the point of it all. That picture...helped keep me going, during those days."

"But why?" Ethan asked, mystified.

Zai looked at him for a long moment. "Sorry," he said, quietly. "If it makes you uncomfortable, I can put it away. Or change the picture."

"I..." Ethan trailed off. He was the guest; it felt strange to ask Zai to change things for him. "I didn't mean...it's fine."

"Are you sure?"

"Yeah."

"Okay. Um..." Zai cleared his throat. "How are you feeling? Yesterday was kind of a trip."

"I...I'm fine," Ethan said, puzzled.

Zai seemed to hesitate. "I know...these past few weeks have been a lot. And the PTSD, and..." He gestured vaguely. "If you, you know, think you might need help..."

"Help?" Ethan echoed blankly.

"I mean someone to talk to, like a therapist, or..."

Ethan's mouth tilted into a humorless smile. "I already don't have a penny to my name. How am I supposed to be able to afford a therapist?"

"You'd think the government would've agreed to donate some money for that," Zai muttered. "Well...there's this great site I heard about that has free counseling. And there are online support groups. You could check those out."

Ethan's mouth twitched. "I don't really think they have support groups for people who get amnesia and then commit crimes."

"I meant...support groups for survivors of sexual assault."

Ethan blinked. He looked at the floor. "Oh."

He'd tried to avoid thinking about what happened for so long, and even though the rational part of him recognized that that wasn't a healthy coping mechanism—that denying it wouldn't and didn't solve anything—the thought of bringing those memories to the forefront made him slightly terrified.

"I think it could help," said Zai, gently. "When you're ready. But no pressure or anything."

"Yeah," Ethan forced himself to say. Deep down, he knew Zai was right. He just didn't know when he'd ever be ready to face it.

Zai didn't push the subject, and Ethan tried to turn his mind to other things. He shuffled back and forth, thinking how best to ask what he wanted to ask.

"Do you want me to leave?" he blurted out.

Zai looked at him, eyes wide with surprise. "What?" he said, sounding shocked.

That was probably the *worst* way to ask. Ethan tried to back up. "I-I mean...I'm really, really grateful for everything you've done, but I—I don't want to be a burden or anything. And I can't pay you back for letting me stay here, eating your food, even borrowing your clothes..."

"Whoa." Zai held his hands up. "Ethan, I'm not doing any of this because I want something from you or expect you to pay me back. If I did, I would've told you. You don't owe me anything. And you're hardly being a burden by hanging around and eating some of the food in my fridge. If you want to leave, you can, of course, but don't feel like I'm secretly annoyed and just being too polite to kick you out." The corner of his mouth twitched. "That's really not the kind of person I am."

Ethan hadn't expected that reaction at all. "But," he said, weakly, "I don't want you to feel like I'm staying *forever...*"

Zai waved dismissively. "Don't worry about it. Just take as long as you need to rest and get back on your feet."

So Ethan stayed, taking on some cleaning duties in a meager attempt to feel less guilty for taking up space and food. He spent a lot of time looking through his old uSpace profile and peppering Zai with questions, trying to glean information about his old self, devouring every word Zai said.

He memorized every fact and anecdote about himself. His birthday was on April twentieth. He and Zai had been born in the same year; he was older than Zai by a few months. He was born in Orphis City and lived there his entire life. But no matter how much he memorized, it became obvious to him that learning about himself wasn't filling the constant sense of hollowness in his chest. The stories that Zai recounted from their college days felt distant, like listening to stories from the life of a stranger. Nor did his uSpace profile, with a hundred and twenty-one friends, feel like it belonged to him. It felt like it belonged to some happy, idealistic college student he couldn't imagine ever having been.

A nagging voice in the back of Ethan's head told him that he *did* have somewhere else to go—back to his family. But the idea made him anxious, so he avoided thinking too much about it. It was easier to believe Zai's assurances and continue staying somewhere familiar, somewhere he'd begun thinking of as safe.

ZAI APPARENTLY HAD an eclectic collection of video games. Ethan browsed through them with some interest—there were quite a few indie games that featured simple-sounding goals set against artsy, psychedelic graphics. He found himself in the middle of one in which he had to move bubbles from one end of the level to the other. The problem was, it was difficult to avoid all the sharp corners that kept popping the bubbles, and he ground his teeth every time he failed a level and had to start over. Why were the bubbles so damn *fragile*?

He heard the front door open. Was the workday over already? Time went by fast.

"How was your day?" he asked, trying to navigate the bubbles around a particularly jagged spot.

"Oh, it was great."

Except the voice that answered wasn't Zai's.

Ethan shot to his feet and spun around. The person standing in front of the door was dressed sharply in a well-tailored gray suit, with a briefcase strap hanging over one shoulder. He wore thick-rimmed glasses, and wavy, dark-brown hair framed his face.

He looked just like Ethan had from the old pictures.

"Who—who the hell are you?" Ethan asked, trying to keep his voice from shaking.

His doppelganger spread his arms. "I'm *you*, Ethan. Well, the better version. The version that *should* have been."

Ethan stared blankly at him. "I—I don't understand—"

"I never went to war," his other self said smoothly. "I finished my bachelor's. Went on to law school. Now I'm working for the Civil Liberties Union, bringing lawsuits on behalf of those who are too poor and powerless to seek justice themselves. Saving the world, one case at a time." Other Ethan tilted his head to the side, regarding him with a pitying expression. "And what do you do? You're so traumatized and messed up, all you can do is sit on the couch, playing video games and trying not to think about how messed up you are."

Ethan's hands clenched. "Shut up," he hissed, stepping around the couch toward him. "You don't fucking *know* what I—you don't know what the fuck you're talking about—"

"My, what a mouth." Other Ethan's eyebrow arched. "Mom and Dad must be so disappointed."

Ethan froze, his anger evaporating into confusion.

"That is, if they can tolerate having a son who worked as a *contract killer*." Other Ethan smiled coolly. "You know I have dinner with them every week? Rachel calls me regularly, too. It's so nice to be close with your family. And they're so proud of me and the work that I do."

Ethan looked down, swallowing hard.

"This could've been your life," Other Ethan went on, "if only you'd let Zai pay that exemption fee. It's your fault, you know."

"No, I—" He pressed his fingertips to his brow. "I didn't—*ask* for this—*Atali* was the one who screwed me over—"

"In more ways than one, am I right?"

Ethan jerked up. "Don't—don't you *dare* blame me for that, too," he snarled. "Don't you fucking *dare*—"

"I'm just saying. You could've avoided all this. Could've kept your memories. And you know what else you could've kept?"

"What?"

As if on cue, the door opened, and Zai walked in. He, too, was dressed in a suit, his black hair slicked back.

"Hey, Zai," Other Ethan said, with a smile.

"Hey," Zai said, smiling back at him.

They met with a deep, passionate kiss, and Ethan had to look away, biting down hard on his lower lip.

"Since he never became depressed, he went on to get his MBA," Other Ethan said.

Zai moved away, walking to the bedroom, and though Ethan's eyes followed him, he never once glanced at Ethan. As though Ethan wasn't there.

"Now he's working for Meridian. Doing very well, too. Who knows, he might even become CEO one day, when his mom retires. And he's on great terms with his parents. He's not estranged from them. He sure as hell isn't in *debt* to them." Other Ethan's voice turned icy. "Maybe you don't care about screwing up your own life, but you should at least feel guilty about screwing up *his*."

"But I..." Ethan barely whispered, "I didn't...mean to..."

"You almost *murdered* him."

He recoiled. "I know...I'm sorry..."

"It's no wonder he can't love you. Not the way he loves me."

Ethan caught movement out of the corner of his eye. Other Ethan held his hand up, showing off a silver wedding band that glinted in the light. The sight of it made Ethan's breath hitch, a painful lump throbbing in his throat.

"He proposed. We were married. Just celebrated our third wedding anniversary earlier this year, in fact."

Ethan covered his eyes. *No. Stop. Please...*

"Face it, *Vax*." Ethan heard a click and looked up to find himself staring at the muzzle of a gun. "You're a waste of space, and you're better off dead."

The gun fired—

Ethan woke with a gasp. Where—what—he was—

He was in Zai's bed. Right. He realized he had his knife held out in front of him, and, shaking, he put it back into the drawer of Zai's nightstand. He leaned his head against his hands, trying to catch his breath. It was a dream. Just a dream.

He lay back down on his side and curled up, wrapping Zai's comforter around himself. Sleep only came to him in restless spurts, and no matter what he did, vivid fragments of his dream kept replaying in his head in a constant, torturous loop.

This could've been your life.

Just celebrated our third wedding anniversary.

Maybe you don't care about screwing up your own life, but you should at least feel guilty about screwing up his.

It's your fault.

You're a waste of space, and you're better off dead.

ETHAN HEARD THE bedroom door open in the morning. *Zai*, he thought. And then he realized he couldn't face him. Not with his dream self's accusations still rattling around in his head, and not with that goddamned image of his doppelganger and Zai locked in that openmouthed kiss seared into his mind.

"Ethan?" Zai called, in a low voice. "Are you awake?"

It seemed rude not to reply, but part of Ethan still hoped Zai thought he was asleep. Before he could respond, though, Zai went on.

"I'm just going to get some clothes. I'm going out to work today—I've got some video conferences and stuff."

Thank God, Ethan found himself thinking. Not because he didn't want Zai around, but because that saved him from having to face him...at least for the moment. If there was one thing Ethan was a pro at, it was avoiding his problems.

Zai quietly went to the closet, fabric swishing softly as he looked for clothes. Then he left, just as quietly. Only when Ethan heard the front door close did he let out a breath.

The dream, and his restless sleep, had left him exhausted. The day passed in a featureless blur, with him alternating between trying—unsuccessfully—to nap, aimlessly surfing the internet, and occasionally grabbing something random to eat when his stomach reminded him it still existed.

Mostly, he brooded. And he berated himself. Why was he still getting so emotional over the fact that he and Zai weren't in a relationship anymore? Was it because he liked the *idea* of being in a relationship, after being treated like shit for years? Or was he confusing his gratitude toward Zai for a crush? Either way, he had to stop.

But...was that really what it was? He did like Zai as a person. He admired his drive, and he also appreciated Zai's open honesty about his own mistakes. He trusted Zai. He felt safe around him...

He had to stop thinking before he lost what was left of his sanity.

In the afternoon, the front door opened, making Ethan jump from where he was sitting at the kitchen table. He didn't expect Zai to be back already.

"You're back."

Zai shrugged, setting his messenger bag down. "I finished everything I needed to do."

His eyes went to the bag of shrimp chips in Ethan's hands, and Ethan suddenly felt self-conscious. He slowly pushed the bag away.

"Uh...I was hungry," he muttered.

"It's fine," said Zai. He sat next to Ethan at the table, his eyebrows knitting. "You okay?"

Maybe you don't care about screwing up your own life, but you should at least feel guilty about screwing up his.

Ethan shrugged, hoping Zai didn't notice the way his throat tightened. "As okay as I can be, I guess."

"You look tired. And you seem...stressed."

"Stressed?"

"Well." Zai nodded at the bag of chips. "If your eating habits are anything like they were in college, the less happy you were, the more junk food you ate."

Ethan's shoulders slumped a little. Sometimes he still forgot Zai knew him so well.

"You know..." Zai hesitated. "If you ever want to talk—about anything—I'm here. I might not be a therapist, but... I'm willing to listen. No matter how dumb or embarrassing or terrible you might think your thoughts are."

Had he returned early because he'd been worried about Ethan?

As if you hadn't screwed him over enough.

"I...sorry," Ethan whispered.

Zai blinked. "For what?"

"For..." Ethan swallowed. He stared at the table and went on, in a small voice. "Don't you ever...hate me for fucking up your life?"

"What?" Zai sounded strangled. "No, I—never. Why would you ever think that?"

"Because of me..." Ethan leaned his forehead against his clasped hands. "You're estranged from your parents. You're broke, instead of working for Meridian and living a cushy life, or whatever. Fuck, you're in *debt* to them, and it was all—all for nothing."

"Ethan—no. First off, I'm not *broke*. It's a lot less money than I grew up with, but it's still more than many other people have. Secondly, if we never tried the operation, we always would've been left wondering and obsessing over what things might be like. Besides..." He sounded as though he were trying to smile. "Better to be in debt to my parents than to a bank. At least they don't charge interest."

If that was meant to be funny, Ethan didn't feel like laughing.

"I *chose* to go into journalism after you—after I thought you died. I knew what I was getting into, and I never regretted it. Hell, I thought I was trending up. Actually doing something meaningful with my life, for once. So don't—you don't have any reason to feel bad."

Ethan raised his head. Zai's expression was warm. Calm.

Just celebrated our third wedding anniversary.
This could've been your life.

He massaged his forehead. *Stop thinking about what you can't have before you drive yourself insane.*

"You've got enough to deal with," Zai went on. "You don't need to worry about me on top of all of that. Really."

"Yeah, I, um..." Ethan rubbed his face. "Sorry. I don't mean to..." He made a helpless gesture. "You must be sick of dealing with my freak-outs by now."

"Nah. What else are friends for?" Zai said, with a crooked smile.

Friends. Right. Frankly, he was lucky Zai even considered him a friend and hadn't just run away in the opposite direction.

"Trust me, if I feel like I'm starting to burn out, I'll tell you, and we'll find a solution. And, well...when I was depressed, there were well-meaning people who said unhelpful things, and..." Zai shrugged. "I told myself that if I were ever in the position of trying to support someone else, I'd do better. But, you know, don't hesitate to tell me if I'm saying something wrong or if there's anything else I can do to help or whatever."

Are you kidding? Ethan wanted to say. Zai was already a saint by his standards. Letting him stay there, listening to him ramble, worrying about him...it was far more than he deserved.

This couldn't last forever.

Cold certainty settled in his veins. Even if they were friends now—even if Zai were willing to consider them *best* friends, which sounded so ridiculous he nearly laughed—eventually, Zai would get tired of listening to him, or putting up with him. Eventually, his patience would run out, or he'd finally burn out, or...whatever. Besides, Ethan already owed him too much.

His thoughts turned to his family, whom he still only knew as faces from the pictures. He'd put off thinking about them for so long, because he'd been convinced they would reject him. But...if they didn't, maybe they would take him in again. That was what family did...right?

"Zai?"

"Yeah?"

Ethan took a deep breath. "Where does my family live?"

Chapter Sixteen

ETHAN STARED AT the apartment door. They'd made their way a few miles across town to an older apartment building, and now he stood in front of the Tromers' unit.

"So this is it, huh?" he muttered.

"Yep," Zai answered. He'd been the one who'd called ahead to make sure they'd be at home, after Ethan had turned down the offer to make the call himself, out of anxiety. Zai had also asked Ethan if he wanted to meet his family alone, but Ethan had stopped just short of begging him to come along. If he'd gone by himself, there was a good chance he would chicken out entirely and bolt.

Safiya Bahur. Daniel Tromer. Rachel Tromer. It felt...wrong, that he'd had to memorize the names and faces of his own family members, but that was one of the perks of having no memories. The night before, he'd practically grilled Zai for information about them—his mom's family were Coptic Christians from Egypt and she worked as a public school teacher; his dad was Jewish and a social worker; his sister was about to start her senior year at college.

And now they were waiting on the other side of the door.

Ethan realized his heart was beating very fast. He didn't even remember his family, and he was practically sick with anxiety at the thought that they'd reject him.

"You can do this," Zai said.

Ethan took a deep breath, and then he stepped forward and rang the doorbell. The building was so old that it still had antique-style buttons.

A long moment passed. Then footsteps sounded from the other side of the door, getting closer. Closer.

The door opened, revealing a young woman with dark-brown hair and olive skin. He recognized her from the pictures—Rachel, his younger sister. Her eyes widened as she looked at him.

"Who..." Her voice was a whisper. "Who...are you?"

Ethan swallowed. *Keep it together.* After all, it couldn't be easy to see the face of one's dead family member.

"It's me," he said, his voice wavering a little. "It's...Ethan."

God, his name sounded so strange when he said it out loud. He still wasn't used to it—still had a paranoid fear that someone or something was going to swoop down on him and expose him for an imposter.

"*Ethan?*" she breathed.

He nodded once and tried to smile. "It's...it's me, Rachel. I'm alive."

She stared at him for a moment longer before she threw herself at him, wrapping her arms around him in a crushing hug. He staggered back from the impact.

"Oh my God," she said, "oh my God...*Ethan...*"

Unsure what to do, he settled for awkwardly patting her back as she stood there, hugging him as though she was afraid he would disappear. Her shoulders started to shake, and he realized, with a jolt, that she was crying.

"But y-you were dead," she sobbed against his chest. "You d-died...how are you...?"

"It's a long story," he said with difficulty, overwhelmed by her emotional outburst.

Finally, she drew back, wiping tears from her face, now smiling so widely he thought her face might crack. "I can't believe it. I can't—*Mom*! *Dad*!" she yelled into the apartment. "*Come quick*!"

He barely had time to catch his breath before his parents appeared in the hallway. They looked the same as they had in the pictures, except with more silver in their hair, but it was still a shock to see people who looked like him—to see that he had his mother's nose and his father's eyes. Like Rachel, they too looked stunned at the sight of him.

"Ethan?" Safiya whispered. "Is...is it really you?"

"Yes." He had a lump in his throat, and suddenly he was blinking back tears. "I'm—I'm here."

They both hugged him. Ethan lost track of time, cocooned in his parents' warm arms.

"Come in," Daniel finally said, keeping one hand on his shoulder. "We want to hear everything."

Ethan stepped inside and glanced at Zai over his shoulder. None of his family members seemed to have noticed him. "Uh...Zai's here, too."

"Of course." Safiya gave Zai an embrace. "It's good to see you again, Zai."

"You too," Zai said with a smile.

As Ethan followed his family through the narrow hall, he saw the digital picture frames hanging on the wall, and he stopped dead, staring at them. By now, he'd seen plenty of pictures of himself from five, six, seven years ago, but these were ones of him as a gap-toothed child. As a curly haired, chubby-faced toddler. Evidence that, once upon a time, he really did have a normal life—a life now completely lost to him.

"Ethan?" someone called.

"Y-yeah." He tore his eyes away from the photos. "Coming."

They sat around the dining table, and Safiya insisted on boiling them some tea. Ethan breathed deeply and looked at his father, mother, and sister. They all looked as though they had a million questions on their tongues, but no one spoke, and an awkward silence settled over the table.

"I..." Ethan swallowed. "I'm...sorry for what you all must have gone through when you thought I was dead."

Safiya put a hand on his arm, and he fought the instinct to draw away, already starting to feel frazzled. "We just want to know where you've been. Why didn't you tell us you were alive?"

Her voice was gentle, but Ethan still winced.

"A lot of...really bad stuff happened. I didn't...I didn't want you to know what I'd done, or what had happened to me, or...what kind of person I'd become," he finished, his voice trailing off into a whisper.

"You're our son," Safiya said. "We'll always forgive you."

Ethan almost uttered a choked half laugh, half sob. *You wouldn't say that if you knew...if you knew what I'd become...*

Zai's hand brushed against his.

"You don't have to do this now," Zai murmured to him.

No, he would've loved not to. But then he'd keep living in fear, pretending to still be someone he wasn't, dreading the day his family finally found out, one way or another.

"No, I...I owe you all the truth."

He took a deep breath, glancing at their expectant faces. Fear seized him, freezing him. Could he really do this? Break their hearts, the way he broke Zai's?

Don't think. Just do it. Rip the band-aid off in one go.

"I've killed people," he choked out.

There was the briefest of pauses before Daniel said, "We know, Ethan. You were a soldier in a war. We understand."

His shoulders hunched. "No, that's...not what I meant. I mean I..." He cringed and spoke to the table. "I was working as an assassin, these past four years."

Dead silence.

"I'm sorry." He didn't dare look up to see their expressions. "That's...the truth. I know it's...horrible, and I did awful things, and I...if you can't forgive me...I'll understand."

More silence. He swallowed hard and braced himself for the inevitable *You're not our son, you're not Ethan, get out and don't come back.*

"How?" was all Safiya said, her voice shaking. "How did it happen?"

Oh. Well. Maybe they were just too shocked to process right now. Time for bombshell number two, Ethan thought to himself. He leaned his forehead against his clasped hands.

"I didn't...remember who I was," he whispered. "Actually...I still don't. Remember anything, I mean."

Still more silence. Zai's hand slowly slid up and down his arm, in a reassuring gesture.

"Wait." Rachel sounded choked. "You don't remember...your childhood? Us? *Anything*?"

"No." It still killed him to admit it, to say it out loud. "I've tried. I've looked at pictures. But everything beyond the last few years is just...blank."

No one else said anything. He heard a small, stifled sob, and he realized it came from himself.

"I'm sorry," he whispered.

Someone gathered him in their arms. His mom.

"Oh, Ethan..." Her voice was filled with sadness. "Ethan..."

"I'm so sorry," he mumbled into her shoulder.

"Shh. It's not your fault. Shh…"

He didn't know how long he stayed like that, with Safiya gently rubbing his back. Finally, he pulled away. Her hand lingered on his shoulder, but he kept his gaze lowered, not wanting to see her expression.

"Ethan," she said gently.

He raised his eyes, reluctantly. She was giving him a soft, tentative smile.

"You're alive," she said. "That's the most important thing. Everything else…we'll figure it out."

"Okay," he whispered.

"What happened?" his dad asked. "Was it some kind of head injury?"

"Um." Ethan fidgeted with his fingers. "The short version? Someone stuck a neural implant in my brain that caused permanent damage."

It was silent for a second—and then the table exploded.

"*What*?"

"What kind of person would do something like that?"

"Tell us who did this—"

He hadn't been prepared for their reactions of pure outrage, and he was left speechless in the face of it all. Maybe he should've thought of some more tactful way of putting it.

"Guys—*guys*—" Ethan shrank down in his seat and almost covered his ears. "Please—can you stop shouting?"

Their voices quieted, but he could still see the shock and anger in their expressions. God, he hadn't expected this. He had no idea what he was supposed to do.

"Ethan." Safiya's voice had a hard edge. "Who did this to you?"

Shit. This had been a mistake. A really, really bad mistake. Seeing the grief and pain in their expressions somehow made everything so much worse than it had been when it was only in his head.

"He's—he's already being investigated," Ethan stammered, trying to backpedal. Trying to steer the conversation away from Atali and everything that had happened. "There's nothing more you guys—or anyone—can do, so can we just move on?"

"But who was it?" Rachel demanded.

Ethan shook his head. He didn't feel like he deserved all this outpouring of righteous anger on his behalf. They didn't even *know* him. Not the person he currently was.

"Hey, um…I know you guys are upset," Zai broke in, gently. "But Ethan's had a stressful couple of weeks, and it's still a lot to process. He'll tell you guys when he's ready."

Ethan gave him a grateful look. *Thank you.*

His family didn't look satisfied, but apparently Zai was persuasive enough, because they let the issue go.

"One question," Rachel said. She looked between Ethan and Zai. "If you didn't have any memories, how did you find Zai? Or was true love *actually* stronger than amnesia?"

"That's not how amnesia works," Ethan muttered. His irritation was drowned out by the sense of guilt and shame that overwhelmed him whenever he thought back to their first, and nearly lethal, meeting.

"It was a total accident, kind of," Zai said, after an awkward pause. "It might have involved a gun and a bullet hole in my wall." He frowned. "Speaking of which, I should really fix that. It's a major eyesore…"

Ethan stared at him, unable to comprehend how Zai could sound so chipper about the fact that he'd nearly been *killed*.

"Wait." Rachel turned wide eyes to Ethan. "You mean you *shot* at him?"

He wanted to protest, but there was nothing he could say in defense of himself. He sighed, slumping over the table, mumbling, "Yeah."

"That is *so* not romantic," Rachel said under her breath.

"Well, then I knocked him out with a taser and tied him up, so I'm pretty sure we're even," Zai added apologetically.

"Not really," Ethan mumbled.

"*Anyway*, the point is, we're all alive and everything worked out fine," said Zai, with slightly forced cheer. "More or less."

Silence settled over them once more. Ethan wasn't sure if he was supposed to talk, or what he was supposed to say.

"So, um," Rachel began, "you don't know...anything about yourself?"

"I...know the basics," Ethan said, hesitantly. "Zai's told me some things. And I read my obituary..."

Everyone at the table winced. Damn, he'd forgotten how weird that sounded when he said it out loud.

"But you don't know what happened since you...uh, almost died, right?"

Ethan shook his head.

"Well, Grandpa died two years ago," said Rachel.

"Oh." Ethan felt strange—a sense of loss, but also a sense of not knowing what he'd lost enough to be able to grieve. "That's...um...very sad," he said, feeling more and more like a fraud by the second.

"Rachel," Daniel admonished gently, "why don't you start with something less depressing?"

"Oh yeah! Mom won the teacher of the year award last year," Rachel said, her face lighting up. "It's her third time winning the award."

"That's cool," said Ethan, struggling to smile.

"Samar—um, cousin Samar had a baby girl. They named her Hawa. She just had her third birthday a few months ago, she's so cute..."

Ethan kept listening, nodding and smiling whenever someone looked at him, because he didn't know what else to do. Not reacting felt wrong, but acting as though everything they were talking about meant something to him was exhausting him. The more they talked, the farther and farther Ethan felt from the life he used to have, like an unmoored sailboat floundering in the middle of a sea.

Mercifully, Safiya turned to him after a few minutes and said, "You look tired, sweetheart."

"I..." Ethan blinked. The word "sweetheart" made his eyes prickle with an emotion he couldn't name. He managed to get out, "Yeah...I...didn't sleep well last night."

"Oh, you must be exhausted. You'll stay with us, won't you?"

Ethan froze. "Uh...what?"

"We still have your bed, and some of your things," Safiya said. "Where else would you stay?"

His mind went completely blank. He hadn't expected this, and he had no idea what to say. Nor did he have any idea why the idea threw him into such a panic. He should want this...shouldn't he? But it was just...it was so sudden...the thought of moving back in with the family he didn't remember and didn't know...

Zai cleared his throat quietly. "Ethan's been crashing at my place," he said.

Those seemed to be the magic words; the tension in the room broke. "Oh, I see," Safiya said, though she was still looking at Ethan. "Well...you're still more than welcome to come back whenever you want. We'd be happy to have you around," she added, in a soft voice.

Ethan forced himself to smile. "Thank you. I...I'll think about it."

Somehow, miraculously, Zai came up with an inoffensive reason to leave and delivered it with profuse apologies and promises to visit again soon. They said their goodbyes, and Ethan received one last round of hugs, though at that point he was so worn out that all the nerve endings in his skin felt raw, and he tried not to flinch. Then, he and Zai set off back toward Zai's apartment.

"That wasn't so bad, right?" Zai said, with a smile, after they'd left the building. "Told you your parents are super nice people."

They were. Except...they almost seemed *too* nice. Ethan had spent a whole sleepless night worrying about what he would do if they rejected him, bracing himself for the accusations, the disbelief, the *anger*, and now...all that nervous energy was still balled up inside him, wiring him.

"Ethan?"

He couldn't speak. Zai's obvious concern, on top of the sudden exhaustion and still-sharp anxiety he felt, was too much for him. He bolted, not knowing where he was going, running until something bubbled up inside him and burst, and he stopped with his face against a brick wall, stuffing his sleeve in his mouth to muffle his sobs.

He could sense Zai hovering nearby, and he expected Zai to tell him to stop, or ask what was wrong with him. But Zai stayed quiet, waiting. Only once Ethan had calmed down did Zai ask, cautiously, "Are you all right?"

It took a moment for Ethan to find his voice again.

"I don't know, I—" He took a deep breath. "I thought it would be easy to...go back to my old life. But it's not. People look at me like they know me, but I don't know who they are, I don't even know the person they think I am, and I—" He wiped his eyes roughly. "God...I'm sorry. I'm so fucking pathetic."

Zai shook his head. "There's no handbook for what you're going through. There's no right or wrong way to react."

Ethan snuffled.

"I'm sorry I don't know how else to help," Zai said quietly.

"No, don't—don't apologize." He rubbed his eyes again. "It's my problem, not yours. I'm...glad we came here today. It's just...hard," he whispered.

"Yeah." Zai was quiet for a while. Probably thinking about what a pitiful wreck Ethan was, but there was nothing Ethan could do to take back that impression now. Finally, he asked, "You ready to go home?"

Ethan breathed out. "Sure."

THE SENSE OF malaise and disconnect didn't leave him; instead, it intensified during the rest of the day. Zai seemed to sense it, because he kept asking if Ethan was okay.

"I'm fine," he answered flatly.

Zai paused. "It's okay not to be, you know," he said, in a careful voice.

"I'm not made of fucking *glass*, Zai," Ethan snapped back.

Zai flinched, and Ethan's anger deflated as suddenly as it had appeared. God, what was wrong with him? He finally had what he'd desperately wanted for four years, so why didn't he feel better? Instead of feeling happy, he felt more depressed, lashing out and being a jerk to the person whose charity was the reason he wasn't sleeping on the streets. *What the fuck is wrong with me?*

"God, I'm sorry, I didn't—didn't mean it like that," he mumbled. "I'm sorry."

"It's okay." What a lie. Nothing was okay. "Do you... want to talk?"

No. No, I don't what to talk, because there's something really wrong with me and I don't know what it is. What kind of person felt depressed after seeing their family for the first time in four years—or, in his case, the first time he could remember? Why was he recoiling from everything he thought he'd wanted?

"Or...do you want me to give you some space?" Zai asked, tentatively, when the silence grew long.

Panic rushed through him. *No, God no, please don't leave me.* And then he felt even more ashamed. As if he had the right to demand that of anyone, let alone Zai. He was a fucking human disaster, that was what he was, clinging desperately to the one person who'd shown him kindness and generosity with the death grip of a starved leech.

He dug the heels of his palms into his eyes. *Get a fucking grip on yourself.* "Yeah," he forced himself to say. "Yeah, sure. You probably have a lot of work to do, anyway."

That was the wrong thing to say. He could feel Zai's concern mushroom, almost becoming a tangible presence.

"Well, no, not really. It's all manageable. I don't have to go if you need—"

"I'm fine," he repeated. Worst lie of the year, but it was all he could say. "I just...I do need some space," he said, his voice sounding unnatural, as though he'd had to extract the words from his throat with pliers.

Zai didn't look convinced, but he said, "Okay...if you need anything, call me, all right?"

"Yeah," Ethan mumbled to the table. "Thanks."

Then Zai was gone, and Ethan was left alone in the apartment.

Not knowing what else to do, he eventually crawled into bed, even though it was only four in the afternoon. He was tired...tired of thinking, tired of being a collection of mental health issues, tired of being a burden on other people. Himself. All of society.

You're a waste of space, and you're better off dead.

His thoughts drifted, becoming hazy. At some point, he swore he heard Atali's voice.

"See? I'm the only one who ever cared about you. I saved your life."

"You only did that so you could experiment on me," Ethan replied dully. "If you really cared, you would've let me die."

"Well...it's not too late for that."

Ethan rolled over, as though that would make Atali shut up. "Leave me alone."

"Just like how you've chased everyone else in your old life away? Not that they care, though."

"Zai...cares..." Ethan said, faltering.

"Does he really, though? Maybe he just pities you. And even that will only last until he realizes exactly how broken you are and that nothing can fix you. Not therapy, not time...not friendship or love."

"Go away," Ethan mumbled.

"You know it's true. You just don't want to hear it."

"Just go away." Ethan pressed his knuckles to his eyes. "Please, just...go away..."

The sound of a door opening made him jerk awake. He grabbed the knife in the nightstand drawer before he heard Zai's voice call out, "Ethan?"

He exhaled, shakily, and put the knife back. It might be awkward to explain to Zai that he kept his combat knife there just to have a weapon close to him while he slept.

Before he could pretend he was still asleep, the bedroom door opened.

"Oh—sorry, I didn't know you were sleeping. Did I wake you up?"

"It's fine," he said mechanically. Judging by the navy tint to the sky outside the window, it was already evening.

"There's chicken salad for dinner."

"I'm not really hungry." Which wasn't entirely true; he felt the hunger in the pit of his stomach, but he couldn't feel any desire to eat.

Zai paused. "Maybe...just a little bit? Or...there's yogurt in the fridge if you want something easier to digest."

Ethan considered his words, turned them over in his head. He didn't know what to do with them. He didn't know why Zai bothered to care so much.

The bed dipped as Zai sat next to him, though not close enough to crowd him.

"Your parents, um...wanted to know if you wanted to meet them for a meal sometime. Lunch or dinner."

Ethan shrank into himself. He couldn't deal with this right now. Couldn't...deal with *life* right now. It was too much.

"Should I tell them you need some time?" Zai asked softly.

Right, because they'll take that so well from their own son, won't they? Ethan thought bitterly. They'd ask why, and he wouldn't be able to answer, not in a way that would make sense. *Because you don't know me. Because I'm scared. Because I'm a complete mess of a person.*

"It's okay to take things slowly," said Zai.

"Is it?" His voice was flat.

"Of course it is. Sometimes, it takes a while to adjust to a new situation. But you'll get there, in your own time."

"It's not...that easy. They think it'll be so *easy*, but—" The poison crawled up his throat, and he tried to keep it down, hidden, but he couldn't. It wanted out. *"I was going to torture him to death*, Zai. And I still don't regret it—I only feel bad that I *don't* regret it." He stared down at his hands. "What does that mean?"

After a pause, Zai said, "I can't tell you how to feel about him, Ethan. I don't have that right."

"He *liked* hurting me," Ethan said, through his teeth. "He liked—watching me in pain. And then I wanted to hurt him, too. What does that say about *me*?"

"You're not like him." Zai's voice was suddenly fierce. "You're not, Ethan."

"How do you know? You don't know who I am. *I* don't know who I am."

"I know that you're asking yourself this question. I don't think he ever did."

"But that...doesn't make me a good person. I...I guess I used to be a good person. But I'm not...not anymore." He thought for a moment. "Scratch that—maybe I never was one in the first place." *And it hurts when people think I am.*

"What makes you say that?"

A deranged laugh bubbled up in his throat at the obviousness of the answer. "If I were a good person, I wouldn't have believed Atali. I wouldn't have done what he asked. I would've...escaped, found some way to resist, I don't know. And don't—don't say it wasn't my fault. I wasn't brainwashed. I knew what I was doing—especially when I tried to torture him. Maybe I was never that person you thought you knew. Maybe all of this—everything that happened—maybe I deserved it. I'm not worth a second chance."

It was silent in the room, his words sinking through the stillness like stones falling to the bottom of a clear pool. Zai must have agreed. Maybe he'd finally kick him out, deciding enough was enough for someone he barely knew anymore.

"I don't think you deserved it," said Zai, quietly. "And not because of whether you used to be a good person or not. I don't think anyone would've deserved it. It's his fault for lying to you, not your fault for believing him."

Ethan heard the words, understood them, but couldn't quite believe their meaning.

"Your family doesn't think you deserved it," Zai added.

"How do you know?" Ethan's voice came out harsh. "It's just a matter of time before they realize that I'm—"

Screwed up. Broken. Not who they remember. The words lodged in his throat like jagged shards of glass; he couldn't speak them out loud.

"They're not looking for reasons to kick you out, you know. There's no test that if you pick the wrong answer to, you'll fail." Zai paused. "But you don't have to do it all at once. These things aren't always easy. Your fears are real— they're not just in your head."

A shudder went through Ethan.

"But you're not alone. I'm still here for you."

Something broke inside him at those words. He hunched over, curling in on himself. "You shouldn't—you shouldn't be," he mumbled, his voice cracking. "I don't deserve it."

"Compassion isn't something you have to deserve," was all Zai said, quietly.

He didn't know how to respond to that. After a moment, Zai's hand touched his back, lightly but firmly, rubbing slow circles. He closed his eyes and concentrated on the rhythmic sensation, letting it lull and soothe him.

THE NEXT FEW days passed quietly. Zai mostly worked at home, typing at the kitchen table while Ethan sluggishly puttered around, doing nothing in particular—listening to soothing music, surfing the internet, watching random videos, or playing with apps. He looked into the online support groups and free counseling Zai had mentioned, but every time, he stared at the "Connect with a listener" or "Join the discussion" buttons for long minutes before losing his nerve and exiting. Even though he wasn't doing much, he felt exhausted most of the time for some reason, and he often curled up on the couch with his eyes closed or fixed blankly on the wall.

If Zai thought he was a useless, depressed couch slug, he didn't say anything. He only asked if there was anything he could do to help, although Ethan wasn't sure there was anything Zai could do. Every now and then, he'd come and talk to him for a while about random, lighthearted topics, and Ethan was grateful for the distraction.

Some days were better than others. Some days, Ethan could actually believe what Zai said about it being okay to take things slowly, and he could get through the day without feeling completely horrible. At night, they'd occasionally open the video games menu on the TV screen and play a few rounds of Mega Melee Fighters, which was always good for a few laughs and lifting Ethan's spirits for a little while.

One evening, Zai was losing more than usual, and a few good-natured ribs from Ethan only provoked absentminded chuckles. After the sixth match, Ethan finally decided to ask him, "You seem kind of...distracted. Is everything okay?"

"Hm?" Zai shook himself. "Oh...fine. I just got chewed out by my mom over the phone today, that's all."

Ethan's mind immediately went to the debt Zai owed. His heart sank. *Shit. It's all because of me, isn't it?*

Zai must have caught his expression, because he hurried to say, "It's no big deal, just...now that I'm safe and sound, Miki decided to rat me out. So I got an earful of my mom demanding to know why I didn't tell her my life was in danger and lecturing me about how I should've gotten a safer job. Or stuck to sports reporting."

Ethan didn't feel much better.

"It's not your fault," Zai said.

"It kind of is," Ethan muttered.

"Well...if it hadn't been you, I'm sure Norman would've sent some *other* assassin after me. So no, it wasn't your fault."

Ethan didn't have the energy to argue back against that.

"At least your mom cares," he said, trying to focus on something positive. "That's a good thing, right?"

"You'd have to be a *really* heartless parent not to care if your kid is alive or dead," said Zai. "Not that she's heartless. More like the opposite—she gets weirdly overprotective at times. Anyway, don't worry about it. It's just another chapter in the ongoing saga of arguments between my parents and me."

He sounded casual enough, but Ethan wondered if there was something else going on beneath the surface. It was hard for him to wrap his mind around the idea that Zai, who could charm almost anyone when he put his mind to it, couldn't get along with his parents.

"I thought...they'd be proud," Ethan said, his voice faltering a little. He was way out of his depth. "You broke a huge story."

Zai shrugged. "I mean, I'm sure my mom is secretly glad that Cyrex is having a hard time, but...with them, it's always complicated." He paused for a long moment. "I guess you could say they've always had high expectations for me, since

I was the eldest and all. I was supposed to be responsible, dutiful, hardworking. I never met those expectations, and they never quite got over that disappointment."

Ethan frowned. "Even when you became a journalist?"

Zai's sudden burst of humorless laughter startled him. "Oh, you should've been there for that conversation. They were mostly stunned when I told them what I wanted to do, because up till then I had never thought much about my post-college future, except that I'd probably get a job at Meridian. I said I wanted to do something that would make a difference, and they said, 'If you want to make a difference, why not become a doctor like Miki instead of chasing celebrity gossip?'" He made a face. "I can never win with them."

Unable to parse his detached tone, Ethan asked, "Does it bother you?"

Zai glanced at him, looking a bit surprised. Ethan tried to backpedal. "Sorry, I didn't mean to pry."

"No...it's okay." Zai seemed to consider it. "I guess I'm just...used to it by now? It sounds kind of depressing when I put it like that, but...when I was a dumb teenager, I didn't really care about how annoyed and disappointed they were with me. Now...it does sting, a little, but it feels like there's too much past baggage, and no matter what I do to try to make up for it, I'll never redeem myself." He grimaced. "Wow, that sounds *really* depressing."

The music from the game's fighter select screen felt a bit surreal as a backdrop for their conversation.

"I'm sorry," was all Ethan could think of to say.

Zai looked at him. "No—*I* should be sorry. I didn't mean to unload all my problems onto you. I don't usually do that."

"It's okay," Ethan said. "Listening is the least I can do."

Zai fiddled with the corner of a couch cushion. "I guess I sound a bit hypocritical, giving family advice when I don't have the best relationship with my own parents."

"I...well, I don't think you're a *hypocrite*," Ethan said. "No matter what, you're still an expert compared to me. And maybe...they'll come around some day?" He cringed. The words sounded clichéd and generic when he spoke them aloud. Damn, he was awful at trying to comfort someone else, and that made him feel bad.

Zai opened his mouth to say something, but then closed it again, as though he'd reconsidered. "Maybe," he said. "Thanks."

Ethan didn't think he'd said anything worthy of being thanked for. But before he could think of how to respond, Zai said, "Aw, crap. It's ten forty-five already?" He sighed and hit the power switch for the TV on his controller. The music cut out and the screen went dark. "I have a super-early conference call tomorrow that I couldn't weasel my way out of. Stupid time differences and busy schedules," he muttered.

"Oh—sorry," said Ethan. "I didn't know..."

"No worries. I was the one who lost track of time."

They stood and put the controllers away. When Ethan turned, he noticed Zai was looking at him.

"Good night, Ethan," said Zai, in a soft voice.

"Good night," he said.

Zai's eyes lingered on his face, and he gave him one last small smile before turning to the couch. Ethan took this as his cue to retreat to the bedroom for the night.

ETHAN WAS RELUCTANT to leave Zai's apartment, but there was one person he had to see. A few inquiries from Zai led him to discover that Sabela Barros was still in the hospital, so Ethan made the trip to Orphis General.

The nurse let him in, and he found her sitting comfortably in the room, with gauze wrapped around her head, watching some TV program on the opposite wall. When he entered, her eyes met his, and she switched the screen off.

"Hi," Ethan said, uncertainly.

"Hi," she said in return. She didn't seem unhappy to see him, at least.

He sat in the chair next to the bed. "I'm sorry for breaking your arm."

"I'm sorry for shooting you."

They looked at each other for a moment. Her mouth twitched, and Ethan found himself chuckling with nerves. The whole situation felt surreal.

"I, um...I didn't know you were still in the hospital," Ethan said.

"They took out the neural implant, but they're still running tests." She tapped her head lightly. "They don't think the memories will come back, but they don't think anything else has been affected."

"Same here, I think."

Sabela was quiet for a minute. "Do you ever think about all the blank space in your head and everything that's happened, and you can't help wondering...what's the point anymore?"

Ethan exhaled sharply. "Yeah. I...think about that all the time. I know I shouldn't, but it's just...I thought... learning who I was, finding the people who knew me...would make me feel normal again. But it's not that easy."

Sabela nodded. "It feels impossible to think you could ever move on, right?"

"Yeah." She was probably the only person in the world who understood.

"You're still here, though," she said after a pause.

"So are you," he replied.

"Yeah, well…" She shrugged. "I can't pretend it isn't a struggle some days. It feels hard to have faith that the future will be better, but I try to hold on to whatever I can. I guess that's all I can do."

He guessed that was all either of them could do.

"The woman from USABARD said I had family on the East Coast. Once I'm discharged, I'm going to look for them. It's a place to start, at least."

"Good luck," said Ethan, sincerely. "And, uh…if you ever want someone to talk to…" He glanced around before seeing the tablet by her bed. He typed a number into it. "You can call me."

"Thank you," she said softly. "That's very kind of you."

Ethan tried to smile. "I don't know if I can be all that helpful, but…at least I know what it's like."

He stayed for nearly half an hour talking to Sabela—or, rather, mostly listening to her complain about the food and talk about how nice the doctors were. They briefly discussed the ongoing investigation into Cyrex, but they avoided discussing Atali. As he finally turned to leave, she said, "By the way, my name's Sabela. What's yours?"

"Ethan," he said.

"Ethan," she repeated. She smiled at him. "That's a nice name."

"Thank you," he murmured. "So is yours."

AFTER VISITING SABELA, he started thinking more about a lot of things, but one came to the forefront of his mind. It took him a day or so to mull over it and get used to the idea, but once he had, he was determined to tell Zai.

The next morning, he walked into the kitchen, slightly tense with anticipation. Zai was at the table, eating a bowl of cereal and apparently scanning some newsfeeds on his augment, but he quickly switched the holographic text off when he caught sight of Ethan.

"Hey," he said.

"Hey," Ethan replied, a little taken aback. Zai was smiling brightly at him, and the sight of it turned his stomach into a cloud of dizzy butterflies. *God damn it, don't you dare get distracted.* He cleared his throat, keeping his gaze averted. "Uh, so...there was something I wanted to tell you."

"What's up?"

He took a deep breath. "I was thinking...I should take my parents up on their offer and move back in with them. At least until I get a job or something." *A job. Hah. Like anyone would want to hire me for anything.* But he'd figure that out later. First step: get reacquainted with his family. Second step: join a support group and try to improve his mental health. Third step: figure out other stuff.

"Oh." Zai sounded surprised more than anything else. "That's—that's great. Um...when were you thinking of going?"

"Tomorrow, I guess?" Ethan gave a short, humorless laugh. "It's not like I have anything to pack."

"Oh," Zai repeated. He leaned back in his chair. "That's true."

Ethan thought Zai would be relieved, but although he couldn't read Zai's expression, there didn't seem to be a trace of relief in it.

"I just...I've been here long enough, eating your food and stealing your bed," Ethan found himself apologizing.

"You don't have to rush out for my sake," said Zai. "Like I said, it's no big deal."

"Thanks, but...I'll be okay."

"Okay. Whatever you decide." Zai added, "You're always welcome to drop by, if you want to."

"Oh, um...thank you." Ethan was touched by Zai's generosity. "That's kind of you."

"Don't mention it." Zai smiled at him again, bringing the dizzy butterflies back. "It's always nice having you around."

Ethan was about 90 percent sure Zai was saying that out of politeness.

Zai hesitated for a moment, and then asked, "Hey, um, I know this is super short notice, but do you feel up for going out today?"

"Out...where?"

A conspiratorial grin spread across Zai's face. "It's a secret."

Ethan didn't trust that smile. "Like, a pleasant surprise secret, or a 'I'm going to pull a prank on you' secret?"

"Since when have I ever pulled a prank on you?" said Zai, with a mock-wounded expression.

Ethan tilted his head to the side. "*Have* you ever pulled a prank on me?"

"No!"

"You realize I can't tell if you're lying about that or not, right?" said Ethan, his voice dry as dust.

Zai spread his palms. "Believe me, I'm a totally trustworthy person."

Whatever Ethan was about to say fled from his mind at the sparkle in Zai's eyes, a splash of sunlight from the window turning his irises the color of warm buckwheat honey. He sighed.

"Fine. I'll play along."

"Cool." Zai flashed him another grin. "You won't regret it."

"I'd better not," Ethan muttered.

As they took the sky rail downtown, Ethan kept trying to guess where they were going, unsuccessfully. The park? No, they weren't getting off at that stop. Some kind of store? Was Zai a fan of shopping? *Please don't let it be a clothes store.*

They finally got off, and he followed Zai for a few blocks. Then he realized they were standing in front of the aquarium.

He released a strangled laugh and looked at Zai. "Seriously?"

"Seriously." Zai grinned. "Okay, okay, I haven't been here since like, middle school, so I *might* have been looking for an excuse to come, but...you said it was relaxing, didn't you?"

Ethan looked away, unable to hide his sheepish smile. "Good memory."

"Journalist. Comes with the job. Besides, you're not visiting by yourself this time. You're here with a friend." Zai's hand suddenly slipped into his, and Ethan glanced at him, startled. Zai winked. "Or...you can say it's a date?"

Ethan's heart rate spiked, and his face flushed with warmth. An embarrassed laugh escaped him, and he couldn't meet Zai's gaze.

"A...date, huh?" He tried to keep his voice cool. *Date. Yeah. Sure. No big deal.* Because Zai was definitely joking and he didn't mean *that* kind of date. He tried to play along. "You're not...*flirting* with me, are you?"

Zai laughed a little, and Ethan took that as confirmation that he wasn't serious.

"That's what a date is for," he replied with a mischievous smile.

As they reached the entrance, Zai abruptly turned around, fishing out his pod from his pocket and holding it in front of them. "Smile!"

"What?" said Ethan, startled, as he heard the digital click of the camera. So much for smiling. "What are you doing?"

"Taking a picture to commemorate the occasion! Obviously." Zai studied the picture, grinning at the screen. Apparently he liked whatever he saw.

The corner of Ethan's mouth twitched. "I didn't realize you were into taking selfies." His amusement abruptly faded. "Wait...you're not going to post them all over the internet, are you?"

"What kind of appropriately narcissistic twenty-five-year-old would I be if I didn't?" Zai chuckled, and the tense knot in Ethan's chest loosened as he realized Zai was joking. "Don't worry. I'm just taking pictures for a private collection, I promise. C'mon, let's go!"

Ethan practically knew the aquarium by heart, yet it felt like he was seeing everything for the first time. All of the exhibits felt brand-new, as though the aquarium had swapped the lighting or changed the arrangement of the tanks. Yet he knew nothing had actually changed—the only thing that was different was that he wasn't here alone. Zai's questions about the exhibits and which fish he liked best kept him lighthearted the entire time, and for just a few hours, he almost forgot everything that had happened during the past few years. He almost felt...normal.

They found a table by windows that faced the harbor at the aquarium café for lunch. Zai scanned the e-menu, scrolling through the options.

"So, what would you recommend?"

"Me?" said Ethan, startled. "Um…I like their calamari salad, but their clam chowder and seafood burgers are pretty good, too."

"Awesome. Burger and fries for me, then." Zai looked at him. "What about you?"

"Uh…I guess I'll go with the calamari salad again."

Zai punched in their orders and then sat back in his chair. "I'd forgotten how nice this place was," he said. "I should really come here more often."

Ethan tried to think of a reply…and realized he had no idea what to say. It was absolutely ridiculous; he'd been able to talk to Zai just fine while they were hiding from Cyrex and making plans, but faced with having to make normal, pleasant small talk, his mind was now a total useless void.

"Yeah, it is nice," he managed to say, and tried not to cringe at how blatantly terrible his conversational skills were. "The natural history museum's nice, too. It has a lot of dinosaur skeletons and stuff. I mean, if you like that kind of thing…" And now he was rambling. Fantastic.

Zai didn't look perturbed. In fact, he smiled. "That sounds like a good idea. Though I'm guessing their café doesn't have this amazing view."

"No," Ethan agreed, relieved by Zai's unworried reaction. "The aquarium wins on that count."

The table chimed, and they went to grab their orders from the counter at the front of the café. Once they'd returned, Zai took out his pod and snapped pictures of their meal.

"You're really into taking pictures of everything," Ethan commented.

"My PicShare account is pretty dead. Might as well fill it with pictures of food, because who doesn't like pictures of food?"

That reminded Ethan of something he'd always wondered about.

"Speaking of social media, does your Jabber handle mean anything?" he asked.

Zai blinked. "Huh?"

"Isn't it...uh...'z-a-i-z-x-z-l' or something?"

At that, Zai chuckled. "I think you've got an extra 'z' in there. It's actually my name plus my initials."

"Your initials?" Ethan echoed. "XZL?"

"Yep."

"Then...what does the 'X' stand for?"

"Oh." Zai looked oddly sheepish. "It stands for my real name: Xia, X-I-A, Zhao Lumero." He pronounced it like "shya," a soft syllable that glided off his tongue.

Ethan blinked. "I...didn't know that was your real name."

"It's not something many people know," Zai said, shrugging as he dipped a fry in ketchup and ate it.

"But then...where does 'Zai' come from?"

Zai paused. "Honestly? When I was a kid, I didn't like my name. Most people had no idea to pronounce it and mangled it horribly—I mean, no one knows what to do when your name starts with an 'x'—and even when people could pronounce it mostly right, it just...sounded weird. Because most English-speakers can't get the tone right, and stuff. So one day I sat down and started playing with the spelling of my name until I got something I liked. I thought 'Zai' sounded cool, so that's what I started to go by, to my mother's everlasting disappointment and annoyance," he said, in a wry voice. "In revenge, she never stops reminding me that zāi means 'disaster' in Mandarin."

Ethan considered that. "I think 'Xia' sounds nice," he said, tentatively. "What does it mean?"

Zai suddenly looked uncomfortable. He glanced away for a moment, clearing his throat. "Um...it means 'hero.'"

"What, really?" Ethan felt the corner of his mouth slant upward. "That's cool."

"Yeah, well, I don't really like it. I don't feel all that heroic."

Ethan shuffled vegetables and pieces of squid around on his plate before he said, "You kept investigating Cyrex even after you almost died. You pursued a story about people who most of society didn't care about. If that's not heroic, I don't know what is."

Zai pursed his lips at his fries, looking strangely dissatisfied. "Thanks...but I think I still have a long way to go."

For a guy who could radiate confidence, Zai was surprisingly modest.

"Anyway...not that interesting of a story, right?" Zai smiled crookedly. "Other people have like, deep and meaningful reasons for picking a different name. I just wanted something I thought was cool. Story of my life, I guess."

Ethan wasn't sure how to respond to Zai's self-deprecating tone. "No—I mean, it *is* interesting..." He glanced down. "I guess...there's a lot I don't know about you."

"That's not exactly true," said Zai, mildly. "You know all the most personal things about me. Just not...the trivia facts."

That was weird, wasn't it? Ethan thought to himself. It was totally backward from how people normally got to know each other.

He tried to come up with something else to say, but words had once more oh-so-helpfully deserted his head.

God, this was mortifying. He wasn't even—trying to *impress* Zai or anything. It wasn't like they were on a *date.*

"I'm not—good at this," he blurted out, and felt his face flush. *Smooth. Real smooth.*

Zai's eyebrow arched. "Good at this?"

"This...you know. Talking." He cringed. *You're talking right now, aren't you?* "Uh...to people." *What, Zai doesn't count as a person?* "I mean, it's not like I had any friends for a while..." *Yeah, how much more pathetic can you make yourself sound?* "So I just...I don't know..."

"Ethan." Zai's voice was warm. "Don't worry. You're fine."

He didn't really feel like he was fine. Not sure how else to react, he tried to laugh it off, but his laugh came out sounding strained and horribly awkward instead.

"Sometimes I wonder if the neural broke whatever part in my brain is responsible for normal conversation."

Zai winced, giving Ethan the impression that he'd said the wrong thing. But all Zai said was "You don't have to be so hard on yourself. Small talk was never your forte, but that doesn't mean there's something wrong with you."

"It doesn't?"

"Of course not."

Ethan wasn't sure why Zai looked so confused. Fumbling for words to explain, he ended up saying, "I just...didn't think you'd say something like that."

"Why not?"

Because you're actually good with people, and I'm not? "You just...never said I was socially awkward when you were singing my praises. You made it sound like I was a kind, selfless person instead."

"Are those two things mutually exclusive?" Zai asked, gently.

Ethan looked at him, clueless as to how to respond. *I don't know, are they?* He didn't think Zai was making fun of him, but he couldn't quite read Zai's expression, either.

"Hey," Zai said, "want to bet I know more dorky fish jokes than you do?"

Ethan was grateful for the change in topic, even if he wasn't sure he'd heard correctly. "You? Dorky?" he said blankly. "Those two words don't go together in the same sentence."

"What?" Zai feigned offense. "I can *totally* be dorky. I can be the dorkiest. Listen to this." He cleared his throat dramatically. "Why do oysters go to the gym?"

"I don't know, why?" Ethan asked, resigned.

"Because it's good for the mussel."

Ethan stared at him. A snort of laughter escaped from him, and before he knew it he was doubled up over the table. He hadn't laughed this hard in a long time, and it left his stomach aching.

"That," he wheezed, "is terrible."

"Oh, really?" Zai was grinning cockily. "You're laughing, aren't you?"

"Because it's so bad!"

"Uh-huh."

"Oysters and mussels are different species!"

"*Shh.*"

They were smiling at each other across the table. Ethan thought he wouldn't have traded this moment for the world.

ON THE RIDE back to Zai's apartment, Ethan stared out the window, absorbed in his thoughts. Once in a while, he snuck a glance at Zai, who looked equally pensive, his fingers gently tapping against his knee as he stared at some distant point in front of him. Probably still thinking about the fallout from his Cyrex article, or maybe thinking about his next story.

He realized he'd started imagining what it would be like if they did this again—if they went somewhere to have a good time, just the two of them—and closed his eyes, trying to put a stop to that train of thought.

For God's sake, what was wrong with him?

He was literally the walking definition of "undateable," what with his mess of PTSD and memory loss problems and dysfunctional emotions. There was no possible way he could ever hope to compare to his old self, the one he could only glimpse reflected in those smiling photos and cheerful online posts. The one Zai had wanted to marry.

I want to marry you.

But that was in the past. He was grateful for what he had now, and...that was all. Maybe they weren't meant to be, but that was okay. At least, it *would* be okay. He had a friend, and that was more than he'd had these past few years.

His pocket suddenly buzzed. Startled, unsure as to who could possibly be contacting him, he took his pod out and looked at the screen.

It was a message from his mother.

Hi Ethan, how is everything? Are you okay?

Some part of him knew that the message was totally ordinary, just a regular text from a parent checking up on her son. Yet it caught him completely off guard, and he kept staring at it, reading the text over and over again until the letters began to blur in front of his eyes.

Are you okay?

With shaking fingers, he typed back, *Yes, I'm fine. Thank you.*

A minute later, he received a reply. *I'm glad to hear that.* ☺

One text message and a damn smiley face were making him unravel.

He became aware of Zai's gaze on him. "Everything all right?"

Ethan drew a breath. "Yeah. Yeah, everything's fine."

Zai gave him a small smile before turning back to the front. Ethan realized his eyes were lingering on Zai's face in profile, so he turned back to the message on his pod, tracing over the letters on the screen with his thumb.

It was going to be okay.

WHEN THEY GOT back, Zai said, "Hey, could you take out your pod for a second?"

Ethan did so. Zai tapped his pod to Ethan's, and a message flashed on the pod's screen, asking if he wanted to accept the incoming download. Ethan gave Zai a puzzled look; Zai grinned back crookedly.

"I promise it's not a virus."

Ethan tapped the screen to accept. Another message flashed on his screen when the download finished, and Ethan realized Zai had transferred the pictures he'd taken during their trip, including that first one that featured Ethan's comically confused expression.

"I don't know if it helps," Zai said, "but I thought...having the pictures could help remind you that you had a good time today."

That brought Ethan up short. All this time, he'd thought Zai was taking pictures for his own amusement—he'd never dreamed that Zai did it for *his* benefit. To give *him* the pictures.

"I...um...thank you," he stammered, overwhelmed, as he tucked the pod away. "For today, and...for everything."

Zai nodded and smiled at him. "Of course. I just...wish there was more I could do."

"No, you've—you've done enough. More than enough."

"You and I have different definitions of 'enough,' but..." Zai shrugged. "If you ever need anything—if you ever want to talk about anything—I'm here. Always."

Ethan bit his lip. He could always say it later.

And yet...it felt like the moment was now, or never.

"Zai..."

Zai looked at him. "Yeah?"

"I..." Ethan rubbed the back of his neck and averted his gaze. "I don't...I know I don't have any right to ask if you..." He shook his head at himself in frustration. That wasn't how he'd meant to start. "I mean...I *know*. I know I'm not the person you fell in love with, all those years ago. And I'm...I'm still so fucked up from everything that happened, and who would ever..." He trailed off and sighed. "I just...I...want you to know that...I'm sorry for everything you've gone through. Thinking I was dead, almost...dying, because of me...I'm so sorry." He took a slow, deep, shaking breath. He realized his eyes were prickling. "Listen...even though I don't remember much, I...I care about you, and...I hope you can move on. That you can find someone else who can make you happy. As happy as...as you used to be with me." He stared at the ground, blinking hard. "I just...wanted you to know that," he whispered.

There was a long moment of silence, broken only by the sound of their breathing.

"That...means a lot to me," Zai murmured thickly. "Thank you."

Ethan nodded and tried to smile. "What are friends for, right?"

Zai looked lost in thought for a moment, and the silence was beginning to grow awkward, so Ethan went to the fridge and grabbed a bottle of orange juice.

"Actually...I have been...thinking about someone recently," Zai said.

"Oh?" Ethan poured the orange juice into a glass, trying to keep calm. He wasn't jealous, he told himself. Just glad for Zai. "I, um...wow, I didn't know. Good for you."

"I...wasn't sure if it would be a good idea, at first—I thought maybe we both had too much emotional baggage."

"Huh." Ethan frowned a little as he sipped his juice. *Maybe you should stay away from people with emotional baggage, at least for now*, he wanted to say, but didn't feel that it was his place to offer advice. "Well, what's he like? Or—is it a she this time?"

"He." Zai grinned at him. "Well, he's really attractive."

"Yeah?" Ethan's smile felt too strained to look genuine, probably, but he did his best.

"Yeah." Zai ran his fingers along the surface of the kitchen table. "And he's...he's nice. I was worried that I'd screwed it all up because I treated him horribly at first. And I thought...you know, maybe I don't deserve a second chance—third chance, whatever. Not after how much I'd messed up. And a lot of bad things have happened to him, and I wasn't sure if he needed more time and space to process, but..." Zai's eyes met his. "I really care about him."

Ethan's smile slipped, and he slowly set his glass down. His hand was trembling.

"What...what are you saying?" he whispered.

Zai drew closer to him.

"I'm saying that I...well..."

Zai didn't finish his sentence. He looked at Ethan, as though searching for something in his face. Ethan's heart was beating so loudly he thought it would burst through his chest. No, he was sure he'd misread or misunderstood something, because Zai couldn't possibly mean...

Then Zai leaned forward and kissed him lightly, questioningly. Just the barest brush against his lips, yet it electrified his nerves, leaving them seared and tingling. Ethan's mind went blank.

But...but I...what?

"But you...but I...I'm not—who I was, how could you...?"

"It's not about who you *were*. It's about who you are now. You're not a dead memory, Ethan. You're *you*, and..." His breath caught. "And if you want me too, I'd like to be with you."

"You...you don't know that." Ethan's voice shook badly. His world was falling apart around him, because after all this time, after everything that happened—he was afraid to believe. Terrified to hope again and have that hope ripped away.

"I know you have an endearing sense of sarcasm." Zai's mouth tilted into a crooked half grin that then softened. "I know you're ridiculously brave. I know...you care about the people around you. You care about how they feel, and you don't want to disappoint them. That's more than I knew about you when we first started dating, believe it or not."

"That's not..." Ethan let out a breath. "You make it sound like I'm some kind of...selfless person. I'm not—like that." His voice was small. "I just don't want to be alone."

"No one wants to be alone, Ethan."

Ethan shook his head, taking a step back. "But I—I—I can't have sex," he stammered, his face burning with shame.

And not just because of Atali, either. From the start, he thought that it was a side effect of his "head injury" somehow. It didn't bother him personally, except when he wondered how he was going to deal with it if he was in a relationship. If he could even *have* a relationship. Then Atali...happened, and he concluded he was definitely broken after that. Just one more thing that was wrong with him, on top of everything else.

To his amazement, though, Zai didn't even bat an eyelid. "I thought that might be the case." He shrugged. "I'm fine with that. It wouldn't make things that different from how they used to be."

Ethan stared at him. "What?"

It was Zai's turn to look confused. "Uh...back then, you told me you were asexual—you weren't sexually attracted to people, and you weren't really interested in sex either, so..."

"Oh." He repeated himself: "*Oh.*" He swallowed and asked, in a tiny voice, "And...you were okay with that?"

"Well, yeah," was all Zai said, as though the answer were obvious.

His knees felt weak, as though he'd been carrying a weight all this time and hadn't even noticed anymore until it was suddenly gone. All these years, he'd been terrified of either being too uninterested in sex for anyone to want to be in a relationship with him or being forced to engage in something he really didn't want. To hear someone say that it was fine, that it wasn't an issue, left him light-headed with euphoric relief.

Still, that wasn't his only concern. "I—I'm still too fucked up. PTSD, depression, and...whatever."

Zai was looking at him. "Ethan," he said, carefully, "if you don't want this—if you're not ready, or it makes you uncomfortable—you can say so. It's okay."

It took a moment for him to parse Zai's words, to wrap his mind around the idea that *it's okay to say no*. But that wasn't the problem. Not this time.

"I...no, that's not what I..." He leaned back heavily against the counter. "I just meant...no one would want a relationship with someone who's..."

"Mentally ill?"

He was going to say *someone who's that fucked up*, but that worked, too.

"I used to think so, too," Zai said, quietly. "About myself, I mean. And every time a relationship blew up in my face, I blamed myself. It was my depression that scared them away. No one was going to want to stay with me as long as I couldn't *get over it*." He paused. "But...these kinds of things are a two-way street, you know? Being mentally ill doesn't automatically disqualify you from being in a romantic relationship—not if you want one. And maybe it won't be easy, but the worthwhile things in life rarely are." He gave Ethan a small smile. "I know what you've been through; I know you're still trying to sort some things out. It doesn't change the way I feel about you."

Ethan hardly dared to believe what he was hearing.

"But that's not all...you know the things I've done. The things I...wanted to do."

Zai's expression sobered. "Yes, I know. And I also know that you regret it, and you wouldn't have done it if you'd been given a real choice."

"That—that doesn't make up for what I did," Ethan ground out. "If this is your guilty conscience acting up again—don't. Please, don't. You've already apologized, and you've already helped me more than anyone would reasonably be expected to."

Zai sighed. "I mean, did I feel guilty and want to try to make up for the way I acted toward you? Yeah. But that wasn't all it was—you were suffering, and I couldn't ignore that. I couldn't *not* care, knowing everything that you'd gone through." He swallowed. "I know a little of what it's like to fall into an endless black pit and feel like you're never going to be able to crawl out. I couldn't stand by and watch you go through something similar without trying to help. And then as time went on, I began to think..."

He trailed off, without finishing. Ethan watched him, aware of his heart beating loudly in his ears.

"Ethan..." Zai winced. "I know...you think that the only person I could possibly care for is the person you were, all those years ago. And you feel like no matter what you do, you can never measure up to that. But that's not...that's not how it is." He raised his head, his dark eyes shining. "I'm not looking for someone to idolize, someone to put on a pedestal. Hell, *I'm* so far from perfect it's not even funny. I know that, right now, you might think that the things you've lost, the things you've done, and the things that happened to you—that those are the only things that will ever define you. But they're not, Ethan. You're more than that. Even if you can't see it right now...it's what I see when I look at you, every day."

Ethan was at a total loss for words. A long moment of silence passed.

"I'm sorry," said Zai, in a quieter voice. "I shouldn't have—I don't want to pressure you at all. I know you've got a lot on your mind right now, obviously, and maybe you'd feel weird about being in a relationship given all this history you can't remember, and I'm not—I don't want to make things more complicated..."

"I don't...feel weird about it," Ethan said, slowly. It wasn't like Zai compared him to his past self anymore, except to tell him that he wasn't as broken as he thought he was. He'd never felt threatened or creeped out. But just the fact that Zai was asking about his feelings moved him. Fragile hope battled with certainty that saying yes would be an act of selfishness on his part.

"It's your choice," Zai went on. "And I'm happy to remain friends if that's what you want."

"I..." Ethan swallowed, his mouth dry, his voice shaking. "I just...you...you deserve someone better," he whispered. "You deserve someone who can make you happy."

Zai looked at him. He smiled—a soft smile, with somber gravity and deep empathy.

"I've already found him," he said.

The world shattered and reformed around those words, and the way Zai was smiling at him with bright eyes. Eyes that seemed to pierce through his skin and see into his soul, into all the ugliness and pain there, and yet still held no judgment, only compassion.

"What about you? What do you want?" Zai asked kindly.

"I..." No. He couldn't answer. He was too afraid. Too afraid to speak the truth, to make it real—to make it into something that could be broken, or crushed.

"It's okay," said Zai. "It's okay. You deserve to be happy, too."

Ethan lost it, then, his last walls of doubt and fear crumbling away. He kissed him.

This time, Zai didn't push him away; his arms wrapped around Ethan's neck, pulling him closer. Zai's hands moved to his face, cradling it as though it were something precious. For one moment, it didn't matter, what had happened, where he'd been, or what he'd done.

He was here, and he wasn't alone.

And that was all that mattered.

ETHAN HEARD THE approaching footsteps before a knock sounded on the bedroom door. He turned around from where he was sitting on the bed to see Zai leaning against the doorframe.

"Not that I'm in a rush for you to leave," Zai said, in a wry voice, "but it'll be nice to sleep in my own bed again."

"Sorry," Ethan said sheepishly, even though he knew Zai was teasing. "I'm surprised you didn't kick me out sooner."

"Considering you slept on that really uncomfortable couch for weeks, I would've felt like a total jerk if I did that."

Ethan huffed a quiet laugh.

"Anyway, I just wanted to say good night. Since this'll be the last time...well, for now."

"I'm only going to be a few miles away," Ethan said. "And it's not like we won't be seeing each other, or anything."

"I know." There was a wistful slant to Zai's mouth. "Guess I got used to having you around."

"You can visit," Ethan said impulsively. Then his brain caught up to his mouth, and he added, "I mean...uh, if you have time, or if you want to..."

Zai smiled at him. "I'd like that."

Before Ethan had a chance to think, he added, "Do you want to stay tonight?"

Zai blinked, looking stunned, and Ethan wondered if he'd said the totally wrong thing.

"I mean not to—to *do* anything, obviously," he stammered. He looked at the scrunched-up comforter in his hands, suddenly finding the burgundy fabric fascinating. "Just to...um...sleep. Together. In the literal sense. Unless it's too weird. Is it weird?" He was babbling again. He had to stop doing that.

"I figured that's what you meant. And no, it's not weird." Zai gave him a reassuring grin before his expression sobered. "Just...you're really okay with me being here? I don't want to freak you out in the middle of the night or anything."

Ethan vividly remembered what happened last time, and his good mood came crashing down.

"As long as you don't—touch me while I'm asleep, I think I—I won't freak out." He shook his head. "No, you're right, it's a stupid idea. I don't want to hurt you."

"I can manage not to touch you while you're sleeping. The bed's big enough," said Zai. "But it's your choice. I trust your judgment."

"*I* don't trust my judgment," Ethan muttered.

"You're the only one who knows what will make you comfortable," Zai said.

Ethan looked at him. Comfortable...he couldn't remember the last time he was allowed to make himself comfortable. He *was* afraid, a little, but...he was pretty sure they'd be fine. And he wanted this.

"I'd...like to try it," he said.

"Okay," said Zai.

He came over, switched the lights off, and then slid onto the bed next to Ethan. Ethan settled under the covers as Zai stretched out and released a long sigh. All of it felt so unfamiliar to him—the slight tug on the blankets, the second cadence of breathing, the gentle heat radiating from another body next to him.

"How is it?" Zai asked.

"Uh...new?"

"If you change your mind at any time, just let me know."

Zai's concern touched him. "I think I'm good," he said softly.

"And don't hog the blankets," Zai added with mock sternness.

Ethan chuckled a little, turning to face him. "Right back at you."

Zai moved closer to him, lacing their hands together, and for a while, neither of them spoke. Ethan lay there, breathing slowly, feeling the way Zai's fingers fit between his own, as though the spaces had been made just for him.

"Do you ever...wonder how things would've been?" Ethan asked. "If...none of this crap had ever happened."

Zai hesitated. "I used to. Used to think about it all the time. Though..." He shrugged. "That was back when I still thought you were dead."

Ethan breathed out. "I keep thinking about—about how we would've been so much happier, if only..."

"Hey." Zai's voice was gentle. "You can't keep thinking about that, or you'll drive yourself insane."

"Yeah, but..." Ethan swallowed. "There are so many things I'll never remember. After everything I've lost— everything that's changed—how can things ever be the same?"

"They don't have to be," Zai said, after a pause. "They don't have to be the same. Maybe things are different. Maybe you're different. Maybe—no, hell, I *am* different. I'm definitely not the same person I was when we first met. But different doesn't have to be bad."

"You really think so?"

"Of course I do." Zai smiled softly at him. "We can make new memories. Together."

New memories. The thought was...liberating, though scary at the same time.

"What if this doesn't work?" Ethan whispered.

Zai's thumb brushed against the side of his. "We can at least give it a try, can't we? I don't know about you, but the fact that we're both alive, and *here*—that alone is a miracle to me." His eyebrows drew together. "I mean, not that I'm trying to give a bullshit speech about silver linings and things happening for a reason. What you went through was awful and pointlessly cruel. You didn't deserve any of it, and I—I wish none of it ever happened. I wish the world wasn't such a terrible place." He drew a breath. "But after everything that's happened—all we've been through—I *have* to believe there's still hope. For the world to right itself, one day. For everything broken to be healed. And...hope for both of us."

Hope. It was such a strange, fragile idea.

"At least, that's what I think," Zai murmured.

"It's...a nice thought." He wasn't sure if he was nearly that optimistic. Maybe one day...maybe.

"It's okay if you don't believe it." The backs of Zai's fingers ran along the side of his face, as gentle as a bird's wing. "I can't promise that everything will be easy or ideal from here on out, but...things won't always be as bad as they've been, either."

"I know," Ethan said. His voice cracked, and he tried to clear his throat. "I know that, despite everything, I've been...lucky, in some ways. And I'm grateful for that, and I do...I want to get better. Not stay in that dark place forever."

"You're doing your best," Zai said. "That's enough."

Something deep inside of Ethan relaxed. Zai touched their foreheads together, his fingers tracing soft, soothing patterns through Ethan's hair.

"Hey, Ethan," he said, after another long moment of contented silence. He spoke in a soft tone, as though they were meeting for the first time in a long time, as though Ethan had just come home after a long, exhausting, wayward journey.

"Hey."

Zai smiled at him. It was the kind of smile that almost made Ethan dare to believe again—in the future, in love, in hope.

"I'm glad you're here."

Those four plain, simple, heartfelt words brought tears to his eyes.

"Me, too," Ethan whispered, smiling back. "Me, too."

Acknowledgements

It's been a long road from when I wrote the first words for *Eidolon* to its final publication, and I'm grateful to all of the people who helped make this dream a reality.

I'd like to thank the team at NineStar Press, especially Sam and Raevyn, for giving *Eidolon* a home, and Natasha Snow for designing the cover.

Thank you to my parents, for the unending love, support, and enthusiasm. Thank you as well to Tom Early for generously looking over an early draft.

Last, but certainly not least, thanks to Rachel and Stephanie for the detailed comments, for cheerleading me on, and for believing in this story from the beginning.

About the Author

E.S. Yu is a writer of speculative fiction and a geek who lives for video games, superhero comics, and all things sci-fi/fantasy. E.S. is a recovering law school graduate who lives off green tea and dreams of writing full-time; for now, she follows wherever her muse takes her to places sometimes dark, sometimes quirky, but always hopeful.

Email: esyuauthor@gmail.com

Twitter: @aetherquill

Website: www.esyuwrites.wordpress.com

Also Available from NineStar Press

Connect with NineStar Press

Website: NineStarPress.com

Facebook: NineStarPress

Facebook Reader Group: NineStarNiche

Twitter: @ninestarpress

Tumblr: NineStarPress